Dedication

I dedicate this book with gratitude to my family for their support and encouragement. I'd also like to dedicate this book to the inspiring young black girls out there, reminding you that you too can be princesses, embracing your softness, femininity, and elegance. These traits do not diminish your blackness. Remember, there is no one way to be black; you define your own identity, and that's a power no one can take from you!

BY ADE OLUOKUN

Copyright

Chapter 1

I strolled into school with a big grin on my face, determined to make the most of the day. Despite the series of unfortunate events that had happened earlier - waking up late, stepping in dog poop, and narrowly avoiding a car accident - I wasn't gonna let them get me down. I had always been the glass-half-full type of girl.

Entering the school building, I made my way to my Bio class just as the bell rang, blending in seamlessly with my classmates. Taking my seat, I let out a contented sigh, though I had to admit that Biology wasn't exactly my favorite subject. I was still ready to tackle whatever came my way.

After class, I made a quick stop at my locker to grab the books I needed for my next class. As I hurried along the hallway, I bumped into Simran Bakshi, who had held a grudge against me since our kindergarten days. To this day, I couldn't quite understand the reason behind her animosity. In fact, I vividly remembered us playing together on our first day as kids and hoped we'd become friends. But her attitude had swiftly changed a week into school and she'd hated me ever since, leaving me puzzled.

Whenever I shared my concerns with my dad, he would assure me that Simran's behavior stemmed from jealousy. I found it hard to believe seeing as she was one of the most popular girls in school, always surrounded by admirers. Smart, good-looking, with beautiful black wavy hair and flawless brown skin – why would she envy me?

"Watch where you're going, Rore-whore." Simran snapped, using her annoyingly creative name she had made up for me. Despite her not-so-friendly words, I decided to rise above the negativity and kept on walking, not giving her the satisfaction of a reaction.

However, under my breath, I muttered, "My apologies, Sim-ran-through."

Suddenly, I felt a firm grip around my wrist, and before I knew it, I was forcefully pushed into the lockers. The abrupt confrontation caught me off guard, and I winced at Simran's choice of words, as I had always held a distaste for profanity. Her words came out in a high-pitched, hostile tone, "What in the fuck did you just say, bitch?"

It wasn't often she physically grabbed me so I wasn't expecting it, my comment must have really got to her. It was a name my neighbour, Kiyana, had come up with for Simran after I had told her about her fun nickname for me but I had no idea what it actually meant.

"Simran, what the fuck? Relax," one of her friends interjected, pulling her away from me. "We don't do physical violence, we're ladies."

"Fuck that, did you hear what she said to me?" she seethed, glaring at me. I straightened my dress still in shock from being attacked.

Her friend shook her head.

"She called me 'Sim-ran-through.' The nerve—"

Before she could finish, her friend burst into laughter. "I'm sorry, but that's actually pretty funny." She turned to a guy at a nearby locker. "Hey, Cody, listen to what this girl just called Simran."

Simran, red-faced, called out, "No, don't!"

I seized the opportunity to slip away, heaving a sigh of relief, and continued on to my next class, well aware that I was probably late, as usual.

Lunchtime was a welcome break from the day's drama. I headed to the cafeteria, and my spirits lifted when I saw Mrs. Peters, the lunch lady. I greeted her with a warm smile, thankful for her kindness in a school where most people seemed to ignore me.

She beamed at me. "Hey, Aurora! What can I get you?" she asked.

"Just some fries and Jell-O, please. I love your hair by the way, it really suits you!"

Her face broke into a smile, and she shook her head playfully, her new bob bouncing. "Funny how you noticed it before my own husband did."

I chuckled in amusement. "Well, how could I not? You look amazing!"

She laughed in response. "You know, whenever I see you, my day instantly gets better."

Blushing slightly, I waved my hand dismissively. "Oh, come on, Mrs. P, you're too kind!"

Our light-hearted exchange was suddenly interrupted by an impatient voice from behind me. "Can you speed it up? Some of us are hungry here!"

I exclaimed, laughing, "Whoops! Bye, Mrs. P!" I waved enthusiastically as I walked away, and she replied with another cheerful laugh and a wave of her own.

Leaving the cafeteria with my tray, I made my way outside to the bleachers, my favorite spot to sit. It was like my personal sanctuary.

As I arrived at my usual spot, my ever-present smile faded when I noticed someone sitting there.

"Excuse me," I politely began.

The guy glanced up, his expression turning sour upon seeing me. I was a little taken aback by his unwarranted annoyance since we were complete strangers. My eyes traveled down his outfit. He wore loose black cargo pants that hung comfortably on his hips and a black tank top that clung to his torso, showcasing his toned physique beneath. On his feet he wore a clean pair of white Nike Air Force 1's. A black leather jacket was casually draped over the seat in front of him.

"What?" he snapped, the sunlight reflecting off his nose ring. His sharp features accentuated his intense demeanor, causing a wave of intimidation to wash over me.

Ignoring his attractive appearance, I composed myself. "That's actually my seat," I said, clearing my throat."

Furrowing his eyebrows, he glanced around at the countless unoccupied seats before returning his gaze to me.

"Your seat?" he questioned, raising an eyebrow, his voice deep and smooth.

"Yes," I confirmed.

Clearly annoyed, he asked, "Can't you just sit somewhere else?"

I stood my ground, refusing to back down. "No, because that spot is perfect. It gives me a great view of the cafeteria, so I can see if

I'm running late and people are leaving. The sunlight hits me just right, making it super comfortable. Plus, I can discreetly watch the hot football players on the field without drawing attention!" I defended my cherished spot passionately.

"You think you're Sheldon Cooper or some shit?" he asked, with an arched eyebrow.

"Move, please!" I shot back.

His response was defiant. "No."

"Please?" I pleaded, trying to reason with him.

He smirked. "Nah. I think I like this seat too," he taunted.

Frustration bubbled up inside me, a rare occurrence for me. I prided myself on being a patient person, but there was something about this guy that just pushed all the wrong buttons.

"Just get up!" I insisted.

"No! Now fuck the hell off—"

I gasped. "Stop swearing!"

He squinted at me as if contemplating if I had lost my mind. "You can't tell me what to do. I straight up just met you."

"I don't care. I just don't like it when people swear," I retorted firmly.

Surprisingly, his expression softened, showing a hint of regret. "For real?" he asked.

I nodded, standing my ground.

"In that case..." he trailed off, a mischievous smirk playing on his lips. "Damn, bitch, fuck—"

Cutting him off before he could finish, I quickly started singing. "I'm happy! I'm happy! I'm always happy! I'm always happy and never angry!" I sang in a slightly exaggerated manner.

He stared at me as if I were a complete lunatic. "What on earth is you doing?"

I cheerfully explained, "That's my happy song. I sing it whenever I feel anger creeping in, and it magically calms me down. See? Now I'm happy again!" I beamed at him.

His eyes scanned my face, clearly questioning my sanity. "Okay, bye," he muttered, diverting his gaze back down to the novel in his hands. As my arms started to ache from holding the lunch tray, I pouted.

With a sigh, I reluctantly conceded that sitting beside him wouldn't be so bad after all. I settled down, but the sun was now shining directly into my eyes, causing me to growl in frustration. In response, I turned the other way, edging closer to him.

"What the fu—" he quickly caught himself.

"—flip are you doing?" he snapped angrily.

"Sorry, but the sun was blinding me. And hey, you didn't swear! Yay!" I exclaimed cheerfully.

"Because I didn't want to, not because you said you don't like it." he said, angling himself away from me.

Deciding to occupy myself, I reached for a fry and started to munch on my lunch. However, I quickly grew bored when I realized that the football players weren't on the field today.

Out of curiosity, I glanced over at the guy next to me to see what he was reading. It was *Sophie's World* by Jostein Gaarder. Before I could really examine the book cover, he grunted.

"Oh, fu—come on now!" he exclaimed, abruptly closing his book.

"Hmm, I'm pretty sure you stopped swearing for me," I remarked casually.

"Can you just let me be?" he retorted, his irritation evident in his tone.

"I'm not doing anything," I replied defensively.

"Yeah, except you're all up in my bubble. Ever heard of personal space?" he shot back, his annoyance mounting.

"It's not my fault you're sitting in my spot!" I argued, frustration creeping into my voice.

"You're annoying as hell, like what the fuck—" he started to say.

"I'm happy! I'm happy—" I began to sing, trying to lighten the mood.

"It might be the bleach in your hair seeping into your brain, but you do realize that acting preppy, dressing like that, and dying your hair blonde won't earn you more respect in your suburban neighborhood," he quipped, his gaze scanning my baby blue sundress embellished with daisies.

My smile faded, and I glanced downward. I was sick of this dumb narrative that everyone seemed to force on me. People always seemed to think I was 'trying to be white', but I wasn't.

I could acknowledge that growing up in a predominantly white area might have influenced some aspects of my identity, but I wasn't trying to be something I wasn't; I was just being myself. There was no one way to be a black girl.

"My hair colour is natural." I whispered.

He gave me a flat look. "Don't do that. It's just sad."

I felt my anger surge at his audacity. "How dare you? You don't freaking know me. My hair is naturally blonde and I'm just being me. You don't see me making assumptions about you."

"You know what? Whatever. I just realized I don't really give a shit." He abruptly stood up, grabbed his bag, and sarcastically bowed while gesturing toward my spot, "You can have the seat, Princess."

I scowled. "Princess? What's that supposed to mean?" I called after him as he stormed away.

"Figure it out," he retorted over his shoulder.

Chapter 2

I heard a persistent voice calling from outside my bedroom door. "Aurora, get your butt outta bed!" I groaned, reluctantly throwing off my warm covers.

Ever since I arrived late to school last week, my dad had taken it upon himself to be my personal alarm clock. The only problem was that he insisted on waking me up two hours before school started!

I brushed my teeth without much enthusiasm and then let the warm water from the shower wake me up. As the droplets cascaded down my body, it felt like a refreshing splash of energy. After stepping out, I wrapped myself in a towel before changing into a sundress.

After styling my tight blonde curls, I looked at my reflection in the mirror and smiled. It's not every day you come across someone with my dark complexion and naturally blonde hair. When I was younger, I used to hate it, especially when other kids accused me of coloring my hair, like that jerk had done the other day. They'd say things like: "Black girls can't have blonde hair; it must be fake!" or even, "You're trying so hard to be white with that dyed hair!" Those words used to sting, but now I was growing to love and fully embrace my uniqueness.

I gave myself another once-over, smoothing down my forest green sundress before making my way downstairs for breakfast.

"Morning, sleeping beauty!" my dad greeted me with a cheeky grin. He'd always enjoyed comparing me to my namesake Aurora, she was a Disney princess who was literally known for sleeping, and I did love my sleep.

I mumbled a response and slumped into a chair. Mornings were the only time when I could be a little grumpy. An hour after waking up, I'd be back to skipping around and singing like a bird.

"Lucky Charms?" he offered, holding out a bowl. I snatched it from his hand and started devouring the cereal.

"Alright then," he sighed and retreated to fetch his own breakfast. My dad was a morning person, which, quite frankly, annoyed the heck out of me.

After breakfast, I still had an hour or so before school started, so I decided to catch up on some assignments.

"How's school?" my dad asked from across the kitchen island, sipping his coffee.

I shrugged indifferently. "Fine."

"Anything new? Friends? Boys?" he inquired.

"No, Dad, you don't have to worry. There are no boys," I replied, a playful giggle escaping my lips as my grumpy mood began to fade.

"Good, that's my girl," he said with a proud smile, taking another sip of his coffee.

"So basically, you're saying you're proud that no one wants to date me," I chuckled. "Which means you're proud that I'm ugly."

His face briefly contorted in thought, but he soon broke into a wide smile. "True."

"Hey!" I exclaimed, playfully tossing a pen at him.

He swiftly ducked and burst into laughter. "Just playing around, baby. You're beautiful, and I'm sure there are plenty of guys who'd be interested in you. But, you know the drill, no dating until you're eighteen..."

His voice trailed off as he realized something, causing a mischievous smirk to spread across my face. "Eighteen? Like in two months when I turn eighteen? I think I can handle waiting that long."

My dad, who had been reiterating the "no dating until you're eighteen" rule for years, frowned again. "I changed my mind. Let's make it twenty. No, twenty-four!" he declared, his brow furrowed in mock seriousness.

I laughed. "It's a little late to change it now, Dad. Besides, I don't think you'll have much say in my dating life once I'm eighteen."

He raised an eyebrow. "You do realize we're black, Aurora? As a Jamaican man, make me make it clear now, me ago have a say inna yuh dating life as long as me choose to."

"But, Dad!" I whined. "I'll be an adult."

"No, no, no. We not deh pon dat "once yuh eighteen yuh na mi kid" ting, yuh a mi chile forever."

I rolled my eyes. "It's not like anyone is lining up to date me anyway, so you're in the clear."

Before he could speak, I headed to the hallway to grab my bright yellow converse.

"I gotta go now, Dad," I announced, slinging my school bag over my shoulder.

"Alright, but throw on a jacket, too. I can't figure out how you wear sundresses all year round," he chuckled, amused.

"I can't help it, Dad. I just love them!" I twirled around playfully, nearly losing my balance under the weight of my bag. Laughing, I looked up at my dad.

He gave me his trademark look, the one that always seemed to ask, "Are you out of your mind?" Poor guy, having to put up with me.

I hurried up to him, giving him a peck on the cheek, and then headed out of the house. Walking to school was something I cherished. It offered a chance for reflection and deep thoughts. I never took rides from my dad, even on rainy or snowy days. I just loved being outside.

As I skipped along the road, my bag bouncing with every step, I couldn't help but ponder how silly I must appear. But that thought only made me laugh even more – an almost grown woman happily skipping along in a flowery dress and sneakers.

Arriving at school, I greeted everyone with a wide grin. Some people responded with smiles of their own, while others opted to ignore me. But that didn't put a damper on my spirits at all. I continued to beam even wider, trying to spread joy wherever I went.

"Excuse me! That's my locker. Could you just move a little to the left?" I asked the couple who seemed to have chosen my locker as their ideal makeout spot.

Initially, they ignored me, absorbed in their own world. However, as I persistently tapped the guy's shoulder – with my eyes firmly shut—I wanted to preserve my innocence, thank you very much—they finally moved.

With a contented sigh, I opened my locker and grabbed the books I needed for the day. After homeroom, I made my way to Calculus class.

Upon entering the room, I noticed that the only other person present was the guy who had taken my seat at the bleachers. Prior to last week, I hadn't noticed him at school ever. But now it seemed like he was in almost all of my classes.

I opted to take a seat at the back of the classroom, as far away from him as possible. Every time I happened to glance in his direction, he seemed to be glaring at me.

With a sigh, I opened my textbook and attempted to concentrate. Out of sheer boredom, I turned to look at him, only to find him glaring at me once again. I locked gazes with him, my warm brown eyes meeting his intense, piercing hazel ones. His eyes, a stark contrast to his velvety, brown complexion.

In an attempt to be friendly, I offered him a small smile, just as I did with everyone else. His response was an eyeroll before he returned his attention to his novel. I couldn't help but notice that, like me, he appeared to have no friends. I could understand why, though – he came across as rude and unapproachable.

However, even though I was the complete opposite, it seemed that no one liked me either.

Before things could become any more awkward, the classroom started filling up with other students. Simran walked in, and as soon as she spotted Mr.grumpy, she took a seat behind him – something I had noticed before. She always seemed to choose a seat either behind him or in front of him.

I had a feeling she was trying to get his attention, but he appeared unfazed. It wasn't surprising that she was interested in him; he was extremely attractive – more than that, he was downright hot. He had the looks of a model, or even a Greek god.

His shoulders were broad and sculpted, and even from my seat I could see how his snug black tank highlighted his well-defined chest as he awkwardly squeezed his tall frame into the combination desk.

His sharp jawline, those envy-worthy cheekbones, his plump and perfectly pink lips, and his hair – his luscious dark brown curls that sat beautifully on his head...

Suddenly, he turned to look at me, raising an eyebrow, and my eyes widened in realization. I had been blatantly staring at him for half the class. Flustered, I quickly offered another one of my smiles before hurriedly looking away, my cheeks burning.

As soon as the class finally ended, I practically bolted out of the room and made my way to my next class, hoping to leave that rather embarrassing moment behind me.

During lunchtime, I grabbed some food and greeted Mrs. P before making my way to my usual spot. I was excited because the boys' football team had practice, and although I knew other girls would come to watch, my seat was further up where I could eat in peace.

However, my excitement quickly turned to frustration as I discovered that the same guy was sitting in my seat again. After he didn't show up again last week, I had hoped he wouldn't return at all, but there he was, purposefully sitting in my seat and engrossed in his dumb book.

"Why?" I asked in frustration. He glanced up at me and flashed a smirk.

"Why what?"

"Why are you sitting in my gosh darn seat again?" I huffed, irritated. When I so much as glanced his way in class I was met with death stares but here he was purposely trying to be around me.

"Gosh darn? Do you mean 'God damn'?" he questioned, seemingly enjoying getting under my skin.

I wasn't used to getting frustrated by someone and I definitely didn't appreciate it. "Come on, could you just move?" I pleaded, my frustration growing.

He let out an exasperated sigh and rolled his eyes before reluctantly sliding into the seat next to him.

"Thanks," I mumbled, "Try not to insult my blackness this time."

He scratched the back of his head with a slight grimace. "I wanted to apologize about that. I might have crossed a line."

"You were also incorrect," I pointed out, trying to hide the surprise on my face at the fact that he had apologized.

"Yeah, I really shouldn't pre-judge anyone. I deal with enough of that myself. Sorry."

I nodded and went back to contentedly observing the football players goofing around on the field while savoring my Jell-O.

"Oh, by the way, I'm Aurora," I introduced myself to him.

"Jeremiah," he replied, not lifting his gaze from his book. "Maybe you could try and stop staring at me like you wanna eat me when I'm tryna focus in class, it's creepy."

I froze in horror mid Jell-O scoop.

Suddenly, a shadow cast over us, and both Jeremiah and I looked up. Simran stood there in a thigh-length denim skirt, white kitten heels, and a pink and white baby tee that read 'barbie', a bright smile on her face as she directed her attention toward Jeremiah. Then, her expression shifted into a scowl as she turned to glare at me.

"Why are you sitting here?" she asked, her tone dripping with disapproval. I glanced around briefly in confusion before looking back at her.

"Because I can. I always sit here," I responded, quietly.

"You always sit next to Jeremiah Summers, huh?" she questioned, her tone laced with accusation.

It finally struck me that she wasn't inquiring about my choice of seat but rather my proximity to her precious crush.

"No, but I didn't ask him to sit here, so why don't you ask him yourself instead of acting like he isn't right beside us?" I responded, taking a sip of my juice to signal my disinterest. It was bold of me but I was hoping she wouldn't try anything with Jeremiah around.

"Go away," Jeremiah suddenly interjected, though he hadn't looked up from his book, making it hard to tell who he was addressing.

"You heard him," Simran declared, crossing her arms with a smug expression.

Exhausted by the conversation, I started to rise from my seat when suddenly, a hand shot out and forcefully pushed my shoulder, urging me to stay seated. I was caught off guard as I was firmly planted back in my seat.

"You, go away," Jeremiah reiterated, his gaze fixed intently on Simran, leaving no doubt that his words were directed at her.

Simran opened her mouth, then promptly closed it, appearing somewhat baffled, her glare intensifying. She spun on her heel and stormed off in frustration.

I couldn't help but let out a small giggle at the sight. Jeremiah looked up, raising an eyebrow at me, and I immediately stifled my laughter, feeling slightly self-conscious. He returned his attention to his book.

For some reason, I found myself wanting to avoid getting on his bad side. There was a certain intensity about him. Nevertheless, despite his rudeness, when he was engrossed in his book and not speaking, he actually made for decent company.

"Do you like Jell-O?" I asked him, attempting to strike up a conversation.

He closed his book with a sigh. "Why do you ask?"

"Because it's amazing! Why did you close your book?" I inquired.

"I shut my book 'cause I barely got through two pages with all the commotion, and if you keep throwing these little questions my way, I doubt I'm gonna get any more reading done."

"Hey! First off, it's not my fault Simran approached us, and second, I'm just trying to get to know you," I explained, coming to my own defense.

"You're trying to get to know me, and the first thing you ask about is Jell-O?" he remarked, raising an eyebrow.

"Yep," I replied, a grin tugging at my lips.

He rolled his eyes once more. "You sure like rolling your eyes," I noted.

He shrugged. "Only when you're around."

I huffed. "I'm not that bad!"

"Trust me, you are. Like that whole singing-about-being-happy thing? That ain't normal," he insisted.

"Hey, people have their little chants or rituals to pep themselves up or motivate them, right?" I explained. "I sing."

"No, you're weird," he retorted.

I couldn't help but beam. "Thanks!"

He rubbed his hand over his face and then tilted his head back, appearing thoroughly exasperated. "Someone kill me now."

I burst into laughter. "Oh, come on, I'm really not that bad!"

"You're like a unicorn vomiting rainbows, cotton candy, and flowers," he muttered under his breath.

I beamed at him. "I love unicorns! And rainbows, cotton candy, and flowers!" I exclaimed, clapping my hands together in delight.

"Imma leave," he declared abruptly, getting up.

"Alright, see ya, Jerry!" I called out cheerfully.

He turned around slowly, fixing me with a menacing glare. "Don't call me that."

I playfully pouted. "How about Jeremy?"

"No!" he replied firmly, walking away.

"Jer?" I tested, calling after him.

With no response, a triumphant grin spread across my face. "Jer it is!"

Chapter 3

"Hey, Jer!" I greeted him with a smile as I settled down beside the antisocial boy.

We had been sitting together for the past few days, and even though he mostly immersed himself in his books, I enjoyed his presence. It was just nice not to be alone. While he rarely spoke to me, except when he wanted to throw a snide remark my way, I had a feeling that he didn't mind having me around either. Otherwise, why would he keep coming back here day after day?

He gave a curt nod in acknowledgment and returned to his reading, this time it was *Catch-22* by Joseph Heller. It was crazy how fast the guy could run through a novel. He had only been half way through his last book when we first met but here he was, on to the next.

Today, I had forgotten to bring money for lunch, but since my dad had treated me to breakfast to celebrate his recent job promotion, I wasn't too bothered. Things were finally looking up for us financially since my mom's passing a few years ago.

With no luck in sight and the guys not playing on the field, I had nothing to occupy myself with. Turning to Jer, I spoke up.

"Hey, Jer?" I started.

He didn't react, so I pressed on. "What's your favorite color?" I asked, genuinely curious.

"I don't have one," he replied flatly.

"What? You have to have a favorite color! Everyone has one color they prefer," I insisted.

"Can't you just leave me alone?" he groaned, clearly irritated.

"After you tell me your favorite color!" I said, crossing my arms.

"Black, okay? It's black!" he finally relented.

"Like your soul," I whispered under my breath, thinking he might not hear me. But of course, he rolled his eyes in response.

"Now, can I get back to my book?" he asked, sounding slightly exasperated.

"You know, most boys like you don't spend their time reading. They flirt with girls, go to the gym and get drunk off weed," I pointed out.

He burst into laughter, surprising me. My eyebrows furrowed in confusion. I didn't understand what was so funny. It was quite strange seeing him laugh, but I couldn't deny that it was kind of cute—okay, really cute. His eyes crinkled at the sides, and his white teeth were on full display as he brushed his curls away from his face.

"What?" I asked, intrigued by his reaction.

"You said 'drunk off weed'!" he chuckled, trying to stifle his laughter.

"Yeah, I know," I frowned, my cheeks heating up.

His face dropped. "Wait, so you meant it?" he asked.

I nodded slowly in confusion and he burst out laughing again.

"And." he heaved."I'm guessing boys like me also get high off alcohol?" he asked.

I smiled. Now he was getting me. "Yes! Exactly!"I nodded.

He heaved again. "Stop! Just stop! You're killing me!" he breathed out.

I folded my arms. As nice as it was seeing him smile, he was starting to piss me off, excuse my language. Darn it! He was making me swear too!

After a while, he got up and wiped his eyes. "You are too funny." he sighed and shook his head.

"Okay?"

He chuckled again and picked up his book. "I can't believe you're real."

I watched him walk away, still utterly stomped on what I had said that was so funny.

✧

Ever since the encounter with Simran, she had been extremely cruel towards me. I made sure to never be alone with her and her friends.

But today seemed to be a particularly unlucky day for me. As I sat in my social studies class, waiting for the lesson to begin, Simran and her friends entered the room. Once she spotted me, a malicious smirk appeared on her face. She strutted over, looking like she had just stepped off the runway. She wore a beige strapless mini dress that clung to her figure, featuring ruffles on the front and a cascade of ruffles at the hem. A fabric rose adorned her left hip, and she finished the look with brown knee-high heeled boots.

"Rore-whore! Just the bitch I was looking for," she sneered, striding over to me. "So now you feel special, don't you?"

Confused, I responded, "What?"

Rolling her eyes in annoyance, she continued, "You feel special because Jeremiah Summers sits with you at lunch," she stated, her glare fixed on me.

I chose to remain silent, not wanting to engage with her any further. She scoffed at my lack of response. "Well, I hope you don't actually believe he likes you. He's only taking pity on you because no one else likes you. He's just trying to be nice. I've watched you guys, you know."

Okay, 'cause that's not creepy.

"And it's clear that you annoy the crap out of him. Sooner or later, he'll realize he's had enough and leave you, just like everybody else. Ian left you, your so-called 'friends' left you," she taunted, her smirk growing devious. "And so did your dead mom."

I sucked in a breath.

"Ms. Bakshi!" Mr. Turner's voice echoed through the hallway as he entered the scene, having heard the end of the exchange. He stood at the door with some students, including Jeremiah. "Principal's office now," he commanded in a stern and unwavering tone.

Simran's smug composure faltered, and she let out a sigh before reluctantly leaving the classroom. Mr. Turner walked further into the room, clearing his throat.

"Everyone, to your seats now. And Aurora, you can leave the class for a few minutes if you need to," he instructed.

Feeling dazed, I walked out of the classroom and started down the hall. Lost in my thoughts, I was brought back to reality when I heard Jeremiah's voice.

"Hey uh... Av-Am—what was it? Um... Princess?" he stumbled over his words.

I snapped out of my state, a shaky voice escaping my lips. "W-what are you doing out of class?" I asked, slightly taken aback by his presence.

"Turner said that someone should go out and make sure you're good, and I offered," he explained.

I managed a weak smile. "Thanks."

He shrugged, and we began walking down the hall together. "Wanna talk about it?" he asked, scratching the back of his neck uncomfortably. It was clear that he wasn't used to doing this kind of thing. I still appreciated his effort though.

"I—we..." I sighed, struggling to find the right words. "What she said was wrong. They... they didn't leave me, not by choice anyway... well, maybe my friends did, but not my mom and Ian."

"Ian?" he inquired.

"Yeah, he was my best friend when we were kids. He moved away, but it wasn't his choice," I explained, my voice tinged with sadness.

"And my mom, sh-she... she loved me. She wouldn't leave me," I added, my voice breaking slightly.

"I know, I know," Jeremiah reassured me. He reached out, grabbing my arm to stop me from walking, and hesitantly pulled me into a hug. I clung to him, finding comfort in his presence as tears welled up in my eyes. I despised feeling this way. I despised being sad. I was always happy and cheerful, and that's how I liked it. It just seemed like these past few weeks, I hadn't been able to maintain my usual happiness.

"Don't listen to her, okay?" Jeremiah whispered softly. I nodded, wiping away my tears.

I pulled away from his embrace, my gaze falling to his shirt. "I'm sorry for getting your shirt wet," I apologized.

He chuckled. "It's fine."

"Jer?" I said quietly.

"Hm?" he responded.

"My name's Aurora," I smiled. He smiled sheepishly and scratched the back of his head.

"Oh yeah, forgot."

After wandering the halls in silence for a while, we returned to class. It was evident that I had been crying, and as I made my way to my seat, I could feel the weight of many eyes on me.

I let out a sigh as I slumped into my seat. For the rest of the day, I decided to allow myself to be a bit less of the happy Aurora that everyone expected.

After that class, I made the decision to go home early and give myself some rest.

When I arrived home, I grabbed a tub of ice cream and settled in to watch some CSI on Netflix. It was the perfect way to spend the evening.

✧

I woke up suddenly, glancing around to see that my dad had closed my laptop and taken away the tub of ice cream I had been snacking on.

I felt relieved that it was Friday, as it meant I could finally sleep in over the weekend.

After taking a shower and brushing my teeth, I changed into a white sundress and held my black Chuck Taylors in hand. As I walked downstairs, I saw my dad cooking eggs in the kitchen.

"Good morning baby, how you feeling?" he asked with concern.

I had told him I felt sick yesterday so that I could sign out of school. "Fine, just cramps," I muttered as I sat down.

"Ah," he nodded in understanding. "Need some Advil, love? Or should I buy you some pads?" he offered, wanting to make sure I had everything I needed.

I chuckled. "No, Dad, I'm fine now." Most girls might find it awkward to talk to their dad about their period, but for me, it was a normal part of life. My mom wasn't around when I had my first one, so my dad had been there to buy me pads and endure my mood swings ever since. It was just something we dealt with, and there was no need to feel awkward about it, according to my dad's perspective.

"Okay. Eggs?" he asked, preparing to cook them for me.

I nodded eagerly, licking my lips in anticipation. He knew how much I loved eggs, so he always made sure to give me a generous portion.

After a satisfying breakfast, I made my way to school, reflecting on the events of the previous day. I realized that I shouldn't have let Simran's words get to me. I was feeling better now and understood that her negativity didn't define me.

I silently hoped that she had received appropriate consequences for her actions. It might not be the nicest thing to think, but she deserved to face the repercussions.

As I walked into the Chemistry classroom, I caught a glimpse of Simran chatting with her friends. She appeared to be the same as yesterday, with no signs of having faced any significant punishment.

Taking my seat in the third row, I pulled out my books, ready to focus on the lesson.

"Don't think this is over, Rore-whore. Because of you, I have a month of detention, and you're gonna pay for it," Simran hissed, leaning over my desk.

I remained silent, refusing to engage with her, and instead looked down at my books. My parents had always advised me not to entertain bullies, hoping that if I ignored her long enough, she would eventually leave me alone. But I had been doing that since kindergarten, and she still persisted.

What frustrated me even more was the fact that no one seemed to do anything about it. People either watched silently or turned a blind eye. I couldn't understand why everyone seemed to neglect me. I had always been kind and friendly, yet it seemed like I was invisible to them. I had always been the most approachable person in our grade, maybe even the whole school but yet after Ian left no one seemed to want to be my friend anymore.

"Bakshi, back to your seat," Ms. Erickson called out, redirecting Simran's attention. The class began, and I tried my best to focus on the lesson, pushing aside the unsettling thoughts and emotions stirred up by Simran's presence.

Chapter 4

"Alright, folks, today marks the beginning of a new project that carries twenty-five percent towards your final Literature grade. So, let's buckle down and put our best efforts into this one. It's a great opportunity to secure some marks, especially if you're unsure about the upcoming written exam. Now, let's form pairs," Mr. Dermott announced, concluding his speech with a sharp clap of his hand.

As soon as he mentioned pairing up, that familiar sense of dread washed over me. I watched as everyone quickly gravitated towards their friends, leaving the loners like me awkwardly looking around. I wished that, for once, the teacher would assign partners instead of letting us choose.

Feeling dejected, I sighed and slumped into my seat, deciding not to stress myself about it. Whoever was left without a partner could join me.

Thinking I'd be waiting a while for a partner, I was surprised when seconds later the chair beside me screeched back, and someone sat down with a sigh. When I finally mustered the energy to look up, my eyes widened, and a grin took over my face.

"Jer!" I cheered, genuinely happy to see him. He, on the other hand, rolled his eyes and rested his head in his hand, seemingly unimpressed. I had completely forgotten that he was in this class. He was always so good at blending into the background, almost like a master of invisibility.

"Alright, now that everyone is paired up, let's dive into the details of the project," Mr. Dermott began.

But my mind was wandering outside, longing to embrace nature rather than being stuck in a classroom.

"Princess?" I heard Jer's voice, and my attention snapped back to him.

"Huh?" I replied, caught off guard.

"Do you daydream often?" he asked, raising an eyebrow in curiosity.

I shook my head, still somewhat mesmerized by his perfectly shaped eyebrows. I couldn't help but wonder if he put any effort into grooming them or if they were just naturally that perfect.

"What?" I asked, realizing I had spaced out again.

He rolled his eyes. "Let's focus on the project, okay?"

I nodded, trying to shake off my distraction and concentrate on the task at hand. "Sure, let's do this!"

"Great. So, first, we need to choose a play," Jer said.

"Wait," I interjected, feeling lost, "before we dive in, could you explain what exactly the project entails? Because, honestly, I'm not entirely sure what Mr. Kermit said."

Jer looked at me, a puzzled expression on his face. "Mr. Kermit?"

Oops, did I say that out loud?

"Okay, so I know it's not nice, but doesn't Mr. Dermot sound just a tad like Kermit the Frog?" I whispered, trying to suppress a laugh. His nasally voice was starting to get on my nerves, but I didn't mean any offense to Kermit, of course.

Jer couldn't help but smirk, attempting to stifle his laughter. "You're something else," he said, shaking his head.

I grinned. "Thanks!"

Turning our attention to the project, Jer explained the task at hand. "For this project, we have to pick a Shakespearean play and give it a modern twist or adapt it to our lives."

My enthusiasm waned as I groaned, "Ugh, I've never been a fan of these kinds of projects."

"Don't worry, we've got this," he reassured me with a confident smile. "I enjoy reading, and I'm pretty good at writing, so we'll make it work."

"Oh, quite the modest one, aren't you?" I mumbled under my breath, half-joking. Jer frowned.

"Alright, let's focus on picking a play first," he said, shaking his head lightly. I thought for a moment before a spark of inspiration hit me.

"Romeo and Juliet?" I exclaimed with excitement, only to be quickly shut down by Jer.

"No. Too Cliché."

Deflated, I slumped back into my seat. "Fine, fine. Any ideas then?"

After some contemplation, Jer finally suggested, "How about 'Merchant of Venice'? It's got some intriguing themes and characters we can work with."

I shrugged nonchalantly, not particularly caring about the choice. "Sure, sounds good to me."

We jotted down 'Merchant of Venice' on our sheet, and Mr. Dermott seemed satisfied with our decision, moving on to the next group.

"Now, don't just sit there, get those creative gears turning! Think about the plot, character traits, and the differences between Shakespeare's time and now. And don't forget to find similarities as well. Let your pens dance on those papers!" he encouraged.

"Since the original play has quite a large cast, I don't think we should include as many characters. It might get confusing."Jer said, making notes on the sheet of paper

"And there are a few scenes we can definitely do without," I added, trying to streamline our adaptation.

Jer nodded in agreement, "For sure. We can trim the story down to keep it interesting and impactful."

"What do you think about giving the characters more modern names?"

After lunch, I caught up with Jeremiah as he was about to head to his next class.

"Hey, hold up a sec," I said.

"What?" he snapped back.

"We need to work on our project after school," I told him quietly, confused by his tone.

He let out a sigh, realizing the truth in my words. "Yeah, you're right. Let's meet up after school."

"I'd offer to do it at my place, but my dad is pretty strict about having boys over," I explained, feeling a little embarrassed.

Jeremiah raised an eyebrow. "Even for schoolwork? We can't do it at my house either."

"Why not?" I asked, crossing my arms.

His expression hardened as he replied, "It's just not an option, okay? I can't have you come over."

I followed him as he walked, still puzzled by his response. "Alright, but where can we work on it then?" I questioned.

"The library," he suggested.

"We can't, it's under renovation," I pointed out.

Jeremiah thought for a moment before clarifying, "The public library. There's one like fifteen minutes away."

"Oh," I sheepishly admitted, "I'm actually banned from there."

His eyes widened in disbelief. "You're banned from the library? Why?"

I rolled my eyes playfully. "Apparently, singing and skipping around in the library isn't allowed. Go figure."

He looked at me like I was crazy. "There's definitely something wrong with you."

"Thank you!" I said with a grin. "So, where else could we go?"

"We'll have to head downtown," he suggested. "Are you free after school?"

I responded without hesitation, "Yep, I'm always free after school."

With our plan set, we agreed to meet outside the school later in the day.

After school, I practically skipped down the stairs of the entrance, my excitement for the project bubbling within me. As I scanned the area for Jer, I couldn't spot him anywhere. So, I leaned against the stairs' railing, patiently waiting.

I couldn't help but feel a tad hopeful about this project. Jer was known for his perpetual frowns and constant anger, but I couldn't help but wonder if spending time with him would somehow soften his rough edges. I know, I know, it's a typical "trying to change a guy" scenario, but I couldn't help myself.

Lost in my thoughts, I didn't notice Jer approaching until I heard his voice, calling me "Princess." I turned to see him walking down the stairs.

As he passed me, I followed him, feeling defensive. "Hey, my name isn't that hard to remember. You keep calling me Princess. But I don't act like one!"

"Trust me, you do."

I whined, "I don't!"

He didn't seem to be taking my protest seriously, just shrugged, and continued walking. "Well, that's just my opinion. And since I'm letting you call me Jer, I get to call you whatever I want."

I huffed, realizing there was no point in arguing with him. I quickened my pace to catch up with his longer legs, genuinely curious about his choice of transportation.

I wondered if he had a cool car or maybe even a motorbike. We finally stopped in front of a sleek black Nissan, and I couldn't hide my disappointment. Although it was a decent car, I had secretly hoped for something more adventurous.

"Quit standing around and get in!" Jer snapped.

I quickly walked around to the passenger side and got in. "Always so grumpy."

He got into the car, and I fastened my seat belt, sighing as I leaned my head against the window. The silence inside the car started to get to me, making the ride feel monotonous and dull.

"You good?" Jer's voice broke the silence, and I looked over to find concern etched on his face.

I shrugged indifferently, not wanting to admit that him randomly snapping at me all the time affected my mood. He let out a sigh.

"I'm sorry," he mumbled, and I couldn't help but be taken aback. Jer didn't seem like the type to apologize often but here he was saying sorry to me again.

"For snapping at you," he continued, "If we're going to work on this project together, I need to be nicer, I guess. I'm just used to being alone."

His admission made me smile, and I replied, "It's fine."

Deep down, I knew Jer wasn't a bad person. He had proven that when he came to comfort me after what Simran had said, and he always put up with my quirks, even though I knew I annoyed him at times. He had a kind heart beneath that gruff exterior.

"We're here," he announced as he turned off the engine. "Try not to get us banned, okay?"

I rolled my eyes. "I'll do my best."

Exiting the car, we made our way towards the building. It was much bigger than the one closer to us, but I couldn't help but feel a sense of loyalty to our local one, which had its own charm, despite them banning me.

Jer held the door open for me, and I appreciated the small gesture. We found a vacant table and settled down, taking out our materials to work on the project.

"So, any ideas for Antonio's character profile?" Jer asked, starting the discussion.

"We could change his name to Anthony," I suggested.

"Okay, what about the other characters? Are we changing all their names?" he inquired, jotting down notes in his notebook.

"Um, no," I said, smiling. "I think Portia and Nerissa are cute names. We can leave them as they are."

"And Bassanio?" he questioned.

"Oh, we definitely need to change that. How about... Ben?" I suggested.

Jer looked puzzled. "How do you go from Bassanio to Ben?"

"It's completely logical!" I argued. "B for Bassanio, B for Ben."

He facepalmed, rejecting the idea. "We're not using Ben."

"But—"

"No."

"But—"

"No!"

✧

"Just drop me off here, please. I don't want my dad to see your car," I said to Jer as he pulled over a couple of houses down from mine.

"No problem. Seems I was somewhat right about you, living in a boujee neighbourhood." Jer mumbled, looking around.

"Stop, not this again." I sighed.

He held up his arms in defense. "All I'm saying is it must be nice. Anyway, I want to get this project done as soon as possible, so we gotta go to that library every day after school, cool?" he stated with determination.

I groaned. "Ugh, fine. Bye."

He nodded, and I closed the car door as he drove off. As I unlocked the door to my house, I heard someone calling my name from behind me. I turned around and couldn't help but break into a wide smile. A girl, dressed in a stylish purple cropped cardigan and a charming purple and pink checkered skirt, hurried over to me.

"Kiyana!" I shrieked.

Kiyana lived across the street from me and was my only friend. When you're the only two black girls living in a predominantly white neighbourhood, you tend to gravitate towards each other. Unfortunately she attended a private school close by as per her parents wishes. As she ran towards me, her braids bounced around her face.

"Hey, babe!" she said, hugging me. "What's up?"

We both walked into my house, and I couldn't help but tease her. "Okay, so you come running out of your house calling frantically for me, and then ask me what's up?"

She laughed. "I just really have something to tell you, but I'm kinda embarrassed."

I became intrigued. "What is it? Is it about a boy?"

She twirled one of her braids with her finger, looking down.

"Yeah...kinda."

"Tell me!" I demanded, playfully smacking her arm.

"Okay, so remember how I started taking dance classes?" she asked. I nodded, trying not to discourage her even though I wasn't sure dancing was her forte.

"Well, I was struggling in class, and the instructor's brother, who was helping out that day, offered to help me after class," she grinned. "We kinda hit it off, and guess what? He actually goes to your school!"

"Really? What's his name?" I asked, taking a cup of chocolate pudding from the fridge.

She grabbed a spoon and snatched some of my pudding. "Hey! Get your own!" I whined, but she just stuck her tongue out and ate it.

"His name is Ryan Olssen," she revealed.

"I think I know him," I said, though truth be told, I only recently noticed Jer in my classes, so who knows.

"Cool!" she clapped her hands. "I'm so happy! I really like him, and I think he really likes me. We're actually moving pretty fast."

"That's great, Kiki! I'm happy for you," I smiled.

She beamed. "So what about you?"

"What do you mean?"

"You know what I mean," she said, poking my shoulder. "Come on, Rory, you must have something to tell me. You never seem to."

I let out a sigh. "Well, there is something," I admitted.

"What?" she asked excitedly. Kiyana and I were both pretty energetic people, and my dad hated when we hung out around him. He said it was like torture.

"Okay, so I just met this guy named Jeremiah—"

"Hold up a second! A guy?" she asked, and when I nodded, she screamed. "Oh my gosh, Aurora, you've never told me about a boy!"

"Well, we're only friends Kiyana, if you could even call it that, but he sits with me at lunch and we're doing a project together."

"Do you like him?"

"I'm not sure. I definitely want to get to know him. He seems really interesting."

"Well I'm happy you're finally making friends in school." she said.

"Me too."I said grinning back. "By the way, your little nickname for Simran got me in trouble the other day."

Her eyes widened. "Don't tell me you actually used it on her."

I nodded slowly and she grimaced.

"Oh no, Rory," she shook her head, patting my cheek. "You poor, naive girl."

"What does it even mean anyway?" I asked, slapping her hand away. "What is 'ran through'?"

"It means she's had multiple sexual—"

"Oh my! That's enough, I don't want to know. I can't believe you made me say that." I grabbed my chest in horror.

"Girl, I never told you to say it to her face. That's on you."

"Okay lesson learned, do not repeat Kiyana's insults." I sighed, rubbing my forehead. "How about we watch T.V?"

She nodded, following me into the living room. "Sounds good."

"Disney?" I asked, plopping down on the couch.. I know, I know a seventeen-year-old watching Disney Channel? Well, I don't care. I will love Disney *forever.*

"Sure." she laughed.

Chapter 5

For the past week, Jer and I had been working non-stop on our project. He was really determined to get it done as soon as possible, and he even tried to convince me to work on it during lunch, but I protested, of course.

"Hey, Jer!" I greeted him with a smile as he sat beside me for lunch. "You're usually here first. What took you so long?" I asked, curious about his delay.

"Nothing," he replied quickly, but something seemed off. I furrowed my eyebrows at him, noticing a strange scent.

Shaking it off, I began eating my fries, but I couldn't shake the feeling of someone's gaze on me. I looked up to see a guy staring directly at me as he walked past the bleachers. His eyes then shifted to Jer, and he shot him a glaring look before focusing back on me again. He looked familiar, but I couldn't place where I knew him from.

Jer remained unaware of the guy's presence, still looking down. "Jer?" I asked, concerned.

He glanced up briefly, and his eyes were bloodshot red. "A-are you okay?" I inquired further.

He threw his head back with a groan and then giggled a little to my surprise. "It's all gucci," he whined. "Relax, homie."

I arched an eyebrow in surprise; this wasn't how Jeremiah spoke, he seemed somewhat out of it. He looked disheveled, his gray baggy cargo pants hanging lower than usual, the buttons of his black flannel misaligned. Sweat trickled down his forehead, his hair clinging damply to his face.

"Have you ever wondered why the fruit 'oranges' are named after their colour but other fruits aren't? Like why aren't bananas called 'yellows'?"

I hesitated for a moment, unsure of how to respond, before stuffing a few fries into my mouth.

Jeremiah's eyes gleamed with interest as he spotted my tray of food. Without asking, he reached over and grabbed a handful of my fries, swiftly devouring them just as I had done.

"Damn, these fries are so good. Now I see why you always ordering them," he mumbled in surprise. I nodded in agreement, subtly shifting my tray out of his reach.

We didn't exchange much more during lunch, and when the bell rang, I got up and turned to him. "You sure you're fine?" I asked, wanting to make sure he was okay.

"Yeah, baby," he smiled, rubbing his temples before slowly getting up. I offered my support as he swayed slightly, giggling again. He grabbed his bag and walked past me, leaving me bewildered by the whole ordeal.

Throughout my next class, I couldn't help but worry about him.

Later, when I went to my locker to grab some books, I noticed Jer's locker from a distance. I watched as he sluggishly put books into his bag, but my view was suddenly blocked by someone standing in front of me—a tall guy with sandy blonde hair and broad shoulders, dressed in casual gym wear.

He smiled and brushed his hair out of his face. "You're Aurora Winters, right?" he asked.

I nodded, slightly surprised that he knew my name. "Yes, that's me," I replied, extending my hand.

"I'm Ryan Olssen, Kiyana's friend," he introduced himself.

My eyes widened in recognition. "Oh, you!" I responded.

Ryan chuckled. "Yeah, me. I wanted to talk to you," he said, his expression turning serious.

"Oh, okay," I replied hesitantly, not sure what he wanted to discuss.

He sighed, clearly concerned. "I'm only telling you this because I care about Kiyana, and you're her friend. It's about Jeremiah."

Curiosity piqued, I asked, "What about him?"

"He's not someone you want to hang around with, Aurora. He's bad news. You noticed he was acting weird at lunch, right?" he questioned. I nodded in agreement.

"That's because he was high."

"What?" My shock was evident, struggling to believe what I was hearing.

"He was with a bunch of guys smoking at the back of the school, saw him with my own two eyes. This may just be a rumour but apparently he also deals drugs, like the harder stuff. He's involved in gambling and gangs and other messed up stuff. He isn't the kind of guy you want to be friends with."

I stared at him, blankly, not sure how to respond to such a revelation.

Ryan continued, "A few years ago he also got in a fight with my uncle Ronny, I wasn't there so I don't really know much but Jeremiah stabbed him and I remember him being rushed to hospital. Ronny won't speak of the incident so I can't really elaborate but I just thought you should know."

"Jeremiah?" I asked, needing to confirm if he had the right guy.

Ryan nodded solemnly. "Like I said, I care about Kiyana, and I feel obliged to help her friend out, so that's why I'm telling you this. You don't have to listen to me, and you can still hang out with him if you want, but I just wanted you to know so be careful."

"Thank you," I whispered, feeling grateful for the warning. Ryan gave me another small smile and squeezed my shoulder before walking away.

Feeling overwhelmed, I slumped against my locker. Everyone else was already in class by now. I couldn't believe what I had just heard. Jeremiah, the quiet guy who loved to read and be by himself, was allegedly involved in drugs and a stabbing?

The drugs? It seemed impossible, but his strange behavior at lunch made it plausible. But stabbing someone? I couldn't believe my ears. He was everything I was against if it was true, and I didn't know how to process the information.

I was supposed to meet him at the library after school, but now I was torn between avoiding him or confronting him about what I'd heard.

In a bit of a daze, I walked to my next class, my mind consumed with thoughts and uncertainties.

"Ms. Winters, why are you late?" Ms. Rowe asked, with a sigh.

"Sorry, I felt a little sick. I was in the bathroom," I replied quietly.

"Are you alright now? Do you want to go see the nurse?" she inquired. The great thing about being a good student was that teachers always believed you and trusted your explanations.

I considered telling her I was fine, but then an idea struck me. If I went to the nurse and asked to call home, I could leave school early and avoid going to the library with Jer. I had never missed a class before, it was kind of exhilarating actually!

"I think I'll go see the nurse," I decided, adding a pained expression for good measure.

Later that day, Kiyana came over after her dance class and sank down beside me on the couch.

"Hey, Ryan told me everything about you and this Jeremiah guy," she said, placing her arm around my shoulder, trying to show her support.

I brought my knees up to my chest. "I don't know what to do, Kiyana. I can't believe he would do that kind of stuff, but it's not like I know him well enough to say that he doesn't," I sighed, feeling torn and disappointed.

She rubbed my arm gently. "It's not fair, is it?"

"No, it's not," I sighed again, feeling overwhelmed. "I finally had a friend, and he just had to end up being a drug dealer or...stabber? Or Whatever."

Thankfully, tomorrow would be Saturday, so I didn't have to face Jeremiah for at least two days. Maybe I'd even pretend to be sick on Monday to avoid him.

"Rory, whatever you decide to do, just be careful, okay?" Kiyana advised, expressing her concern.

I nodded, appreciating her presence.

After staying home from school on Monday and Tuesday, my dad thought it was time for me to go back.

Which meant I was feeling extra grumpy this morning.

"Hey, honey! Pancakes?" my dad asked, trying to cheer me up.

I nodded groggily and slumped down in a chair. "You feeling better?" he asked, showing genuine concern for my well-being.

"No."

He sighed, a hint of frustration evident in his voice. "Aurora, you're my daughter. I know you. I know you're not really sick. What are you avoiding? Is it Simran again?"

I groaned. "Dad, no, it's nothing. I don't want to talk about it right now," I mumbled.

He didn't press further, leaving me to think about what to do when I got to school. What was I going to do about Jer?

Arriving at school, I quickly walked to my first class after visiting my locker. I had managed to avoid Jer so far, but it was only first period, so that wasn't saying much.

Entering the classroom, I felt relieved to see that I didn't have this class with Jer.

However, the next period was American Literature, and I felt distraught. On one hand, I didn't want to skip class because I never did that; it was a bad thing to do. But on the other hand, I dreaded working on the project with Jer. Going home wasn't an option since my dad had forced me to attend school.

Ultimately, I felt stuck with no good choices.

As I slowly walked to Lit, dreading going inside, an idea suddenly popped into my head. I quickly approached the teacher with my famous pained expression.

"Um, sir?" I said quietly, trying to appear distressed.

He looked up, furrowing his eyebrows in concern. "You okay?"

Scanning the room, I spotted Jer sitting in his seat, engrossed in his book, *The Fortune Men* by Nadifa Mohamed. A pang of guilt washed over me; after all, this was an important project, and avoiding him might not be the best solution.

"Uh, I'm on my period and my cramps are really bad. Can I go to the restroom?" I whispered discreetly, touching my stomach and scrunching my face to make it believable.

He winced sympathetically and nodded. "Yeah, sure. Take as long as you need," he said, allowing me to leave the class. I gave him a pained smile before scurrying out to the restroom.

During lunchtime, I decided to go to the study hall instead of sitting in my usual spot at the bleachers, knowing he'd be there. By the end of the day, I had successfully avoided Jer.

Feeling relieved, I walked out of the school, ready to head home, when suddenly someone grabbed my arm.

"What the hell are you doing?" Jer demanded, spinning me around to face him.

I removed my hand from his hold and took a step back. "I-I'm walking," I stuttered, trying to avoid the situation.

"You know that's not what I meant, Princess," Jer replied.

"What do you mean, then?" I asked, dumbly.

"You haven't been in school for the last two days. When you finally show up, you skip Lit, you don't come to lunch, and now you're going home when we're supposed to work on our project," he pointed out, concern evident in his voice.

"W-well, I was feeling sick," I shrugged, not wanting to reveal the real reason for my absence.

"You don't look sick to me, Princess. Just tell me what's going on," he urged.

I rubbed my arm, looking up at him. It was hard to believe that this guy, who seemed to care about school and education, could be involved in something as serious as dealing drugs.

His expression shifted, like a realization was dawning upon him. "What?" I asked quietly.

"You heard something, didn't you? About me? That's why you're avoiding me," he said.

I stayed silent, nervously biting my lip.

He sniffed, nodding with understanding. "Wanna know how I know? The way you're looking at me. I thought you were the one person who didn't think of me like I'm some delinquent. You were the only person who talked to me while everyone else was too scared to. You were the only one who stood up to me," he said, his voice tinged with disappointment.

"On that first day, you walked up to me and told me to get up from your seat. I was surprised; no one in this school has ever talked to me like that. I thought I had finally found someone who saw me as an actual person, but I guess I was wrong."

He turned away, but I pulled him back before he could distance himself further.

"Jer, what was I supposed to think, huh? Last week at lunch, were you or were you not high?" I asked, crossing my arms. Aware that people were staring as they walked by, I didn't care.

He bit his lip and looked down, admitting, "Exactly." I whispered.

Frustration rising, I turned my back on him, but he swiftly spun me around again.

"Okay, I—" he stopped, noticing the prying eyes around us, and then pulled me into a corner for more privacy.

"I was high, but, but you need to let me explain," he pleaded, desperately seeking a chance to clarify.

"Why? Why should I believe anything you say? There you were, making me feel bad when you actually are dealing drugs," I stated, feeling hurt and betrayed.

"Hey, hey, who said anything about dealing drugs? I admitted I was high, not that I dealt drugs," Jer clarified defensively.

"So you don't deal them?" I asked, seeking further clarification.

"Well, technically I do—" Jer started to explain, but I interrupted him, feeling frustrated.

"Okay, I'm leaving. You're just trying to waste my time," I said, not wanting to listen to any excuses. Before I could turn away, he spoke up.

"You're not my mother, Aurora. What does it matter if I deal a bit of weed? It's legal in a lot of places. You're acting like I killed someone!" Jer retorted defensively.

"Well, apparently you stabbed someone too, so who knows? Maybe you have," I shot back, my emotions getting the better of me.

His mouth shut instantly. "I didn't expect you to be the type of girl to listen to rumours, Aurora," he bit out.

"Well, Jeremiah, I didn't expect you to be the kind of person involved in illegal activities, but here we are," I replied.

I understood that maybe selling weed wasn't such a big deal, but the gambling, gangs and stabbing someone too? I didn't know if I could be friends with someone like that.

"You're not being fair, just let me explain," he pleaded, attempting to stop me from leaving.

I crossed my arms, indicating that he had my attention but that he needed to provide a convincing explanation.

He sighed, a mixture of guilt and sincerity in his eyes. "My cousin, Derrick, deals, and he asked me to sell at our school. I know it's wrong, but I was just helping him out, and I dunno why I smoked too, I just did. I'm sorry, but that was the only time I've ever been high," he said, making eye contact to convey his honesty.

"Really?" I asked, still skeptical.

He nodded earnestly. "Yes, I swear."

"And the stabbing?" I inquired, still unsure if he was being truthful.

"I don't really wanna talk about that. It's a hard topic. Just know that me and the guy involved are on really good terms," he replied.

I sighed, understanding that some things might be difficult for him to discuss. I couldn't expect him to open up fully so soon. While I was still wary, I wanted to give him another chance. After all, he was my first friend in a long time.

"Okay, I believe you," I whispered, hesitantly.

"Will you stop ignoring me?" Jer asked, hoping for a resolution.

"Will you stop selling drugs for your cousin?" I asked firmly.

He groaned, throwing his head back.

"Do you wanna continue our project or not? I know you care about your grades but I will not be canoodling with a dealer. It's just not my thing."

He rolled his eyes and sighed. "Yeah, fine. I promise."

I smiled. "Okay, let's get on with that project then," I said, ready to move past this whole issue and focus on our school work.

He blew out a relieved breath and nodded. "Agreed. Let's go."

As we walked towards the car park, I couldn't help but notice how empty it was, in the time we had been arguing, most people had left for home. My eyes landed on a vehicle that made my heart skip a beat.

"Oh. My. God," I said, stopping in my tracks.

Jer whined, "What now?"

"Is that yours?" I whispered excitedly, pointing towards a sleek black and gray motorbike.

I think he mistook my excitement for fear and groaned, "Please don't tell me you're scared."

"Scared? No way," I replied, running over to the motorbike and admiring it. "Shiny!" I exclaimed, thrilled by the unexpected sight. "Don't touch," he said, pulling my hand away as I reached out. I went to use my other hand. "Princess, stop!"

"But it's so shiny," I pouted, unable to resist the allure of the sleek motorbike.

He gave me a flat look. "Here," he said, passing me a helmet from the helmet compartment.

I took the helmet and placed it on my head as Jer grabbed another one for himself before closing the compartment.

Once he was on the bike, he held out his hand to help me get on. I squealed with excitement and clapped my hands. "This is so exciting!"

"Would you just wrap your arms around my waist? Don't want you flying off," he said, reminding me to hold on tight.

As he revved the engine, we took off, leaving the parking lot behind. I couldn't help but notice Simran, standing with her friends by her car, watching us as we rode away. I knew this wouldn't sit well with her, but I was too caught up in the thrill of the moment to care.

The wind ran through my hair, and the world around me became a blur of streaks and lights. It was exhilarating, and I couldn't help the wide grin on my face.

Eventually, we arrived at the library, and I was a little sad that the ride was over.

"Hey, could you maybe let go?" Jer asked, bringing me back to reality.

I realized I was still holding onto him tightly, even after we had stopped.

Blushing, I quickly let go and tried to dismount the bike, but I ended up falling face-first onto the ground. To make matters worse, my sundress had blown up in the fall, barely covering my butt and revealing my Spongebob knickers.

I felt like disappearing from the face of the earth. How could I have embarrassed myself that much in just a few seconds?

As I lay on the ground in shame, two strong arms pulled me up by my armpits. I didn't dare to turn around and just stood there, mortified.

"You okay?" Jer asked, concerned.

I nodded but still didn't dare to look at him.

"Are you sure?" he asked, walking in front of me.

I nodded again, keeping my gaze down.

"Okay," he said with uncertainty. "Let's go then."

I followed him into the library, trying to forget what had just happened. At the door, he stopped and turned to face me.

"Hey, Princess?" he called.

"Yeah?" I replied, still feeling embarrassed.

"Spongebob? I dunno, I just felt like you were more of a Hello Kitty type of girl," he teased with a smirk.

My face turned bright red, feeling both mortified and caught off guard by his comment. He held the door open for me, and I quickly walked past him, keeping my head down.

When we felt satisfied with our progress on the project, we decided to pack up and head home. I was pretty excited about going on the motorcycle again, secretly hoping I wouldn't embarrass myself this time.

I gave Jer my address, and we were off.

A few houses away from my place, he slowed down to a stop. Before I could attempt to dismount, he stopped me.

"Let me help. Seeing your cartoon-themed underwear once today was enough for me," he teased.

"Oh, shut up," I said, blushing. He held out his hand, and I grabbed it to jump off the bike.

I pouted as I stared at his motorcycle. "What?" he asked, curious about my expression.

"I wish the ride to my house was longer," I confessed.

"Why? Because you love spending time with me?" he asked, a cocky grin on his face.

"No, Jer, because I really enjoyed the bike ride," I clarified.

"Well, how about I take you to school on it tomorrow?" he offered.

"Really?" I asked excitedly.

He nodded. "Yeah, sure."

"Yay!" I clapped my hands in excitement. "Thanks, Jer."

"No problem," he said, amused by my enthusiasm. "I'll see you tomorrow?" he confirmed.

I nodded eagerly. He revved the engine, getting ready to leave.

"Bye!" I said, raising my voice over the noise, and he nodded before zooming off.

I grinned, watching him ride away, and then continued walking the rest of the way home.

Chapter 6

The next day, I waited for Jer a few houses before mine, ensuring that my dad wouldn't be able to see us leave on the motorcycle.

As I stood there, I realized it would have been a good idea to get Jer's number since I didn't know when he would come by.

I didn't have to wait for long; after less than ten minutes, his bike slowed to a stop in front of me. He opened the bike compartment and handed me his spare helmet. With his help, I got on, wrapping my arms around him securely.

"Hey!" I greeted.

"Hi," he replied, and without further ado, he zoomed off.

I was once again both exhilarated and a little upset when we arrived at school. Sighing, I let him help me off the bike.

He got off as well, skillfully kicking the stand down. After taking off our helmets, he placed them back in the compartment.

"Enjoy the ride?" he asked, looking at me with a small smile playing on his lips.

"Yep!" I smiled back, grabbing my bag from him. "Thanks for offering to pick me up. It was really sweet of you."

He shrugged nonchalantly. "I pass by your house anyway, so it's no big deal."

I raised an eyebrow, skeptically. "Right."

We walked side by side towards the entrance, but as I looked around, I noticed people staring at us as we walked past them. The pace of my steps slowed as more and more people stopped to gawk.

Jer seemed to notice the staring too and turned to me with a raised eyebrow, silently questioning the situation.

"Have any idea why more than half of these people are staring at us?" Jer asked.

"Not entirely sure, but it might have something to do with us walking into school together," I replied.

"We sit together at lunch, and you're my project partner. People already see us together a lot," he pointed out.

"Yeah, but not many people sit outside, especially in this weather. And Lit doesn't really count; that's just for school work. This is like the first time people have seen us together outside of our usual spots," I explained.

"The two school 'loners' united, and now everyone is talking about it," he muttered.

✧

I groaned, leaning back in my chair. "Jer, we've done loads! Can't we stop?" I asked, feeling a little overwhelmed with the project.

"Come on, Princess, let's just finish this scene," he insisted.

I sighed heavily. He rolled his eyes and placed his pen on his notebook.

"How 'bout I make you a deal? For every scene we finish, we can do something fun – your choice, of course," he suggested.

My eyes widened with excitement. "Really?" I asked.

"Yeah, right after we're done with the scene, we can leave and do whatever you want," he confirmed.

"And you'll actually participate?" I asked skeptically.

He nodded, looking exasperated. "Yes, I promise."

"Just to clarify, you'll have to spend even more time with me," I pointed out.

He rolled his eyes again. "I know that. What's the big deal? We're friends, right?" he said casually.

I nodded and smiled, happy to hear him say that. We had been acting more like friends and we're a lot less at each other's throats recently, and I wasn't entirely sure if we were friends or not. Now, I had my confirmation.

I clapped my hands happily. "Okay, let's get this scene done!"

"Shhh!" someone hushed me from afar.

I made a face at the back of their head, not caring about the interruption, and we got back to work.

I hadn't been paying as much attention to the project as I should have because I was busy thinking of what we could do for fun. Ideas raced through my mind, and then it hit me.

"Ice skating!" I announced with enthusiasm.

"Ice skating?" he asked skeptically as we walked to his motorbike.

"Yes! It'll be fun!" I said, my excitement evident. "I haven't been ice skating in a while."

"I've never been ice skating," Jer admitted.

I gasped, genuinely surprised. "Never?"

"Never," he answered, sarcastically. "Believe it or not, skating on ice isn't really my thing."

"Oh wow, this is more important than I thought," I muttered, ignoring his tone. "I must teach you how to skate. Don't worry, I'm pretty good, so you'll learn quickly."

"Oh, how modest," he teased, mimicking my voice.

I stuck my tongue out playfully at him as we put on our helmets.

I directed him to the closest ice skating rink. When we arrived, he slowed to a stop and helped me off his bike before getting off himself.

I grabbed his arm and excitedly dragged him inside. "I can't wait! I can't wait! I can't wait!" I repeated with excitement.

He shook his head, amused, as I pulled him along.

Inside, we got our boots and started putting them on. I waited for Jer as he struggled with them.

"Do you need help?" I asked, genuinely concerned.

"Nah, I'm a grown man. I know what I'm doing," he grumbled, trying to get the boots on.

After a little while, he let out a frustrated sigh. "Maybe I need a bigger size."

"Well then, get one, Jer! We don't have all day!" I said, trying to hide my laughter.

Finally, when he had the right-sized boots on, we stepped onto the ice.

"You know what, I'm not so sure about this anymore," Jer said, wobbling on the ice and quickly latching onto the railings for support.

"It's too late to back down now," I playfully told him, grabbing his arm and steadying him. "Now come on."

After ten minutes of me trying to drag him along the ice, he groaned.

"I can't do this," Jer said, frustration evident in his voice. He wobbled, and I reached out to steady him.

"Yes, you can. You're just not making an effort," I said, crossing my arms.

"Hey, don't let go! I'm on the ice, what else do you want from me?" he retorted, trying to reach for my support again. "If anyone I knew caught me doing this shit, I would be clowned for the rest of my life."

"Who cares? It doesn't matter what other people think, Jer. Just have fun," I insisted, holding out my hand expectantly. He sighed and reluctantly grabbed my hand. I tried not to let it show, but my heart was racing. He was holding my hand. My hand!

It was large and callous, yet surprisingly soft, and it fit perfectly around mine. I kind of wanted to squeal with excitement.

"Hey, you good?" he asked.

"Hmm?" I asked, trying to act nonchalant.

"You look like you're having trouble breathing," he remarked.

I scoffed, trying to regain my composure. "No, I'm, like, totally chill," I shrugged.

"Uh-huh," he said, sounding unconvinced.

As we continued to skate, I couldn't help but notice that we were both gliding on the ice now. Jer was actually skating! He seemed to have found his balance.

"Hey, you're doing it," I pointed out happily.

He scrunched his eyebrows and looked down, surprised by his newfound skating ability. "Oh yeah, I am," he said. "I honestly didn't even notice."

"You're a natural," I praised, genuinely impressed.

"Thanks," he said with a slight smile.

"Crap." he muttered after a while, his expression changing.

I furrowed my eyebrows, concerned. "What's up?"

"Her," he replied, nodding his head in a particular direction.

I turned to look and saw Simran Bakshi standing there with a few of her friends. She didn't look happy at all. On the other hand, her friends appeared utterly shocked to see us together, ice skating, while holding hands.

I knew the way it looked. She probably thought we were on a date. Simran's presence always bothered me, and now with Jer thrown into the mix, I didn't feel like skating anymore. Simran had been a lifelong bully, mostly through hurtful words, but they still cut deep. Finally finding a friend was a relief, but why did it have to be someone she had a crush on?

I wished Simran would just leave me alone.

Jer looked at me curiously, and I forced a smile despite feeling sad. "Maybe we should call it a night, what do you say?" I suggested, slowing down.

"Sounds like a plan," Jer agreed. "Enough excitement for one day."

As we passed Simran and her friends, I kept my head down, and Jer shielded me from their view. We walked together to the parking lot in silence.

"Is she bothering you again?"

I looked down at the ground, thinking about his question. I didn't know whether to put on a brave face or tell him the truth about how she treated me. After all, we are friends now, right?

Before I could answer, Jer reassured me, "You can tell me; I'm here if you need to talk." We stopped at his bike, twirled a strand of my hair, feeling uncertain.

It felt strange. Jer and I had grown closer, but I hadn't expected this level of openness. Could I confide in him? I gazed at him thoughtfully, biting my lip as the lamp post illuminated his face, revealing his expectant expression.

"She's basically been bothering me my whole life," I finally admitted.

"Wait, for real?" he asked, surprised. I sighed with a nod.

He clicked his tongue in disapproval. "I didn't realize it was a regular thing."

Silence hung between us. Jer broke it, saying, "You know, I kinda miss your upbeat energy right now, seeing you like this is weird. What if I talk to Simran and try to sort this out?"

I hesitated, worried it might make things worse. "I don't know if that's a good idea, Jer. Confronting her might just make her angrier."

He seemed determined to help. "Well, she likes me, doesn't she?" he asked with a hint of humour.

I nodded slowly, not sure where he was going with this.

"So, I'll just work my charm on her," he said with a playful pose and a hand through his hair. It made me giggle, it was cute that he didn't mind looking silly to cheer me up.

"Charm, where?" I teased.

He playfully pushed my arm. "Hey! Bottom line is, I'll get her off your back, okay?"

I nodded, not entirely convinced but willing to give it a try. Jer handed me a helmet and smirked.

"Now," he said, helping me buckle it, "Get your pretty little ass on the bike."

Chapter 7

"Jer, wait!"

"What now?" he asked, sounding exasperated.

"Um..." I hesitated, thinking of something to say.

"Princess, stop stalling. I'll be real quick, just a minute," he assured me.

"But—" I tried to protest.

"Aurora, I'm just trying to help. Let me handle this, okay?" The use of my actual name silenced me.

He got up and walked down the bleachers toward where Simran and her friends sat, their attention divided between the football team's practice and us. It seemed like Simran was more interested in observing our interaction.

I watched intently as Jer stopped in front of her, his expression unreadable. He spoke to her slowly, almost like he was talking to a child, and pointed in my direction a few times, causing my cheeks to burn as people started to notice. Simran glared at me every chance she got while Jer continued with his very...very long warning. When he finally finished, he let out a sigh and returned to me.

"Well?" I asked anxiously.

"She promised to leave you alone."

"Really?"

"Yes, really. Now," he said, pulling out a tattered copy of *To Kill a Mockingbird* out of his bag, "let's enjoy our lunch in silence. You can eat, and I'll read, okay?" This time, he spoke to me as if I were a child.

I nodded and went back to eating my grapes.

Despite the brief resolution, I couldn't help glancing at Simran. She was already staring at me, and when our gazes met, she smirked.

I knew it wouldn't be so easy to get her off my back.

It was the period after lunch and I was walking to my locker to get my books but before I could two arms latched onto mine. I looked to either side of me to see Simran's friends. My face paled and I started to struggle.

"Woah, calm down." the blonde one said.

"Yeah, I'm Mona and that's Chrissy, we're not going to hurt you." said the one with jet black hair.

Chrissy turned to her. "Why would you introduce us? What do you think this is?"

"I dunno, I've never kidnapped someone before!" Mona said through gritted teeth.

While they were distracted I tried again to pull my arms from their hold.

"Listen. If Simran can't get Jer away from you, she's going to get you away from Jer. She has something she wants to show you and you're coming whether you like it or not." Chrissy said. They forcefully pulled me along until we reached the back doors of the school.

I was terrified of what could have been waiting for me behind the doors and pleaded once more. "Please let me go."

"We're only trying to help you." Mona told me softly.

Knowing my efforts were in vain I stopped trying to struggle and closed my eyes accepting my fate.

Chrissy pushed open the squeaky metal doors and pushed me out. I heard male voices and my eyes flew open once I heard Jer's. What I saw made my heart break just a little.

He was with a group of guys and they were sniffing something, a white powder.

"Jer?"I asked in a quiet voice but I knew he still heard me because he quickly turned in my direction, his eyes widening. He quickly wiped his nose.

"Aurora..." he tried to walk towards me but I stepped back. I shook my head and pushed past Simran's minions.

I couldn't believe it. He was lying to me the whole time. I should have known he was lying when he told me getting high was just a one-time thing. But even though I had some doubt I pushed it to the back of my head because I finally had a friend. What's worse is that it wasn't just weed, I didn't know a lot about drugs but whatever that was he was sniffing was definitely a lot worse and illegal in all places.

Feeling broken inside, I slowly entered my Biology class, twenty minutes late. The teacher saw the look on my face and simply told me to sit down. Frowns were rare for me, and everyone knew not to bother me when they saw one.

I tried to listen in class but my thoughts always went to back to seeing Jer sniffing that poison. How could he put that in his body?

After class, I hurriedly packed my stuff, eager to leave and get through the rest of the day. Mr. Roger called out my name, asking me to wait for a moment, so I let out a sigh and stayed behind as the rest of the students filed out.

With only three people left in the class, he spoke to me, "Hey, Aurora, are you okay?"

I nodded, not wanting to dwell on it.

"Just try to get to class on time, okay?" he advised gently.

"Yes, sir," I mumbled before making a quick exit.

Walking into Lit, I wasn't surprised to find Jer absent. He was probably up to no good again. I felt icky saying that, especially with how he hated being judged but how could he be mad if what they were saying was true?

After school, I left with my head down, hoping to avoid any unwanted attention. However, I heard someone call my name.

"Hey, Rore-whore!" I turned to see Simran smirking at me with her friends by her car. Chrissy wiggled her fingers at me mockingly, while Mona offered an apologetic smile. "Looks like this 'friendship' between you and Jer is over."

I shrugged, trying not to let her get to me, and turned to walk away. "It's too bad, Aurora. It just means that no matter how hard you try to be sweet and happy, no one will ever be your friend. You'll be forever alone!" she called out dramatically, laughing as I walked out of the school compound.

I let out a sigh, knowing she was trying to get under my skin.

Once I got home, I called Kiyana to come over.

"What's up?" she asked as I opened the door for her.

"Jer," I replied, leading her to the couch.

She grimaced. "What has he done now?" she asked, concerned.

"He lied to me. He said the drugs thing was a one-time thing, and I believed him. I feel so stupid. He was my first real friend at school since Ian, and I was happy. He even stood up for me against Simran!" I poured out my feelings to Kiyana.

"I know, I know. It's not fair, but Rory, you can't blame yourself for believing him! I genuinely think Jer is a good guy, but maybe he's just caught up with the wrong people. Ever thought of that?" she offered, trying to comfort me.

I considered her words, hoping there was some truth in them. Jer seemed like a smart guy, and maybe he was just mixed up with the wrong crowd, considering he mentioned his cousin being involved in drugs. However, that still didn't excuse the fact that he lied to me.

"I guess you're right, but that doesn't change the fact that he lied to my face. I can't trust someone who could look straight into my eyes and deceive me like that," I explained to Kiyana.

She nodded understandingly. "Hey, how about we forget that idiot, watch a few movies and stuff our faces with junk food?" she suggested.

"Disney movies?" I perked up. She nodded, and a smile finally crossed my face.

"Okay," I whispered, appreciating her attempt to cheer me up.

Kiyana hurried back to her house to grab as much junk food as she could, while I changed into my pajamas, even though it was just four in the afternoon.

We enjoyed a delightful movie marathon with Frozen, Mulan, and Pocahontas before my dad arrived home with a box of pizza. Kiyana joined us for dinner before heading back to her house.

"So how was school today?" my dad asked while we washed and dried the dishes together.

I shrugged. "Fine, I guess."

He paused and looked at me intently. "Since when does Aurora Winters reply to that question with a shrug and 'fine, I guess'? Usually, it's 'Omg Dad! It was, like, so amazing!'" he mimicked the last part in a high-pitched voice.

I couldn't help but giggle; my dad always knew how to lift my spirits, even when he didn't fully understand what was bothering me.

"I know, I know, just feeling a bit down," I admitted.

"Hm, it seems like you've been feeling down quite a bit since school started this year... any particular reason?" he asked, concerned.

Jer.

"To be honest, Dad, I don't even know."

"Okay, how about I finish up here, and you go get some rest," he suggested, taking the dishcloth from me. I nodded before giving him a quick kiss on the cheek.

"Night, Dad."

"Goodnight, sweetheart."

Chapter 8

Jer hadn't come to school since that day, and it had been a week.

I was angry at him, but I couldn't help but worry. He could have been in trouble.

Since Jer and I had met, he hadn't missed a single day of school.

It could have been because of what happened last week, but for some reason, I couldn't shake off the feeling that it was more than that.

I sighed as I walked to the bleachers, eating lunch on my own while Simran and her friends sat below, throwing me smug glances, as they had been doing the whole week.

I was starting to think that maybe Jer's absence was related to the drug business.

Perhaps he got into trouble for selling drugs, or maybe he was involved in selling them right now. Or maybe, as an absurd thought crossed my mind, flying ninja monkeys captured him on his way to school on Monday.

That last one was a silly notion, but my concern for him was genuine.

As I made up my mind, I got up from the bleachers. I decided that I needed to find out where Jer was. I couldn't call him since I didn't have his number, and I didn't know where he lived. However, I knew one person who might have some information about Jer.

"Feeling lonely, Aurora?" Simran taunted as I passed her group.

I rolled my eyes. "I'd rather be lonely than hang out with a bunch of people who secretly hate me but put up with me because I'm popular," I shot back, refusing to let her words get to me.

Her mouth shut instantly, and her smug expression vanished. Some of the girls were shocked, while others tried to conceal their laughter. Mona offered me a smile and a little wave. I smiled back at her and walked away, thinking she seemed nice, I wondered why she was hanging out with Simran.

"Hey, Ryan!" I greeted as I met him at his locker.

"Hey, Rory!" he smiled, giving me a quick side hug.

Lately, I had been spending more time with Ryan and Kiyana, which was both fortunate and unfortunate. It was fortunate because they were awesome to be around, but unfortunate because I often felt like the third wheel. However, Ryan and I were growing closer as friends.

"Sooo..." I started, unsure of how to bring up Jer, knowing how much Ryan hated him.

Ryan turned to me expectantly.

"I need your help," I admitted, offering a sheepish smile.

His eyes narrowed suspiciously. "With what?"

"Nothing major... I just need to ask a couple of questions."

"Shoot."

I took a deep breath, trying to find the right words. "It's about Jer."

Ryan instantly frowned. "Of course, it is," he sighed, clearly not thrilled with the topic.

"Hey, don't be like that. I just really want to make sure he's okay," I defended myself.

"Why? He's literally cokehead!" Ryan said, displaying his disapproval.

I was about to deny it, but I realized I couldn't because, in truth, I wasn't entirely sure.

"I know you don't like him, Ryan, and I understand why, but I can't help how I feel about him," I confessed.

His eyes widened in surprise. "How you feel—"

"—as a friend! I mean as a friend!" I quickly clarified, my cheeks burning.

"I don't understand you, Aurora. You know the truth about him, and yet you still care so much for him? He's willingly throwing his life away!" Ryan exclaimed with concern.

"Ryan, I don't want to argue about this. Just please tell me if you know where he'd be. You seem to know so much about him anyway," I pleaded.

He let out a sigh. "Not by choice, Rory. It's my uncle's fault."

"The one that he allegedly stabbed?" I inquired, grimacing.

"Yeah," Ryan explained quietly. "I have no idea why, but he's still cool with Jeremiah even after what he did."

"Jeremiah said there's a good explanation behind that, that's why they're still friends."

"Is there ever a 'good reason' to stab someone, Aurora? Let's be real here."

"Where do they usually hang out? Where would Jer be if he was with them?" I asked, changing the subject.

Ryan sighed, giving me a hesitant look. "Please, Ry," I urged.

He sighed again. "Fine," he said reluctantly. "They're probably going to be at Murphy's, in the basement."

"Murphy's?" I repeated, unfamiliar with the place.

"It's a bar downtown. I believe Derrick works there, and they use the basement for all their illegal stuff," Ryan explained.

"Oh," I said, lost in thought. So this was real... Jer was really involved with this stuff.

"Give me the address," I said, determined to find him.

Ryan gave me an incredulous look. "No way, it's dangerous!"

"Ryan, stop being so difficult! Just give me the address!" I insisted.

"Rory, can't you see I'm trying to look out for you here? This isn't a good idea."

"Fine then." I turned, ready to leave, thinking I could just search up the location.

"Okay, okay, wait," Ryan said, gripping my arm.

"What?" I sighed, looking at him.

"I'm coming with you," he declared firmly.

I narrowed my eyes. "You said—"

"Look, I know that if I don't give you the address you'll find another way to get there, let me at least take you, so I know you're safe."

"Yay!" I exclaimed, clapping my hands while jumping up and down.

"I would consider what you're doing there weird for someone your age, but Kiyana's worse, so I'm not even surprised."

I laughed. "She's very lucky."

He furrowed his eyebrows as he retrieved his keys from his pocket. "How so?"

"Because she has such an amazingly caring boyfriend," I replied, sincerely meaning it.

He gave me a small smile before rolling his eyes playfully as he ducked into his car. Even though he disliked Jer, I couldn't help but notice how similar they were in some ways.

✧

"That's it?"

"That's it."

"That one?"

"Yep."

"Are you sure—"

"Goddammit Rory, that's the bar!"

"Okay, okay! No need to swear," I pouted. It was just hard for me to believe that the nice-looking bar we were staring at had a basement with illegal activities going on.

I had pictured an absolute dump, not this fancy Irish-themed establishment.

We got out of his car and approached the bar. When we walked in it felt like stepping into a cozy Irish haven. The place had a warm, dimly lit atmosphere with wooden furniture and walls adorned with old Irish souvenirs. The smell of fresh bread and hearty stews from the kitchen filled the air, making me hungry.

"Bruh, how are we supposed to get to the basement?" I asked, feeling a little uncomfortable just standing at the entrance.

Ryan rubbed the back of his neck and turned to me slowly. "I'm not exactly sure."

I rolled my eyes and looked around. We didn't even know where the basement entrance was, and even if we did, it's not like we could just waltz in.

Just then, I heard someone shout out Ryan's name.

We turned to see the bartender waving him over.

He was a very attractive man with his shaggy blonde hair and inviting warm green eyes.

"Derrick." Ryan's voice held a touch of annoyance as we halted in front of the bar.

My eyes widened in disbelief.

This was Derrick?

I had conjured up an image of someone with a somewhat intimidating aura, covered with an abundance of tattoos and a wild, unsettling look in his eyes. This, however, was quite the opposite.

Considering Jer was biracial, I guessed that Derrick likely came from the white side of his family; their sharp, distinct features were the only resemblance between them.

"Hey bro, what's up? I never thought I'd see you here! You're not even allowed to drink yet." His gaze turned to me. "And you brought a hot chick!"

My cheeks warmed instantly. "Wha...?"

"Aw, she's cute," he said, giving me a wink.

"Okay, that's enough, you flirt. We're looking for someone," Ryan interjected.

Derrick's kind expression changed, and I could tell he knew we were talking about someone who might be sitting beneath our feet right now.

"Who?" he asked, crossing his arms.

"Jeremiah," Ryan said bitterly.

"Jeremy?" Derrick asked, his shoulders relaxing. "Why?"

"Beats me. Ask Aurora over here."

My eyes widened as the attention was turned to me.

I gulped. "I just need to see him," I said quietly.

Derrick gave me a skeptical look. "Well, that's a first, someone looking for Jeremy. He barely speaks to anyone."

"I and Jer are friends... well, we were friends."

"Why 'were'?"

"I stopped being friends with him once I was sure he was selling drugs for you." I bit out boldly.

Derrick's eyes widened. "Keep your voice down!" he said, moving closer and smiling tightly at nearby customers. "And what do you mean selling drugs for me? He was the one who got me into this shit. It's more like I'm selling drugs for him! And I regret ever agreeing to help, letting him and those idiots use the basement." He sighed, his eyes shifting to the wall behind us, lost in thought.

I used that moment to process what he had just revealed. Jer was the one who got Derrick involved in drugs. It was even worse than I thought.

After a few seconds, Derrick's eyes snapped back to me. "Look, I can't let you go down there."

"What? Why not?"

"It's dangerous, no place for a sweet girl like you. Besides, if I let anyone down there without asking Boss, I'd get my ass kicked."

"Let's go, Rory," Ryan finally spoke up.

I shook my head firmly. "I came here to see Jer, and I'm not leaving until I can," I said, crossing my arms with determination.

"Rory, stop being so childish. Let's go."

"No."

"Rory."

"No."

"Aurora."

"No."

"Guys, you're starting to make a scene. Come with me to the kitchen, and we'll talk about this," Derrick suggested.

I sighed, feeling defeated, and started following him. It was better than nothing. As we were about to enter the kitchen, I noticed a door to the right of me. A man in a black wife beater with tattoos covering both his arms and neck walked out, looking somewhat like how I had imagined Derrick would look. When he caught me staring, he gave me a creepy smirk before slinking out of the bar.

I bit my lip, having no doubt in my mind that the door he had just come out of led to the basement. Ryan and Derrick were already walking through the kitchen doors. I made a quick decision and dashed for the basement door, slipping inside just as it closed.

I blew out a sigh of relief and turned around, taking in my surroundings. I could hear a lot of noise coming from below and loud rap music playing. I bit my lip nervously and slowly descended the stairs.

I knew they were around the corner, as I could hear their voices coming from that direction. I gulped, my heart pounding as my foot met the last step.

It was dark and had a musty air to it. When I finally rounded the corner, I wasn't noticed right away.

I looked around for Jer and wasn't happy with what I found. The place was a mess, with beer bottles and red solo cups scattered everywhere. A few round tables were scattered around the place where men sat drinking, smoking, and gambling. I was pretty sure it was illegal to smoke in here, and it took everything in me not to snatch all their cigarettes and put them out. Random girls were everywhere, wearing short outfits, and some wore close to nothing as they hung off of men's arms or sat on their laps. The music was even louder as I got closer, and I was surprised it couldn't be heard from upstairs.

Jer was at the far end of the room, his legs stretched out in front of him, some blonde girl on his lap, and a cigarette hanging loosely from his lips as he talked to another guy.

"Hello, dear," someone said from beside me. I jumped in fright and backed up, my calf hitting the stairs. This guy looked to be in his thirties. He wore a black short-sleeved t-shirt showing sleeves of tattoos that covered his massive biceps.

"How did you get down here?" he asked, but I had a feeling it was a rhetorical question as he looked at the door above. "That stupid kid can't do anything I ask him to."

I gulped before deciding to speak up. I didn't want Derrick to get beat up because of me. "H-he tried to stop me, but I ran when he was distracted," I said in a small voice.

The man raised his eyebrows. "So you purposely tried to come down here?" he asked, and I nodded.

"Do I know you? What's your name?" he asked, crossing his arms.

"Aurora." I whispered.

"And what can I do for you?" he asked, an amused expression forming on his face.

"I-I—"

"What the hell do you think you're doing here?"

I almost leaped two feet in the air and turned to Jer, who looked beyond furious.

"Princess, answer my question. How did you get down here?"

I kept my mouth shut and bit my lip.

"Princess?" The man asked. "I thought your name was Aurora... unless..." he smirked.

"Is this your girl, Jeremiah?" he asked in amusement, his eyes switching from me to Jer in amazement. "You finally found yourself a lady?"

Jer glared at him and grabbed my wrist, pulling me to him and away from the curious eyes of everyone who had turned to see what was going on.

"I've gotta go," he mumbled and was about to pull me up the stairs before the man stopped him.

"Now Jeremiah, aren't you going to introduce Princess to us? Wait! Weren't you just sucking faces with Stacey over there?" the man asked before bursting into loud laughter.

"My name's Shawna... not that anyone cares," I heard a girl say in the distance.

Jer glared at him intensely, and I forcefully removed his grip from my arm in anger and disgust... and maybe a bit of jealousy.

"Oops!" The man said when he noticed my gesture, covering his mouth with his hand in a girlish manner that didn't really look right on someone like him. "I wasn't meant to say that, was I?" he asked before laughing again, and some of the other men joined in.

I rolled my eyes at the immaturity.

"From the kinda girls you hang around down here, I wouldn't have expected her to be so... dark." he said with a devious smile, his eyes scanning my face. "But I guess the blonde hair still fits the bill."

I gasped as others chuckled in the background.

"Go to hell, Jacob," Jer snapped back through gritted teeth.

"Jeremy, I don't think that's any way to talk to your boss. Or what do you think, Aurora?"

All eyes were on me. My cheeks flushed, and I looked down, feeling embarrassed by the attention.

"Isn't she cute? A little too innocent for you, Jer, don't you think?"

"I'm leaving," Jer seethed, grabbing my wrist again and walking up the stairs.

"See you later, Jeremy. Hope to see you again, Aurora!" Jacob called after us.

Once Jer closed the door, he turned to me with an angry expression.

"What in the fuck were you thinking?" he asked furiously.

I stared him down with my own furious glare. "Don't you dare talk to me like that, Jeremiah. You've lied to me, over and over again. Never mind you telling me to my face that you'd only done drugs once, never mind you assuring me you'd never do it again. Never mind me catching you sniffing hard drugs and not just weed. You had me believe that you were helping your cousin Derrick, and now I find out that it was the other way around! He's helping you."

His expression changed to one of guilt.

"And I finally thought I had a friend, someone I could trust. I really care about you, Jer, do you know that? I'm so hurt and angry at you, but I was still worried about you. I did everything I could to find you, to make sure you were okay! I..." I stopped, shaking my head. "It doesn't even matter; you obviously don't care."

"Aurora, you know I do," he said, walking closer with a pained expression.

"Do I? I mean all you've done since we've met is lie! Every time I think things are going great, something else just comes up and spoils it all because of your lies."

"Princess, let me explain—"

"Explain? Are you really going to explain or just tell me some crap to keep me happy?" I asked.

His words faltered, and I shook my head. "Unbelievable."

"Aurora, do you remember when we first met? You made a comment about how someone like me was supposed to act. One of those comments was about drugs, and, well, you were right," Jeremiah admitted, throwing his hands up in surrender.

"That was a thoughtless thing to say. There's no single way someone like you is supposed to act. You're Jer, the intelligent, funny book lover that I genuinely enjoy being friends with."

"But I'm also Jeremy, the black drug dealer who once stabbed someone. I'm tired of pretending I'm not, I want to be the guy you see, Aurora, but no matter how many books I read or A's I get, that's who I am."

"So you're just accepting that?" I asked, my eyes brimming with tears. "Is that who you want to be?"

"Aurora, you don't understand. I have no choice; I have to do this."

"But why?" I burst out.

"Because..."he trailed off, looking down.

I crossed my arms. "Go on, I wonder what story you'll tell me this time."

He glared at me. "Because, Aurora, I need the money."

"Then why don't you just get a real job?"

"Because I need big money, fast. I wouldn't even earn a quarter of what I need working at a convenience store."

"Why do you need that kind of money?"

"I can't tell you," he mumbled, avoiding eye contact. I sighed exasperatedly.

Ryan and Derrick came out of the kitchen just then.

Ryan glared at me. "I can't believe you went on your own. I tried to go after you but Derrick said you could only open the door from inside unless you had the key."

Derrick glared at me too. "I can't believe you went at all! You've just fucked me over."

I looked around me, seeing three people who weren't so happy with me at the moment.

"Okay, okay. I'm sorry," I said, putting my hands up in surrender. I admitted it was kind of stupid; I mean, anything could have happened when I went down there, especially if Jer hadn't been there.

"I'm gonna get my ass kicked," Derrick sighed in defeat.

"Sorry," I mumbled again. "I wasn't really thinking, I just did it."

Derrick smiled at me. "Hey, it's fine. It could be worse. I couldn't stay angry at such a cutie anyway," he said, winking at me again. I blushed, and Jer grunted.

"Let's go, Princess," he said. I was just about to protest, but Ryan beat me to it.

"No, she's going with me."

Jer gave him a look like he had just noticed he was even standing there.

"I'm sorry, you are?" he asked, sizing him up.

I rolled my eyes. "Ryan. Kiyana's boyfriend."

He seemed to relax with that information. "Well, whatever, she's coming with me."

Ryan's glare hadn't wavered. "I said she was leaving with me. I'm not letting her go with someone who's probably high as we speak."

I knew this probably wasn't the time, but I couldn't help but smile. It was nice to have someone like Ryan. He looked out for me; he was like the big brother I'd never had.

"For your information I haven't smoked all day," Jer gritted out.

Ryan scoffed. "And you expect me to believe that?"

"I couldn't give two flying fucks what you believe, she's leaving with me."

"You stabbed my uncle!" Ryan blurted out in anger.

"What the—where the fuck did that even come from?" Jer asked him.

Derrick sighed and turned to me. "Hey, my shift is done and we've got some leftover Irish bread pudding in the kitchen. Want some?"

I watched Ryan and Jer argue for a second and even though I kinda wanted some more context on this whole 'cousin stabbing', I smiled at Derrick with a nod. How could I say no to dessert anyway?

Chapter 9

"Hey, Aurora?"

"Hm?"

"Are you a magician? Cos every time I see you, everyone else disappears."

I chuckled. "Derrick!" I said, playfully slapping his arm.

"You know I'm not a photographer but I can picture you and me together."

I giggled and shook my head. "Did you sit in a pile of sugar? Because you've got a sweet ass."

I gasped in shock, my cheeks burning.

Jer grunted and crossed his arms from the passenger seat.

After arguing for a while, Jer and Ryan had soon noticed Derrick's and my absence and joined us in the kitchen, where we were indulging in some delicious dessert.

I quite liked Derrick; he was funny and entertaining. Despite the whole drug thing he seemed like such a great guy.

I had refused to go anywhere with Jer, and he had refused to go anywhere without me. Ryan said he wasn't leaving without me either, so Derrick suggested we all go together in Ryan's car.

We all reluctantly agreed, and I sat beside Derrick in the back so I didn't have to sit with Jer.

"Derrick, you need to shut up," Ryan said.

"I surprisingly agree with Mr. Protective over here," Jer gritted out.

"Oh, hush, Jeremy. You're just jealous," Derrick said, throwing his arm around me and pulling me close.

Jer turned in his seat and stared at Derrick's arm around me. "If you don't get your arm off her right now, I swear I'll—"

"If I wasn't comfortable with it, I would say so, Jeremiah. Now turn around and mind your own business," I snapped.

Jer's nose flared, and he gave Derrick one more glare before turning around in his seat, mumbling about how he wished he could disown Derrick as his cousin. Ryan whistled at my assertiveness before leaning back in his chair with a sigh.

"So, I know where Rory and Derrick live. What about you, Jeremiah?" Ryan asked.

"Why the hell would you wanna know that?" Jer spat out.

Everyone went silent.

"Uh, so I can drop you off?" Ryan said in an obvious tone after a few minutes.

Jer relaxed and gave a sheepish shrug. "Yeah, uh just drop me off at Derrick's."

I stared at the back of Jer's head in thought. I remembered when we had just started our project, and Jer had been so adamant about me not coming to his house to work on it.

It made me wonder if maybe Jer was hiding something. Although he did fail to mention he was a drug dealer and whatnot, so I wouldn't be surprised.

"So, who knew you could be so feisty," Derrick smirked as he brought the conversation back to my hostility towards Jer.

"Well, some people just bring that side out of me," I said, crossing my arms.

Derrick chuckled. "Not gonna lie, it was pretty hot," he said. My cheeks burned again, and I looked down. I don't think anyone had ever said anything like that about me.

"Stop the car," Jer said suddenly.

"What? Why?" Ryan asked.

"Do it now," Jer said menacingly.

Ryan groaned before pulling over at the side of the road. Jer got out and opened the back door. He grabbed Derrick by the front of his shirt, who let out a strangled sound, pulled him out of the car, and pushed him towards the open passenger door.

Jer then got into the car beside me with a contented sigh. After standing there with his mouth hanging open for a few seconds, Derrick got into the passenger seat of the car with a pout and crossed his arms.

"Can I go now?" Ryan asked, annoyed.

"You may," Jer said with a false smile.

Ryan rolled his eyes before starting the car again. "Stupid people and their stupid drama," he mumbled.

I sat, still wondering what the heck had just happened. Jer obviously didn't know when to take a hint.

I puffed out a breath before moving to the window seat on the other side. Of course, Jer only smirked before moving to the middle seat.

Damn, now he had me cornered.

"Why can't you leave me alone, Jer?" I sighed exasperatedly.

"How come you don't mind the fact that Derrick is a drug dealer, and you care that I am?" he asked, ignoring my question.

I rolled my eyes. "It's your fault that he got into all of that. And he didn't lie to me." I whispered the last part, looking down.

"Aurora, I know I shouldn't have lied to you, but I knew you would be disappointed in me if I told you the whole truth. Or worse, just stop talking to me." He said, swallowing hard. I could tell it was hard for him to open up to me but he continued.

"I'm not used to anyone caring if the words that come out of my mouth are facts or not. I don't want to lose you 'cause of my dumb lies, Princess."

I cast a fleeting gaze out of the window, trying to collect my thoughts and emotions. Despite the tough act he put up, he cared what I thought. Still, that didn't justify his involvement in illegal activities.

"I don't know, Jer. The choices you're making and the people you're associating with, it just doesn't make sense to me. You're capable of so much more than this," I said, my voice tinged with both frustration and concern.

Jer's gaze softened as it met mine. "You think I'm proud of what I do? You think I chose this? It's not that easy, Aurora. Right now, it feels like this is the only way I can make it through."

A crease of concern furrowed my brows. Why did he need so much money that this was his sole means of survival? "There's truly no other option? What's really happening, Jer? And what about your parents?"

His jaw clenched at the mention of his parents. "You don't get it. My parents are as good as dead. My life is more messed up than you can even imagine. You have no idea what it's like out there."

I leaned closer, meeting his gaze with determination. "You're right; I don't know exactly what you've been through. But I know that taking this path won't lead you to a better place. If you continue like this, you might end up losing everything, including yourself."

"That's damn easy for you to say from up in your big-ass house in your nice-ass neighborhood. I'm not making excuses here, I'm just playing the cards I was dealt."

I remained silent.

"I'm just fucking exhausted. I'm tired of trying to crawl out of my fucked up life. I'm tired of this drug dealing mess. I'm tired of all the judgment. I'm tired of feeling, feeling fucking alone, and it's like no one gets it."

"Then talk to me, Jeremiah, let me in. I want to be there for you," I told him earnestly.

He bit the inside of his cheek, his eyes scanning my face.

"Okay." he answered, nodding.

"Yeah?" I asked in surprise.

"Yeah, tomorrow at lunch, we go to that café close by the school and talk about this. Everything," he proposed.

My eyes widened. "Really? And you'll answer all my questions?"

"Yeah, I'll give it a shot, unless it's something real personal or tough to talk about, then I might have to be kinda vague in my response." he assured me, and the sincerity in his gaze made me believe him although I had believed him before and it hadn't gone so well.

I beamed at him. "No more lies? You don't have to put up a front with me, Jer."

"Yeah, I know that now. No more lies, I promise." He smiled.

"Pinky promise?" I asked, holding out my finger expectantly.

"Fine." he mumbled, rolling his eyes as our fingers locked.

"Yay! Friends again!" I smiled.

I noticed a breath of relief escaping him as he watched me. "I'm glad to see you smiling again."

Before I could respond, he did the unexpected.

Jeremiah Summers, the 'bad boy' and antisocial asshole, hugged me. He pulled me into his warm embrace. I sat shocked in my seat for a moment before slowly returning the hug.

I mean, I loved hugs, but I never ever thought Jer would hug me, at least not unless I initiated. Maybe he appreciated me more than I thought he did. I hugged him closer, resting my head on his shoulder.

Soon after, we arrived at Derrick's place and dropped him and Jer off.

"Bye Ryan, Bye Babe!" Derrick called, waving.

"Bye Derrick," I called as I moved to the passenger seat.

"Bye, Idiot. Bye, Princess," Jer called.

"Bye, Jer," I giggled, while Ryan just glared at his retreating figure. I waved at them enthusiastically until they closed the door to Derrick's massive... massive house. The dude was loaded. I couldn't help but ponder the reasons behind his and Derrick's involvement in drug dealing if Derrick's family seemed to be doing so well for themselves.

Jeremiah spoke like he had no support but couldn't Derrick's family help him? It was clear that there was more to the story than I thought.

I sat back in my seat as Ryan pulled out of their driveway, and he kept shooting me glances as he continued driving.

"What?" I asked after a while.

"You really care about Jer, don't you?" he asked.

My answer was instant. "I do."

Ryan nodded. "I saw you two talking back there, and even though I wasn't sure what you were saying, I could tell from the way he was acting and talking to you that he really cares about you too."

As Ryan's words sank in, I couldn't help but feel a mix of emotions. It was true; there was more to Jer than met the eye, and he was opening up to me, slowly trusting me with his feelings and secrets. And I found myself caring deeply for him too. It was like peeling back the layers of his tough exterior and discovering the vulnerable person underneath.

I turned to Ryan, grateful for his understanding. "I think we're good for each other," I said softly. "He needs someone in his life who believes in him and supports him, and I want to be that person. And I need someone who can put up with my crazy self."

Ryan laughed. "You're a good friend, Aurora. You really went all out today to make sure he was safe."

"And maybe he's not such a bad guy." He shrugged.

My eyes widened and I turned to him with my jaw dropped.

"Really?"

He rolled his eyes before letting out a small chuckle. "I mean, I still think he's making some questionable choices, but he's not all that bad. He does care about you, and I trust that he wouldn't do anything to hurt you."

"Thanks, Ryan, you're an amazing friend too, and I'm really grateful that Kiyana has a boyfriend like you. I haven't had someone looking out for me in a long time, and having you by my side feels really good, like having a protective big brother."

Ryan flashed a warm smile. "I'm really glad you feel that way, Rory. I don't mind looking out for you at all; I've always wanted a little sister." He winked playfully, and I couldn't help but laugh.

He pulled up outside my house, and I gave him a quick hug before rushing to my front door. I turned and waved at him before unlocking the door and going inside. I didn't hear his car pull away until I was safely indoors.

The next morning, I woke up feeling ecstatic. It was the first time in a while that I felt like my happy self, and I wasn't even grumpy this morning.

I picked out a beautiful pink and white floral dress along with my pink Chuck Taylors before taking a refreshing shower and getting ready. I was so elated that I even attempted to skip down the stairs, but my enthusiasm got the better of me, and I ended up stumbling and falling.

Quickly picking myself up from the floor, I blushed with embarrassment.

"Aurora?" I heard my dad's voice calling from the kitchen.

"Yeah, Dad?" I walked into the kitchen, still rubbing my arm from the fall.

"Hon, did you just fall down the stairs?" he asked, trying to suppress a smile.

My cheeks flushed even more. "Maybe?" I replied sheepishly.

He burst into laughter, the sandwich he was eating nearly falling from his hand. I huffed and snatched the sandwich from his grip, tossing it into the trash can.

He immediately regained his composure and let out a groan. "Aurora! That was a BLT! Yuh couldn't at least tek out di bacon first? Jus' a waste good food."

I stuck out my tongue at him before picking up the other plate with a BLT sandwich on it and sitting at the island to eat. I took one-half to eat, and my dad, faster than lightning, snatched the other half.

"Hey, Dad! Give that back!"

He swiftly ran his tongue across it, causing me to scrunch up my nose.

"Of course," he held it out to me.

"No thank you. Keep it," I said through gritted teeth.

"Thanks, baby! You're so sweet."

I scoffed before finishing my half of the sandwich. Then I remembered something and turned to my dad.

"Hey, Dad, can I have some money today?" I asked. It was unusual for me to ask since I had never asked before in my life. Prior to my dad landing his new, higher-paying position at work earlier this year, our financial situation was pretty tight, making it hard for him to manage as a single father.

Yes, my mom and dad managed to purchase this amazing house in a great neighbourhood back in the day, but it didn't mean we were financially secure right now. My dad was determined to hold onto our home, but he struggled with paying the mortgage all by himself.

He had started giving me an allowance when I was twelve, but after a few months, I told him I didn't want it because I knew we needed the money for more important things. I think my dad felt guilty because sometimes he would just decide we were going shopping and try to buy whatever I wanted.

Of course, I had offered many times to get a job myself to help pay the bills but he didn't want me to. He preferred that I focused on being a teen and school. He was a good father to me, and I wouldn't ask for it to be any different, honestly. And fortunately, his well-earned promotion alleviated most of our financial stress.

He smiled at me. "Of course! What for?" he asked.

I couldn't really tell him I was going to lunch with a boy. "Just thought I'd go down to that café near the school for lunch today," I said with a shrug.

My dad stared at me suspiciously before reaching into his suit pocket and pulling out his wallet. With the way I raved about the cafeteria food, I'm sure he was confused as to why I suddenly wanted to go to the café. "How much would you like?"

"Um, ten dollars would be fine."

"Here."

I stared at the fifty dollars in my hand in confusion before looking up at my dad. He smiled at me. "You deserve it."

"Now get to school!"

I grabbed my bag before planting a large kiss on his cheek and walking out the door.

During lunch, I headed towards the bleachers where Jer had told me to meet him. We had exchanged numbers prior to dropping him off at Derrick's house the day before.

I fidgeted with my feet and nervously wrung my fingers. I couldn't help but feel a little apprehensive. I was scared to find out what Jer was going to tell me.

Suddenly, I sensed a presence behind me and turned around to see Jer, who appeared just as nervous as I did at that moment. He cleared his throat and scratched the back of his head. "Are you ready?"

He was asking if I was prepared to head to the café, but I couldn't help but think it had a double meaning, asking me if I was ready to hear what he had to say.

"As ready as I'll ever be," I replied.

We walked to the café, engaging in small talk along the way.

Once seated in a booth near the door for a quick exit to get back to school on time, a waiter approached our table. "What can I get you guys?" he asked.

"I'll have a hot chocolate with marshmallows and chocolate sprinkles, and a blueberry muffin, please," I perked up, scanning the menu.

"And you, sir?" the waiter turned to Jer.

"Coffee. Black," he said.

I rolled my eyes at his order. Of course, he liked his coffee black.

Bleh.

"Your food will be served shortly," the waiter assured us with a smile before leaving.

"So..." I mumbled.

"So..." Jer cleared his throat.

We fell into an awkward silence. I wasn't sure if I should dive right into asking questions or ease into the conversation.

"How about you just start asking me about what you want to know," Jer sighed.

I nodded, trying to gather my thoughts, but I couldn't find the right words to articulate my feelings. I felt frustrated with myself for not having prepared questions, yet desperately wanting answers. Then, I blurted out the first thing that came to mind, blushing immediately after. "Uh...do you get your eyebrows done?" I asked, realizing how trivial it sounded compared to the weight of the situation. But his perfectly shaped eyebrows had been on my mind recently.

He raised an eyebrow in surprise. "Really? That's what you want to know?"

I crossed my arms defensively. "Well, it's one of the things I want to know."

He stared at me blankly.

"What? I just wanted to know if they're naturally that perfect."

He closed his eyebrows and rubbed his forehead. "Aurora, can we be serious here?"

"Okay, okay. Are you a drug dealer?"

He took a deep breath and responded honestly, "Yes."

Of course, I already knew but I just needed his confirmation. I tried not to show my disappointment and moved on. "Are you in a gang?"

He hesitated before replying, "No but we're kind of in partnership with one."

"What do you mean?" I asked.

"We're their suppliers. Jacob owns a few weed farms and we score the harder stuff from our distributor."

The conversation felt strange and uncomfortable, like was this real life? Was this actually a conversation I was having right now? Despite these thoughts, I felt compelled to continue. "Have you killed a person before?"

His eyes widened in shock. "No! Of course not! Like I said, I just deal drugs. If someone doesn't pay up or there's someone dealing on our turf or whatever, I tell the boss, and he deals with it. It's why having connections to gangs is beneficial, we don't do any dirty work."

I fiddled with my fingers, feeling the unease growing within me. "Do you own a gun?"

Before he could answer, the waiter brought our orders to the table, and we fell silent momentarily. Once the waiter left, Jer finally replied, "Yes."

I squirmed in my seat, confused. "But you said you didn't do the dirty work, why would you need a gun?"

He explained, "I need it for protection. I don't want to hurt anyone, but if someone tries to hurt me, I'm not gonna lie, I won't hold back. I also need it to seem intimidating towards customers so I don't get robbed or something."

"I don't like this at all, Jeremiah. Guns? Really?"

He looked down at his coffee cup.

Feeling anxious, I picked at my muffin and asked another pressing question. "How did you get Derrick into this?"

"It was about three years ago—" Jer began.

"Three years ago? You were fifteen, Jer! When did you start this drug stuff?" I interrupted, shocked at the revelation.

"When I was thirteen, fourteen," he shrugged. "Anyway, it was about three years ago, and Derrick and I were hanging out. We were on my block when I spotted Shawn, one of the guys I work with. He came up to me and started telling me about one of his customers, even though I was sending him signals to shut the hell up."

"Then when he finally noticed Derrick beside me, the idiot offered him coke. My uncle, Derrick's dad, is pretty rich, and Derrick's used to a prestigious life. When he found out I was a drug dealer, he wanted in on it too. He wanted some excitement, to see how it would be to live like I did. When he did join, no one really accepted him though; they all just saw him as the stuck-up rich kid with the nice hair. They didn't trust him either, and he hardly did anything for us."

"They've only recently started trusting him with stuff, but I think that might have something to do with the fact that he offered us the basement of Murphy's, which is his dad's best friend's bar. Derrick had just been promoted to manager, and his dad's friend, Rupert, only comes once in a while to oversee everything. That's how we can use the basement with no issues."

"Derrick doesn't seem too happy about drug dealing anymore," I mumbled, taking a bite of my muffin.

"Yeah, he realized my life wasn't as exciting as he thought, and that he could actually do something with his life. He doesn't need this drug dealing stuff getting in his way."

"You too, Jer, you're really smart. You could do something with your life too."

Jer smiled at me sadly. "Thanks, Princess, but it isn't that easy. It might not work out that way. I could get caught at any time and end up in jail. I'd love to be able to go to college and get a good job, but I don't think that can happen now, no matter how much I try," he whispered, staring at his hands wrapped around his coffee cup.

I frowned, feeling my heart ache for him. I had seen the way Jer approached his schoolwork—always eager, ahead in class, and deeply involved in learning. I could picture him attending prestigious (boring) colleges, having intellectual (boring) conversations with equally interesting (boring) people. "Why do you have to do this?" I asked.

He tensed and pretended not to understand what I meant, "Do what?"

"Why do you have to deal drugs? Why do you need the money, Jer?"

He gritted his teeth before staring down at his coffee. "It's complicated," he muttered.

I sighed. "Okay then, just give me a vague answer. You said if you couldn't answer my question properly, you would at least give me a vague one."

"The money is for my dad," he answered, his jaw clenched.

My eyebrows furrowed. His dad? I thought he said his parents were as good as gone? I looked over his tense state and sighed, realizing I wasn't going to get any more than that.

Hesitantly, I reached out and placed my hand over his tightly gripping the coffee cup. His eyes snapped up to me, and I offered him a reassuring smile. He responded with a weak smile in return.

"Are you sure you want to go on?" I asked.

He bit his lip, deep in thought. I couldn't help but watch as he tugged his plump bottom lip with his teeth. I quickly shook my head, trying to focus on the conversation.

"Princess?" he called out, bringing me back to the present.

"Hm?" I asked, slightly embarrassed by my distraction.

He furrowed his eyebrows. "I said you could continue."

"Oh!" I cleared my throat. "I was wondering about the basement. How do people not notice all the dealers walking through? And what about Derrick's co-workers? Don't they wonder what's going on down there? The music, too—it was really loud. How do the customers not hear it?"

"Okay, so as you know, the basement is opposite the kitchen, so it can't be seen by customers. When people see dealers walking through, they're not surprised; a lot of them go there to drink, but it's generally more of a 'rich people' bar. As for Derrick's co-workers, he informed them and Rupert that someone was renting the basement. Rupert doesn't actually know what's going down there but he was pretty happy since drug dealing brings about quite some money, and Jacob, my boss, pays well."

"And the basement is soundproof, so that's how the customers don't hear anything," he finished.

"Why can't Derrick and his family help you out with money or getting a job? You clearly need help and they're loaded."

"To be frank, and excuse my language, they don't fuck with me. Derrick has been hanging out with me behind their back for years."

I shook my head in disbelief. How could they just abandon their own blood like that? It wasn't right. The fact that Jeremiah had to resort to drug dealing when those who should be close to him had more than enough to help made me sick and upset on Jer's behalf.

"I'm sorry, Jer," I said, feeling disgusted by the situation.

He shrugged. "It is what it is. I don't need them anyway. I've been fine on my own."

Jer's resilience and strength were admirable, but I couldn't help the anger and frustration I felt with this whole situation. I wanted to support him, but I also knew I couldn't change his circumstances overnight. All I could do was be there for him and listen.

I squeezed his hand gently. "You don't have to go through this alone, Jer. I'm here for you," I said sincerely.

He looked at me, and for a brief moment, I saw a glimmer of hope in his eyes. "Thanks, Aurora. That means a lot to me," he said softly. "Any more questions?"

"Well, now I'm wondering why Derrick even works if his family has money," I said in confusion.

"His dad wants him to learn a work ethic so he can be successful as well, he doesn't want to just hand everything to him. He pays for his tuition himself and stuff like that," Jer explained.

I nodded. "So Derrick's not in high school?" I asked.

"First year of college."

"Really? Which one?" I inquired.

Jer scowled. "You know you're asking a lot of questions about Derrick."

"No, I'm not!" I retorted and then smirked. "Even if I was, who cares?" I added slyly.

Jer grunted, and I couldn't help but start giggling as I stared at him.

"Why are you laughing?" he asked.

"Are you actually pouting?" I asked incredulously.

"No," he answered quickly, glaring at me instead.

"Yes, you were!" I laughed.

"Whatever. Maybe if you'd stop obsessing over my dumb cousin, I wouldn't be pouting!"

My eyes widened, and I stilled. "What?" he asked.

I smirked, leaning closer. "Are you jealous, Jer?" I teased.

He frowned at me. "What?"

"You're jealous of my friendship with Derrick," I stated mischievously.

He scowled at me. "What friendship? You guys barely met each other."

"So you are jealous," I said, teasingly, before tipping my head back and laughing.

He sighed heavily and stood up. "Well, that cues the end of this conversation."

I got up too and followed him out of the cafe. He stopped suddenly and turned towards me, causing me to crash into his chest. He grabbed my waist to steady me, and I looked up at him. "What's wrong?" I asked.

"Thanks for listening, Aurora, seriously. It felt good to just talk about it. I'm happy I met you." he told me with sincerity in his eyes, his grip on my waist tightening.

I couldn't really think straight with the way he was staring into my eyes and his arms around me like that. I cleared my throat before breaking into a warm smile. "Me too."

He flashed a breath-taking smile, a smile that was rare but very much appreciated.

We continued to stare into each other's eyes with large smiles on our faces until someone walked past us on the sidewalk and almost knocked me over. I snapped out of my trance, my cheeks warming up. Jer steadied me again before letting go of my waist quickly and cleared his throat.

"We should probably get back to school," I mumbled.

Jer nodded, and we turned and headed back to school, the weight of our conversation still lingering between us. I didn't have all the answers, and I couldn't fix everything for Jer, but I hoped that by being there for him, I could provide some comfort and support.

Chapter 10

I didn't know how I felt about this situation.

My mouth hung open wide as I watched Derrick lean against my locker, absorbed in his phone with his Rick Owens clad feet crossed.

After a minute or so, I continued slowly to my locker, aware of people staring, especially girls, at Derrick.

He looked up just as he heard me approaching and grinned. "Hey, babe."

He pulled me into a tight hug, and I struggled to push him off.

"Derrick! What the heck are you doing here?" I asked, as I managed to step out of his embrace.

"I thought I'd take you out for lunch or something. I'm bored, and I have a lot of money to waste."

"How did you find my locker?" I asked curiously as I opened it.

"I asked. Duh," he said, pointing towards a group of girls who were ogling at him not too far away. I was a little surprised that they knew my locker, I always felt like I was invisible around this place.

"You down?" he asked.

"Sure, as long as you get me back in the next forty-five minutes," I said, closing my locker. "I'm not tryna skip school here."

He dramatically grabbed his chest and gasped. "Do you think I would ever try to tarnish your ever perfect record by making you late back to school?" he asked mockingly.

"Yes." I deadpanned with a flat look.

"You think so lowly of me, my love," he said with a sigh before wrapping his arms around me, catching the attention of a few students.

"Let's just go, Derrick." I mumbled.

As we walked out of the school, I noticed Simran and her friends walking towards us, and I groaned. She just had to be everywhere I went, didn't she?

We tried to walk around her big group, but Simran easily stepped in front of us, causing us to stop.

"And who are you?" she asked with a flirty smile directed at Derrick.

"Um, Derrick? Can we help you?" he retorted, arching an eyebrow.

"Derrick," she mumbled. "You're cute. What are you doing with her?" she asked, sneering at me.

Derrick's arm shifted from my shoulder to my waist protectively. "She's my friend."

Simran smirked. "Oh, of course, she's already been friend-zoned." Her friends giggled behind her.

"Why don't you just worry about your non-existent love life," I snapped, arms crossed. It was easier to stand up to her with Derrick next to me.

Her friends gaped in surprise, a few of them even laughed. For people she called friends, they didn't seem to have her back, and that was pretty sad honestly.

She glared at me, walking closer. "Oh, so you think—"

"Oh, hell no! I already graduated from high school; I am not tryna get myself into any drama. Now, if you'd excuse us," he gently pushed Simran aside, and we continued our walk to his sports car. I couldn't help but smile to myself as I heard Simran scoff behind us.

"So, where are we going?" I asked as he pulled out of the parking lot.

"I dunno yet. Let's just see where the wind takes us, okay?"

"As long as we get back by the end of lunch," I sighed. My eyes widened, and I sat up.

"Sugar balls!"

"What's wrong?"

"I forgot about Jer!"

"What do you mean?"

"I sit with Jer everyday at lunch; we just saw each other in second period. He's gonna be wondering where I am. I feel bad now. He's gonna have to eat lunch all by himself."

"He's a big boy. I'm sure he'll be fine."

"I know that. It's just... I'm his only friend at school, and it isn't fair if I just ditch him, for his cousin too."

"Okay, relax. It's not like he's your boyfriend, and you left him for me."

"What? I never said that!"

"Hate to break it to you, honey, but I don't see you that way."

"Just shut up, Derrick. I'll call him," I said, quickly grabbing my phone from my bag.

"No," Derrick whined. "He's gonna wanna come, and I wanted to spend some quality time with my Aurora."

"Derrick, you text me all the time. I spend eighty-five percent of my time texting you."

"Aw, man! I knew I was coming off too clingy. You still love me though, right, Babe?" he asked. I rolled my eyes, ignoring him.

I placed my phone to my ear after dialing Jer's number.

"Hello?"

"Hey, Jer."

"Oh."

"Oh? What's that supposed to mean?"

"I just thought you were occupied with that guy."

"What guy?"

"Don't give me that bullshit, Princess. Everybody is talking about how some hot, rich guy came to the school and swept you off in his flashy car."

I smirked. "Oh really?" I asked.

"Yes, really. Simran even felt the need to tell me personally that 'my girl found herself another man.' She also felt the need to add in 'but you're hotter than him by a mile.' And I don't understand what is so amusing about this, Princess; I can hear you sniggering."

"You know you sound kinda jealous, Jer."

I could practically imagine the scowl that was set on his face right now. "Whatever. Are you with him right now?" he asked bitterly.

Before I could answer, he was talking again. "You could have at least informed me that you were going on a date, Aurora. I had been waiting for you for a good fifteen minutes."

"Would you like to talk to the guy I'm with?" I asked, still trying to control my laugh.

"Um no. Why would I?"

"I think you would," I giggled.

"Aurora, I don't want to—"

"Hey, cuz," Derrick shouted as I brought my phone closer to his mouth and put it on speaker.

Jer remained silent for a few minutes.

"Oh."

Derrick and I burst into laughter. I couldn't believe he had gotten so worked up. I had to admit it was kind of cute, actually.

"Yeah, laugh it up. What were you doing at our school, Derrick?" Jer asked.

"Just wanted to take my favorite girl out for lunch."

"Of course. Thanks for letting me know, Aurora."

"I'm sorry, Jer. I totally forgot, and I called as soon as I remembered."

"So you forgot about me?"

I rolled my eyes and let out a heavy sigh. "Are you being serious right now, Jer?"

"Yeah, Jeremy, you sound like a clingy, whiny girlfriend right now," Derrick added.

"Stay out of this, Derrick."

"Ooh, okay. Aurora, I think it's that time of the month for her," he pretended to whisper.

"I hate you, Derrick." Jer told him.

"I love ya too, little bro."

"Jer, I'll talk to you later, okay? We're still meeting after school, right?"

"I dunno, I'll probably get ditched again, or should I say forgotten."

I let out an exasperated sigh. "Bye, Jer." I hung up before he could say anything more.

"I feel for you, Aurora. I know girls like that. They seem perfectly normal and nice when you first meet them. You start hanging out, you know, the usual—school projects, motorbike rides, ice skating—then BOOM, the next thing you know, they're calling to see where you are all the time and get hysterical if you even look at someone else."

He shook his head. "Girls are crazy, huh?"

I pinched his leg in response, and he let out a shriek before huffing. "Just trying to empathize with you, Aurora. No need to pinch me."

He finally stopped at a restaurant that I had never seen in my life before, not that I was surprised. When you have no friends to hang out with, you don't really go anywhere.

We stepped inside and settled at a nearby table.

"This place is nice," I commented, looking around. It wasn't overly fancy, yet it had a distinct charm.

"Yeah, I know. I come here a lot," he replied, his attention on the menu that had already been placed on the table. "They serve pretty good food."

I nodded, my gaze scanning the items listed on the menu.

A shadow suddenly fell over us, and I glanced up to find a girl about our age standing there. Her black hair with bright pink streaks was pulled into a bun, she sported a nose piercing and multiple earrings on both ears. The orange stud in her tongue caught my eye when she spoke, and she wore dark purple lipstick and a sleeve of tattoos ran down her arm.

"Derrick, I've told you I'm not interested. Can't you take a hint?" she hissed.

My eyes widened, and I turned to Derrick, who seemed both surprised and captivated by her presence. It was unexpected, as she didn't fit the image of someone I thought Derrick would be attracted to, but somehow that made it even more endearing.

He cleared his throat and smirked. "Yes, I can take a hint, and that's precisely why I decided to bring the lovely Aurora here on a date," he said, gesturing towards me.

My eyes widened again as her gaze shifted to me, as if she had just noticed my presence. Her glare was intense, and it unsettled me.

I fidgeted in my seat, seeking help from Derrick, but he was focused on the girl with a mischievous grin..

"Date?" she asked, arms crossed.

"Uh-huh," Derrick confirmed, winking at me. I sank lower in my seat, feeling the weight of her glare.

Thankfully, another waitress arrived at our table. "Oh, hi, Derrick! I was wondering why Sadie was just standing here and not taking your order, but now I see she was chatting with you. Oooh, who's this?" The fast-talking girl turned her attention to me.

"My date, Aurora."

"Aurora? What a beautiful name. I might use that for my daughter when I grow up. Are you named after Sleeping Beauty? I adore Sleeping Beauty. She was my favorite princess, even though my name is Cindy—short for Cinderella. Anyway, I loved her when I was younger. Did you watch Maleficent? I thought it gave an amazing perspective on Maleficent's life and showed her in a new light. Agree? Oh, wait, why am I here again?" She glanced around, clearly confused.

I stared at her with my jaw dropped.

"Cindy! You're scaring Aurora!" Derrick exclaimed, then he gestured to Sadie. "And you're not much better, stop glaring at the poor girl."

Sadie rolled her eyes and walked away, while Cindy continued to smile at me. "You're pretty. I love your hair."

"Thanks," I managed a smile, although it probably came across more as a grimace.

She pouted. "Oh, I really did freak you out, didn't I? I'm sorry, I'll leave," she said before skipping away.

And I thought I was a lot.

"They didn't even take our order..." Derrick mumbled, looking around in confusion.

"I don't even think we have any time left to eat, Derrick. It took like fifteen minutes to get here. How did you expect us to eat and get back in time?"

"Calm down, I forgot you were a nerd who can't even skip the rest of school."

"Skip? Skip school? Are you crazy?"

He rolled his eyes and got up. "Let's just go. I'll drop by while you and Jer are studying after school with some food for you. I feel bad that you didn't get to eat."

"You don't need to do that, Derrick."

"Yeah, I do. I basically brought you here to make a girl I like jealous. Then you got ambushed by that crazy girl while Sadie glared at you for five minutes straight. And you didn't even get a meal out of it."

"Yeah, you're right. Make those two meals. Bring some for Jer."

"Sure."

After Derrick said goodbye to Sadie, who ignored him, we left.

✧

"Gratiano is a funny character; we should make sure he's really witty and stuff."

"Like Derrick!"

"Sure..."

"Are we done yet? This is boring," I whined.

Jer sighed. "Come on, Aurora, we haven't even started writing the story. We're still trying to modernize the characters! Amy Finch and her partner are almost completely done."

I scowled. "Who cares about Amy Finch? She does nothing but work. It's not like she has anything better to do. She has no friends."

Jer raised an eyebrow. "Are you being for real, Princess? You're not one to talk about friends. And since when did you not like Amy? Aurora Winters is incapable of hate—well, except towards Simran."

I crossed my arms. "Actually, I have friends now: you, Ryan and Derrick. That's not so bad. And I never said I didn't like her; she's just annoying."

Amy sat in front of Jer and me in Lit class. She and Jer were constantly talking about the books they read and physics, as they're in the same class for that. She was one of the few people I've seen Jer interact with in this school, and I had a small inkling that she had a crush on Jer... not that it bothered me or anything.

"Really?" he asked, amused. "What part of her is annoying? The fact that she's smart or the fact that she has read *In Search Of Lost Time*—which for some reason you won't—and we talk about it all through class?" he smirked.

I could feel anger rising in me, but I didn't know why. Maybe I was jealous... just a little, though.

Derrick strutted up to us with two plastic bags in his hand.

"Hey, people!" he called.

"Shhh," someone said from behind him, and he responded by flipping them the bird without turning around.

"I have brought gifts! Merry Christmas!" he smiled, placing the bags in front of us.

"Thanks, Derrick."I mumbled.

"Why so glum, chum?" he asked, taking a seat beside me.

I glanced at Jer who raised his eyebrow in curiosity with that stupid smirk still on his face. I quickly turned my frown upside down and shook my head. "I'm fine."

I opened the plastic bag and saw that he had brought us Chinese food. In the box, I found noodles. I smiled, grabbed a fork, and dug in.

"Okay, so someone's hungry," Derrick laughed. "Guess what?"

"What?" I asked, swallowing my food.

"Sadie has been texting me nonstop since we left the restaurant earlier," he said, shaking his head. "I can't believe my plan worked. Ah, women, so predictable. Ow!"

He pouted, rubbing the spot on his arm where I had pinched him.

"Who's Sadie?" Jer asked.

"My girl," Derrick smiled.

"Your girl? Since when?"

"Since this afternoon. I've got her right where I want her," he smirked. "I mean, she might be texting me all the ways she could kill me with her bare hands, but I still got her attention!"

I rolled my eyes.

Ah, men.

"Thanks for the food, Derrick. You can leave now." Jer said, bringing his notebook closer.

"No!" Both Derrick and I chimed in.

"See? Aurora wants me here," Derrick smiled, pulling me into his side.

"Derrick, we have work to do."

"Too bad."

"Go away, Derrick," Jer snapped, his nostrils flaring.

"What's the big deal?" I asked.

"The big deal is that we need to get going on this project, and you haven't been taking it seriously."

I moved out of Derrick's embrace, sitting up and leaning toward Jer.

"Oh, I'm sorry! Would you rather do this project with Amy? I'm sure she'd take it seriously. She shares your interests, she's pretty, and she doesn't annoy you. She looks just like the girls you hung around with in that secret drug lair basement of yours. Why don't you call her up? Huh?" I asked, my tone laced with frustration. I then stood up, walking towards the exit.

I sighed as I leaned against the wall outside. I didn't know what had come over me; I couldn't believe I was actually feeling this jealous.

"Princess."

I turned away from him, leaning against the wall with my shoulder as my cheeks heated up. It was kind of embarrassing how worked up I had become over nothing. I had unintentionally let out my insecurities regarding our friendship and in general, and I didn't know how to feel about that.

"Princess, look at me," Jer said, coming up behind me. I stayed put, shivering as his breath fanned over my neck.

When I didn't respond, Jer turned me around by my shoulders. I stared down at my shoes, waiting for him to say whatever he wanted to say.

"I'm sorry."

I looked up at him in confusion. "For what?" I asked. I was the one that randomly snapped at him for no reason.

"For saying all that stuff about Amy. I didn't mean to make you feel bad. I was just joking around," he said, his hands still firmly placed on my shoulders.

I shuffled my feet. "It's okay, Jer. I was just being silly, anyway."

"No, Aurora. I wish you had told me you felt that way. I don't want you to like the books I read or the kind of things I do. You should be who you are, and of course, we already have a few things in common, and that's enough. That's what friendship is about, Princess. I don't want to be friends with the female version of myself. I want to be friends with you," he stated firmly, his hands sliding down my shoulders to my arms.

"I want to be friends with Aurora Winters. The fun, positive, beautiful girl who befriended me when no one else would," he finished, his hands stopping at my waist.

I was pretty sure I was dreaming. Had Jer just called me beautiful? I was frozen in place, staring at him in shock. He met my gaze with an amused smile.

I cleared my throat and looked down, my cheeks burning.

"So you don't only think girls like Amy are pretty?" I asked.

"I feel like you're asking if I'm only into white girls, and the answer to that is no," he responded. "Like I said, you're beautiful, like really, really—"

I playfully nudged his arm. "Okay! I get it, enough. I was just like, curious, you know? I don't need a man's validation or anything like that..."

"Of course, of course." He chuckled, releasing his hold on my waist, much to my disappointment.

"You know what? How about we go see a movie or something? I did promise you that we could do fun stuff after we worked on our project."

"But we didn't even do that much work."

He shrugged. "Next time we'll work really hard. Right?" he asked pointedly.

I nodded sheepishly. "Yeah."

"Then let's go see a movie! But first, let's grab our stuff. Our Chinese is probably cold by now."

By the time we found our way back to our table, Derrick was just finishing off Jer's food, and mine was left empty on the table.

"Really, man?" Jer asked.

Derrick laughed in our faces, showing us the food in his mouth.

"Gross, Derrick." I pushed him away. "You still owe us those meals."

"What? It's not my fault you guys had to be all dramatic, and you left your food. I couldn't just leave it there to get cold, I had to eat it."

"Imagine buying people food and then eating yourself. How about you pay for both mine and Aurora's tickets and food, we're gonna see a movie."

"Asking your cousin for money for your date? Classy."

"It's not a date!" I said, my cheeks warming as we walked out of the library.

"And you owe it to us, why would I pay when you can?" Jer asked, holding out his hand. "Pay up."

"Hey, how about I come with—"

"—No!" I exclaimed.

"—Hell no," Jer said, shaking his head.

Derrick scoffed. "You guys are mean. I don't wanna hang out with people like you anyway."

"Just shut up and give us the money, would you?"

He rolled his eyes and carelessly tossed two hundred-dollar bills to Jer.

"Thanks, bro," Jer said, smiling down at the money.

"No prob. See you guys later."

"So, Princess," Jer began while helping me with my helmet. "What movie would you like to see?"

Chapter 11

We came to a stop just a few houses away from mine. Jer helped me off his bike and then assisted me in removing his extra helmet.

"Thanks for tonight, Jer. I had so much fun! I can't believe you actually saw a Disney princess movie with me!" I smiled.

He scowled. "Don't you dare tell anybody about that, okay?"

I nodded, giggling.

"I'm glad you had a good time, though," he said, leaning against the handles of his bike with a lazy smile. I smiled back, feeling my cheeks warm.

"Well, I'll see you tomorrow," I said, quickly trying to avoid any potential awkwardness.

"Yeah, bye."

"Bye!" I began my walk to my house, and as I reached my front door, I glanced back to see Jer still watching me, with intense eyes. I waved at him enthusiastically, and he waved back.

I opened my front door and stepped inside, closing the door behind me. I waited until I heard the sound of Jer's bike starting up and zooming down the street before I turned around, letting out a sigh.

"Ah!" I clutched my chest.

"Where have you been?"

I calmed my breathing and gulped as my dad stood in front of me with his arms crossed and an angry expression on his face. I wasn't used to this at all; I couldn't remember when my dad had ever acted like this... probably because I had never really gotten into trouble before.

"I, uh... I mean..."

I couldn't tell him I had been out with Jer. If he found out I was with a guy and that I rode on his motorcycle, I'd be in serious trouble.

"I went to the movies with a friend," I said quickly.

He frowned. "Just a friend?" he asked suspiciously.

I nodded.

"So why did you press your ear against the door when you walked in?"

Shoot! He saw that?

"Well, I thought I heard an ice cream truck, and I was just listening to see if I was just hearing things or if it was actually there." I couldn't believe I was doing this; it was the first time I had lied to my dad in a long time.

My dad raised an eyebrow. "An ice cream truck? At 9PM on a winter night?"

"I know! That's why I thought I was hearing things. I must really be craving some ice cream. Speaking of which, I think I'll just go and get some—"

"Funny 'cause while you thought you heard an ice cream truck, I'm certain I heard a motorbike out there."

My eyes widened, and I gulped again. "Really?"

"Yeah, just about when you came in, actually," he said.

I cleared my throat. "Dad, I don't know what you're implying here. I just went to the movies with a friend. I'm turning eighteen soon; I think I can go out once in my whole life without being interrogated about it." I crossed my arms, assuming the same stance as him.

He uncrossed his arms and cleared his throat. "You're right, baby. I'm sorry. I shouldn't have doubted you. I just... you didn't even call, and I've been waiting for you to come home. You're the most important thing in my life, and I'm not used to not seeing you when I come home from work. You have to understand that."

I felt really guilty for snapping at him like that. "I know, Dad. I'm sorry for not calling. I was just distracted, and I'm sorry for blowing up at you."

I wrapped my arms around his neck and laid my head on his shoulder.

"It's alright, honey. You're almost eighteen. You need your space... you'll soon be leaving me anyway," he laughed, but it came out forced.

I looked up at him. "Dad, no matter what happens, I'll always come back here to see you. You're my best friend. I don't think I'll be able to go a week without you," I laughed.

"I dunno about that, honey. You've always been such a strong girl," he smiled.

I beamed at him.

"Now go get that ice cream you're craving!"

"I will," I said, running towards the freezer.

✧

I was truly happy that I had Ryan and Jer as friends. In the past, I used to always get stopped by Simran and her friends, but now that at least one of them was with me during the day, I hadn't heard from Simran in quite a while.

To make things even better, I think Ryan and Jer were friends now. I saw them walking to Physics together as I entered my Calculus class.

"Hey, best friend," someone said, leaning against the locker beside mine.

I looked up to see Ryan smiling at me. I raised an eyebrow. "You're in a good mood," I said while closing my locker.

"Yep."

He threw his arm around my shoulder and pulled me along with him down the hall.

"What's going on?" I asked suspiciously.

This was definitely not the way to the football field.

"You'll see," he said, sounding excited. Ryan sounded excited. Now, I was really curious.

"Okay..." I said.

We stopped at the main office, and I looked up at him, confused.

"Why are we here?" I asked, noticing Jer walking towards us.

"Just wait a second," Ryan beamed, dropping his arm from my shoulder and rubbing his hands together.

Jer smiled at us he joined, and his arm replaced Ryan's around my shoulder. We stood across from the main office, waiting. For what? I had no idea.

The door to the main office finally opened, and Kiyana walked out with her mom and dad. I stood in shock as my eyes ran over the agenda, school map, and schedule in her hand.

My mouth dropped open.

"No. Way."

"Way!" She beamed.

I squealed and ran towards her, wrapping my arms around her. She hugged me back just as tightly.

"You're transferring to our school?" I whispered in disbelief.

"Yes!" Kiyana smiled as we pulled away from each other.

"I can't believe this," I shook my head. My best friend was coming to my school. We had been begging her parents to let her come to my school for ages since she went to some snobby private school that she hated.

"Thanks, Mr. and Mrs. Joseph!" I said, hugging them. They laughed and told me I was welcome, but I didn't let go because I was so happy. They didn't mind though; I was like a niece to them.

"Group hug!" Kiyana shouted, and she joined us, almost knocking us over. Then Ryan joined, though he was really only hugging his girlfriend.

I looked up and saw Jer awkwardly standing with his hands in his pockets.

I held out a hand to him, and he hesitantly came closer and grabbed my hand. I paused as I felt tingles shoot through my fingers before I pulled him into the hug.

This was the best day ever!

After that, Kiyana and her parents left since she was starting on Monday. Ryan, Jer, and I headed towards the bleachers for lunch.

"I can't believe you guys kept that from me!"

"Hey, we all agreed it would be a nice idea to surprise you. At least now you won't only have us guys to talk to at school," Ryan said.

I nodded happily and then smirked. "And now you can see your girlfriend all day."

He rolled his eyes, but I could see his ears turning pink. I giggled.

"Aw, he's blushing."

"Shut up," he said, elbowing me.

"Ow!" I exclaimed before throwing a piece of my orange at him. It slapped him in the face and slowly slid down. I leaned back, laughing.

Jer chuckled. "If I didn't know any better, I would think you two were siblings."

I paused and exchanged looks with Ryan. "He's white though," I mumbled.

Ryan burst into laughter.

Jer shook his head. "I know, I know. Y'all just have that dynamic."

"She'd be a shitty sister, not gonna lie," Ryan teased.

I gasped, throwing another piece of my orange at him.

"Rory!" he gritted out. He lunged for me, and I quickly got up, running away.

"Definitely siblings!" Jer called out as he watched Ryan chase me around.

After school, Jer and I made our way to the library. We had thankfully started working on our storyline, although Jer, being the creative writing expert, was doing most of the actual writing while I provided input and ideas.

"Are we done yet?" I asked, my boredom evident.

"One more moment, just need to finish this paragraph," he replied, his eyes glued to my laptop screen.

"Jer, you've been saying that for the past twenty minutes!"

"I know, I know. Once I start writing, whether it's a story, an essay, or even an answer on an exam, I can't seem to stop," he confessed.

I scoffed. "Smart boy problems."

"I promise, just a few more seconds," he assured me.

I sighed in exasperation. I had plans for what we could do afterward. My dad was going to his friend's house to watch a game, so I thought it'd be great if Jer came over, and we could watch a couple of movies. Plus, I had loads of junk food at home that needed to be eaten. The only thing was, I hadn't actually asked him yet. I didn't know why, but I felt a little nervous about it.

"Jer?" I began, twirling a lock of my hair around my finger nervously.

"Hmm?"

"Um, do you want to... uh..."

He turned to me, his eyebrows slightly furrowed, waiting for me to finish my sentence.

I wasn't entirely sure why I was so worked up. Maybe it was the possibility of him declining my offer, or perhaps the thought that he might interpret my invitation in a different way, though I couldn't say I'd mind that too much...

"Aurora!"

My gaze snapped back to Jer. "Huh?"

He rolled his eyes playfully and shook his head. "You were saying?"

"Oh," I gulped, my nerves getting the better of me. "Well, y-you know how we usually do something every time we make progress on this project?"

He nodded, a curious expression on his face.

"Would you like to come over and watch a movie at my place?"

His eyebrow raised slightly in surprise.

"Unless you're not interested, I mean, why would you be? I can be pretty annoying and weird, and you probably have better things to do. I don't even know why I asked. It's just that my dad hasn't gone out in forever, and now he finally agreed to hang out with his friend to watch a game. But now I'm going to be all alone at home, and I know it's silly because I'm almost eighteen, but I watched a horror movie last night and I can't stop thinking about that creepy *Annabelle* doll staring at me whenever I close my eyes, and..."

"Aurora, relax," Jer interrupted gently. "Seriously, you need to chill. Of course, I'll come over. I was just wondering why you seemed so nervous. We've hung out plenty of times before, right? What's the big deal?"

I shrugged sheepishly, still feeling flustered.

"By the way, you're not annoying or weird, okay, maybe a little annoying," he teased, and I scowled at him. "But honestly, I enjoy spending time with you. Every time we work on our project, it's something I look forward to."

I felt a warm sensation spread through me, causing my cheeks to flush. I didn't know why, but I'd been feeling differently around Jer lately, especially after our argument about Amy and he told me how much I meant to him.

By the time I snapped out of my thoughts, Jer had already packed up his things and placed my laptop neatly in my bag for me. I hurriedly gathered the rest of my belongings.

"Ready to go?" he asked, standing up.

I nodded, and we made our way towards the library exit, heading for the parking lot.

As we walked, I felt a light touch on the small of my back. My eyes widened as a tingling sensation rushed through me, reaching all the way to my toes.

He gently urged me forward, using his other hand to zip his jacket up the rest of the way. "Let's hurry, it's getting cold."

We picked up our pace, heading towards his motorbike. Once we reached it, he helped me put on my helmet before putting on his own. With a sense of exhilaration, I hopped onto the back of his bike, feeling the engine roar to life beneath us as we prepared to head home.

The motorcycle rides had become quite enjoyable, though my excitement now stemmed more from the prospect of being so close to Jer than from the ride itself. I leaned my head against his back with a contented sigh as we glided down the road.

"Okay. Comedy or Sci-fi?" I asked, scrolling through movies options and the TV.

After we had returned to my place, I had arranged an assortment of snacks on the coffee table, and now I was on a mission to pick a movie. I glanced over at Jer, who seemed more preoccupied with the choice between M&Ms and a Snickers bar.

I was surprised by how his eyes lit up at the sight of all the candy, and as soon as I dropped them on the table, he eagerly began to sort through the treats, searching for his favorites. I hadn't pegged him for a candy kind of person. It was nice to see him act his age for once, he was always so serious.

"Comedy," he answered in a distracted tone.

I shrugged, scanning the list of available comedy movies.

When I found a movie that seemed decent enough, I sank back onto the couch, snuggled under a blanket, with a variety of candies on my lap. Jer did the same, accompanied by a bag of chips.

Halfway through the movie, I felt Jer shift closer—unusually close. He discreetly pulled a portion of the blanket that was closer to him, wrapping it around himself.

"I need some warmth too," he pouted, sensing my incredulous gaze.

I casually shrugged, trying my best not to let on how flustered I was internally. I refocused my attention on the movie, which was genuinely entertaining.

Crunching on a bag of Doritos, I was taken aback when Jer casually stuffed his hand into the packet, snagging a handful of chips.

"Hey!"

"I'm hungry!"

"Get your own! There's literally like six left, and you've already taken two."

"Yeah, but I need more, and the coffee table is too far away," he whined.

"Shhh," I hushed him as a crucial scene in the movie unfolded.

However, my concentration wavered again when I sensed his arm encircling my shoulders. I shot him a questioning look, and he merely shrugged.

"What? I'm cold; I need your body heat," he stated matter-of-factly.

I shot him another incredulous look before turning my attention back to the TV screen. Note to self: never watch a movie with Jer again. I couldn't even recall the title of the film; all I could focus on was the gentle touch of his fingers tracing light circles on my arm.

Frustrated with my inability to concentrate on the movie, I gave up and dropped my head onto Jer's shoulder. In response, he held me a little tighter, and I sighed contentedly. I could definitely get used to this.

"Princess?"

"Hm?"

"The movie's been over for like five minutes now."

I lifted my head and glanced at the screen, realizing that the credits had already rolled, leaving the room in darkness.

A blush crept onto my cheeks.

"Oh."

I had been lost in my own thoughts, particularly how snugly our bodies seemed to fit together. However, I made no move to get up, and neither did Jer.

I nestled my head back onto his chest, and he continued tracing those gentle circles on my arm.

"Aurora?"

"Yeah?" I whispered.

"I-I think I'm going to stop dealing drugs."

I lifted my head again, resting my chin on the hand that was on his chest.

"Really?" My voice held a mixture of surprise and excitement. Although we hadn't discussed it since our conversation at the café, I had been genuinely concerned about Jer and his involvement in drug dealing.

"Yeah. I used to believe it didn't matter, since I thought I had no future plans anyway... but something made me change my mind." His gaze was locked onto mine, intense and unwavering.

My heart began to race.

Before either of us could delve further into the conversation, the sound of my dad's car pulling up outside startled me, causing me to let out a small shriek.

I swiftly got to my feet. "Get out!"

Jer stared at me, taken aback. "What?"

"Did you not hear that? My dad just pulled up outside. You need to go now," I urgently whispered to Jer. He leapt up from the couch, and I grabbed his jacket and his phone from the coffee table, shoving them into his hands. We hurried through the kitchen towards the back door, my heart pounding in my chest. I pushed Jer gently out of the door.

"Okay, I'll see you later, okay?" I managed to say, my voice hushed.

Jer nodded, quickly putting on his jacket. "Bye, Princess."

"Bye," I whispered, watching him disappear into the night.

I heaved a sigh as I closed the door, my mind a whirlwind of thoughts.

Man, I think I really like this guy.

I widened my eyes at my own realization, taken aback by the flood of emotions I was experiencing. With a shake of my head, I shut the back door, finding my dad in the process of tidying up the aftermath of Jer's and my movie night. Guilt washed over me.

"Hey, Dad."

"Hi, my love. You and Kiyana had a movie night? Looks like you two didn't bother with the cleanup," my dad remarked, giving me a pointed look.

"Um, yeah. I was just using the bathroom, and Kiyana just left," I hastily replied, quickly bending down to help him pick up the scattered candy wrappers.

Well, he made explaining this really easy for me.

After we finished tidying, I asked my dad if he enjoyed watching the game.

"Yeah, actually. It was a good time, watching the game with someone who actually stayed awake and enjoyed it," he quipped, giving me a knowing grin.

I laughed. "It's not my fault, Dad! They're so boring!"

"Anyways, he invited me to join him and some friends for a drink next week. Should I go?" My dad inquired.

"Dad! Absolutely, you should go. I'm thrilled to see you embracing life again," I said with genuine happiness, hugging him.

He chuckled, returning the embrace. "Sweetheart, my life will always be enjoyable as long as you're around. No day is dull with you."

"Aw, Dad." I hugged him tighter.

That night, as I settled into bed, only one thought consumed my mind.

Jeremiah Summers.

Chapter 12

"You didn't get in trouble last night, did you?" someone asked from behind me as I closed my locker.

I shook my head, turning around, only to find myself caught off guard by how close he was.

"You okay, Princess?" Jer's voice pulled me from my momentary trance, and I blushed, looking down.

"Yep. I-I'm great. Wonderful," I stammered, sidestepping to regain my composure and create some distance. Jer followed along.

Where was Kiyana's new locker again?

"This way," Jer said, grabbing my hand and guiding me back the way we came. "So, your dad didn't suspect a thing? We kinda left the place in a mess, and I think it was obvious that more than one person was responsible."

However, I was too preoccupied by the sensation of his hand in mine to fully register what he was saying.

"Princess? Hey, are you okay? You seem kind of out of it today."

I swallowed hard, mentally scolding myself.

Pull yourself together!

I took a deep breath, exhaling slowly. "No, I'm fine. Um, my dad just assumed it was Kiyana who had been over."

He nodded. "Look, there she is."

I let out a delighted squeal and dashed up to my best friend. She closed her locker and reciprocated my excitement with a squeal of her own, meeting me halfway for a tight hug. Our hug turned into a goofy dance of jumping and clapping hands. I could hardly believe that my best friend was actually here. People around us stared as if we were crazy.

We were just two happy black girls, my sundress and her mini skirt swaying as we jumped around.

"Oh God, no," Ryan groaned as he joined us. "Dealing with you two individually when you're like this is enough to make me start puking rainbows and butterflies, but both of you together..."

We stopped our antics, dissolving into laughter at Ryan's remark.

"Don't be such a buzzkill, babe," Kiyana chided, playfully smacking his head. "Now take me to my class."

Ryan sighed, rubbing his head. "Fine."

"Okay, see you guys at lunch!" Kiyana called as she and Ryan made their way down the hall. Kiyana skipped while swinging her and Ryan's linked hands, and Ryan tried to keep up reluctantly. I couldn't help but burst out laughing. They were one of the funniest couples I'd ever seen.

"You know what they say, opposites attract," Jer said, shaking his head, basically reading my thoughts.

I nodded in agreement. "Kiyana has to be the only girl I know who is more energetic than me."

"Hey, I noticed you went quiet when we got to Kiyana's locker. Are you uncomfortable around her or something? Because we are basically like the same person, so I don't get how you can deal with me if you can't deal with her."

"No, it's not that," he said, scratching the back of his head.

"Then what?" I asked.

He shrugged. "I don't know, I'm just not used to having so many people around me."

I cocked a brow. "So, you're shy?"

He scoffed. "Where did you pull that out from? I'm not shy."

"Aw, little Jeremiah is so shy, he gets awkward when people are around." I teased.

Jeremiah's annoyed expression morphed into one of disgust. "Please shut up."

"No, really, it's so cute! Jer-Bear is shy!" I giggled, squeezing his cheeks. He glared at me.

"What did you just call me?" He asked, seething.

"Oh? You mean Jer-Bear? Pretty cute, right? I made it up on the spot. I think I'm gonna call you that from now on." I said as I grabbed the handle for my classroom door.

He pulled me back. "Don't call me that again. And I'm a man, don't refer to me as cute."

I pulled out of his grasp and winked. "Sure thing, cutie. See you at lunch, Jer-Bear."

When lunch finally came around, it was clear that things would never be the same. Gone were the days of watching hot guys run around a field while pestering Jer as he tried to read a book.

Kiyana made sure of that.

"Let's go sit in the caf," she said, and we made our way inside.

"Huh?" I asked.

"You know, the cafeteria? Where most students go to eat lunch? It's cold outside, and I don't fancy sitting on a wet seat. Come on."

I and Jer groaned as she grabbed my arm with her left and Ryan's with her right. I quickly grabbed Jer before he could slip away.

Kiyana opened the doors to the cafeteria and looked around like she owned the place. She spotted an empty table and dragged us towards it, effectively capturing half the school's attention.

Two school loners, the new girl, and an ex-popular kid — what a sight.

"So, isn't anyone gonna ask me how my first day has been?" Kiyana asked, pouting.

Ryan rolled his eyes. "How has your first day been?" he asked, opening a bag of chips.

She sighed dramatically. "Okay, so everyone keeps commenting on how weird it is that I moved schools at this time. It's so annoying, like I had a choice! I would have started here in freshman year if I could have. Moving schools for senior year when we're this far in isn't easy!"

She let out a breath then smiled. "But apart from that, it's been pretty great. I made a couple of friends in Cosmo. This girl, Ariel, has her own YouTube channel where she gives makeup tutorials and she has 500K subs. Amazing, right? I could do something like that. Don't you think? Oh, and I met this guy, Jordan, who said he'd help me with bio. Isn't that so sweet?"

Ryan scowled. "I can help you with biology."

Kiyana giggled. "Don't be silly, Ryan. You're helpless."

He grunted, taking an aggressive bite of his apple.

Kiyana finally stopped talking and brought out her lunch.

I almost screamed as I lunged for one of her brownies.

"Jeez, Rory, calm down," she said as she picked one up too.

I moaned at the taste of Mr. Joseph's amazing brownies. It was weird because when it came to cooking, he was helpless, but his baking skills were on a different planet.

Ryan grabbed one too, and I handed one to Jer, knowing that he wasn't comfortable enough around her to ask.

"So, Jer, I don't think I've heard you say more than two sentences since I've met you. You good?" Kiyana asked with a curious look.

"Yeah, what's your deal?" Ryan asked.

Jer paused mid-brownie bite. He then continued eating and swallowed his food to stall.

"I um..."

"Aw, Jer-Bear! No need to be shy; it's just Kiyana. She doesn't bite," I said, pinching his cheek like I did earlier.

He turned red and batted my hand away.

Kiyana snorted. "You're not shy when it comes to dealing cocaine, but you're too shy to talk to me?"

I almost choked on my water, and Ryan's eyes widened.

"Kiyana!" I said, slapping her arm.

"What? It's true, isn't it?"

"Yeah, but you can't just say it out loud like that."

She rolled her eyes. "Alright, alright. I'm sorry, I guess I'm the only one who wants to acknowledge the fact that we have a criminal sitting with us."

Jer stood abruptly, grabbed his bag, and stalked out of the cafeteria, slamming the doors.

"What the hell, Kiyana? That was fucked up!"

Ryan had beaten me to it, although maybe I would have worded it differently.

She sighed. "Guys, let's be real. He deals drugs. I can't just pretend he doesn't like y'all clearly do. I'm sure he's a nice guy, but seriously—"

"—Honestly, Kiyana, I love you, but you can't just say stuff like that to people. You know most people don't just sell drugs for the sake of it. You said this to me yourself a few months ago. Instead of putting him down, we should be trying to help him. You're my friend, he's my friend. I would have hoped you'd respect that. And for your information, he's trying to get out of the drug business."

I got up, throwing away my trash before leaving the cafeteria too.

I looked around for Jer, but I couldn't find him anywhere. I checked the bleachers, his next class, I even checked behind the school.

I sighed. I knew how he was feeling; he was upset that Kiyana saw him as a criminal, a delinquent, he hated being judged.

I checked my phone and saw that there were only ten minutes left for lunch. Just as I was about to give up searching, I saw a figure leaning against my locker.

"Jer?"

He stayed put, looking down at his phone. I walked closer.

"Jer, don't listen to her. You are the most amazing, smart, caring guy I know, okay?"

He gave me a bittersweet smile. "Thanks, Princess. It means a lot that you see me that way. Your opinion is all that matters to me. I don't care about anyone else."

His words stirred a bunch of different emotions inside me, and I found myself at a loss for words.

Releasing himself from my locker, he gently pulled me into an embrace. My initial surprise turned into a warm embrace, my arms naturally wrapping around his waist.

"I'm so grateful to have you in my life, Aurora," he whispered.

The sincerity in his voice made my heart race even faster. I was grateful he was holding me so tight. If he hadn't I might have just melted.

"Hey."

We turned to see Kiyana, looking remorseful.

"I'm sorry for what I said, Jeremiah. I guess I just didn't know how to act around you knowing about all the drug stuff. Aurora's my best friend, and I just don't want her to get hurt or be in danger."

Jer nodded. "It's fine, I understand. But you don't need to worry. I'd die before something happened to Aurora because of me," he said, his gaze fixed intently on me. His eyes held a mixture of determination and protectiveness that made my heart flutter even more.

✧

"HAPPY BIRTHDAY!"

"Fudge!"

I groaned as I got up, rubbing my butt where I had landed after falling off my bed.

"Kiyana," I whined, casting a sleepy glare at my energetic friend. Thanks to her, I had just fallen off my bed.

She giggled. "How does it feel to be eighteen?"

I flopped back down on my bed, burying my face in the pillow. Honestly, I was too tired to contemplate the significance of my age at that moment.

Kiyana settled down beside me and rolled her eyes. "I forgot how grumpy you are in the mornings."

I offered her a halfhearted pout in response. Words weren't really my strong suit before at least 9 AM.

When I didn't reply, she got up. "I'll be downstairs making our traditional birthday breakfast with everyone else..."

Food.

After ten more minutes of resistance, I finally mustered the energy to roll out of bed. I got ready for the day, thankful that it was a Saturday and I didn't have to deal with the school routine.

I settled on my favorite sundress and shook my head in disbelief. This dress had been with me for so long, and it still fit as if it were made for me.

As my foot touched the last step of the staircase, my dad swooped in, scooping me up in his arms.

"Happy birthday, sweetheart," he exclaimed, twirling me around before setting me down gently.

I chuckled, hugging him tightly. "Thanks, Dad."

Together, we walked into the kitchen, where the tantalizing aroma of breakfast greeted me.

The Joseph family was bustling around, preparing breakfast while swaying to my dad's beloved jazz music playing on the stereo. I couldn't help but laugh as Mr. Joseph playfully bumped hips with his wife.

Seeing us, they turned our way, and Mrs. Joseph hurried over, pulling me into a warm hug.

"Happy birthday, baby."

"Thanks, Aunty," I replied, giving her a thankful smile. Even though Melissa wasn't my biological aunt, the culture in me dictated the title. Better not to rock the boat, especially if I wanted to avoid the scolding that came with calling her by her first name.

Mr. Joseph joined in, giving me a hug and then a celebratory high-five. "Ready for some pancakes, birthday girl?" he asked with a playful glint in his eye. I nodded eagerly. His fond laughter followed as he turned his attention back to the pancake batter, whisking away with a smile.

After a delightful breakfast, Kiyana and her parents bid their goodbyes, leaving my dad and me to indulge in our annual tradition of watching Sleeping Beauty. Each birthday, my dad insisted we watch it together.

As the credits rolled, my phone buzzed. Jer's name flashed on the screen. I quickly excused myself from the living room to answer his call.

"Happy Birthday, Princess."

I couldn't help but smile. "Thanks, Jer."

"No problem," he cleared his throat. "So, uh, do you have any plans for the day?..."

I furrowed my brows. "Um, no, not really."

"Oh, cool."

I arched an eyebrow. "Why do you ask?"

"Well, I w-was wondering if maybe, maybe you wanted to hang out?" Before I could answer, he was talking again. "Like only if you want to, of course, it's just that I thought it would be nice to take you out for your birthday and—"

"I'd love to hang out!"

I heard him exhale in relief, and I couldn't help but giggle.

"I'll pick you up in half an hour?" he asked.

"Sure."

I plopped down on the couch. "Hey, Dad, is it okay if I go out with, um, with friends?" I cringed.

"Of course, it's your birthday, have fun!"

I grinned and hugged him. "Thanks, Dad."

Thirty minutes later, I was leaving my house after reading Jer's text saying he was outside.

I made my way down the street to where he had parked.

He grinned at me, leaning casually against his bike.

"What?" I asked, feeling a little self-conscious under his gaze.

"I like your jacket," he remarked.

I glanced down. "Oh!"

I had thrown on my new leather jacket, a birthday gift from Kiyana, over my sundress.

"Now we're matching," he chuckled, lifting the collar of his own jacket.

I giggled, trying to play it cool even though my heart was doing somersaults. "Yeah, I guess so."

"Happy Birthday again," he said, handing me his second helmet.

I met his gaze, feeling a warmth spread through me. "Thanks, Jer."

I held onto him tightly as he started up his bike.

"No way."

I turned to Jer, my eyes wide in disbelief.

He smirked at me. "Yes way."

"You brought me to the zoo?" I grinned, unable to contain my excitement.

He nodded and took my hand. "Yep, let's go."

After paying the entrance fee, he led me inside.

"How did you know I loved the zoo?" I asked, genuinely curious.

He stuffed his hands in his pockets and kicked a pebble. "I don't know, you just strike me as someone who would enjoy being around animals."

"Well, you were right! Thank you!"

"Quit thanking me, this is the third time already. I'm just doing what any friend would do." As we walked, I quickly linked arms with him to steady myself as two energetic kids darted past, narrowly avoiding colliding with me.

"Now let's go see those tigers," he suggested.

"They're so adorable."

"Princess, what are you talking about? Those hippos are so ugly."

I gasped dramatically. "How dare you? Apologize to the poor hippos for calling them ugly."

He raised an eyebrow at me. "Are you being for real?"

I stood my ground, arms crossed. "Absolutely."

"I'm not doing that."

I pouted and put on my best pleading expression. "Jer, come on! You could have really hurt their feelings."

He shrugged, a playful glint in his eyes. "Good thing they can't understand me, right? You know, 'cause they're animals."

"Animals have feelings too!"

He gave me a flat look. "Apologize!" I demanded.

When he ignored me, I decided to employ a different tactic. "Pretty please?" I added a flutter of my eyelashes for good measure.

He looked at me skeptically, then let out a reluctant sigh, turning to face the hippos. My eyes widened in surprise – I didn't expect it to work.

"You're lucky you're cute," he muttered, giving me a sideways glance.

Heat rushed to my cheeks as I grinned back at him.

"Deepest apologies, hippos. You guys aren't that bad looking."

A man standing nearby shot Jer an odd look before walking away, clearly having overheard his conversation with the animals.

I burst into laughter, and Jer scowled. "Thanks, now people think I'm crazy."

I giggled. "Want to grab something to eat now?" he asked.

"Sure."

After we finished eating, Jer drove me home, stopping a few houses away from mine.

"I know you said I should stop thanking you, Jer, but I have to say thank you for taking me out and paying for everything. I had a great time."

He smiled warmly. "Me too. I'm really glad you had fun." He dismounted from his bike and opened the motorcycle compartment, leaving me intrigued and curious.

He picked up something from the compartment, out of my sight, and sighed before turning to me with a slight grin.

"Oh my God, Jer, you didn't," I exclaimed, placing my hand on my chest in surprise.

"I did," he replied, his smile growing, though he seemed a little sheepish. "I'm hoping that's a good thing?"

"Jer, I absolutely love it. How thoughtful of you," I said, touched by his gesture.

He unbuckled the straps of the old black helmet on my head, carefully removing it. He then replaced it with a new sky blue helmet adorned with beautiful white daisies – the design reminded me of one of my favorite sundresses.

"Thank you so much, Jer. I can't believe you bought me a helmet."

He shrugged casually. "Well, I figured since I usually pick you up for school and stuff, I should get you your own helmet. One that actually fits you properly."

I laughed softly. "I'm honestly at a loss for words," I admitted, my heart feeling warm with gratitude. This gift meant a lot to me.

"I'm really glad you like it. I thought about getting a pink one, but when I saw this design, it reminded me of the dress you were wearing the first day we met."

Was he intentionally trying to make my heart race?

"You remember?" I whispered, surprised and touched.

He shrugged, scratching the back of his head. "Uh, yeah, I guess."

I shook my head in disbelief. "Thank you so much, Jer."

"You're welcome."

"Okay, well, I guess I should head inside now," I reluctantly said, even though I didn't really want to leave.

"Bye," he said with a hint of reluctance himself.

I decided to seize the moment, not wanting to miss the chance. I leaned up on my tiptoes and quickly pressed a kiss on Jer's cheek before my nerves could catch up with me.

Swiftly, I removed my helmet and handed it to him without meeting his gaze. "You should probably keep this. I wouldn't want my dad to start questioning why I suddenly have a motorbike helmet."

He cleared his throat, his voice slightly shaky. "Uh, yeah, sure. I'll take care of it."

He took the helmet from me, and I began to walk down the street, but then I turned back to look at him.

He was still standing in the same spot, watching me.

A warm feeling spread through my chest. "Thanks for giving me one of the best birthdays ever, Jer."

He smiled, a big genuine one that reached his eyes. "Didn't I tell you to stop thanking me?"

I waved one last time before continuing down the street, feeling a sense of happiness and contentment that lingered long after I had entered my house.

Chapter 13

"I love you."

"I love you more."

"Um, no you don't, because I love you more."

"Hate to break it to you, babe, but I love you more."

"Well, that's impossible because I love you more than anything."

"No, 'cause I love you more than—"

I rolled my eyes and groaned, before turning to Jer.

"Thank you so much for coming along. I don't think I can stand being the third wheel again, and Kiyana insists I go with them to the movies every Friday. It's torture."

Jer laughed and then grimaced as he glanced up ahead at the bickering couple. "I can tell."

Kiyana turned to us with narrowed eyes. "I can hear you, you know?"

"Great, so maybe you and Ryan can try to be less sickening."
She gasped. "You're just jealous."

I snorted. "Oh, really?"

"Yep, you're just jelly you don't have love like we do." She said, gazing into Ryan's eyes.

I gagged in disgust, glancing at Jer. "Someone please kill me."

He grinned, and we finally arrived at the theater. "You getting anything?" he asked.

And I shook my head. "No, I already asked my dad for money for the movie ticket. I couldn't ask him for more money for food."

Jer nodded in understanding. After Ryan and Kiyana got their food, we headed into the screening room. I turned when I didn't feel Jer beside me.

I saw him waiting behind. "Is everything alright?" I asked.

He nodded and waved me off. "Go ahead, I'll just be a minute."

I shrugged, a little confused. "Okay..."

I followed behind Kiyana and Ryan, finding them near the very top where seats were saved for Jer and me.

"Where's Jeremiah?" Kiyana asked.

"Oh, he needed to do something. He'll be up in a minute," I replied.

She nodded, focusing on her popcorn as we waited for the movie to start.

As the last of the commercials played, Jer sat beside me, and I raised an eyebrow at the large popcorn, two drinks, and mounds of candy he had in his hands.

He wordlessly passed me a drink and the candy.

"Jer—"

"How could I let you sit through a whole movie without any food? It's unheard of."

I laughed. "Thank you so much, Jer, really."

He shrugged. "No problem."

I felt someone nudge my arm, and I turned to see Kiyana wriggling her eyebrows at me.

I rolled my eyes and stuffed some gummy worms in my mouth as the movie started.

✧

After the movie ended, we discussed the cliffhanger it left us with as we strolled aimlessly around the mall.

"Oh shoot! Ryan, I gotta go. My family's having dinner with my dad's boss."

"Oh yeah," he said, glancing at the time on his phone. "Let's leave now and see if we can beat the rush hour traffic, we'll see you later, guys," Ryan said as they headed out.

"Bye!" Kiyana called.

"See you!" I replied.

I turned to Jer. "So what now?"

"Wanna see something cool?"

"Sure!"

He handed me my new helmet, and I beamed at him as he helped me clip the buckle together.

He smiled and winked. "As cute as always."

I blushed and looked down. He put on his helmet, got on the bike, and then helped me on.

My grip on Jer got tighter as we headed towards a part of town I'd never been.

We slowed down to stop at some iron gates.

"Um, Princess?"

"Yeah?" I asked.

"Can you by any chance let go of me?"

My eyes widened. "Oh, sorry!"

I could hear loud music in the distance as my gaze scanned the surroundings. The run-down houses caught my attention. Then my focus shifted back to the iron gates.

"Welcome to the hood." Jer mused. "Stay close." I nodded in acknowledgment.

"Come on," he said as he pulled open the gates.

"Are we allowed to be in here?" I asked as I walked in.

He shut the gates. "Of course, we are. Why wouldn't we be?"

I shrugged. "Well, I don't know, maybe the big sign that said 'No trespassing' is an indication."

He rolled his eyes. "If we weren't allowed, they wouldn't have left the gate open."

He grabbed my arm and dragged me through the grass.

"Why is this grass so long?" I said as I avoided my eye being poked out by a blade of grass. I grimaced at the squelch of my converse in the mud. Ugh.

"Because no one cuts it."

I rolled my eyes and sighed, letting him pull me along. We stopped at a clearing, and I gasped.

We were met with the most beautiful sight. There were so many different types of flowers, so many different colors. I could see sunflowers, daisies, angelicas, anemones, and some I had never even seen before. It was beautiful.

He took off his leather jacket and laid it on the ground, then gestured for me to sit down.

"Thanks, Jer. You're too sweet," I chuckled before taking a seat. He settled beside me and shrugged nonchalantly.

"Well, don't get used to it," he replied, absently picking at the grass.

"Too late, I already am," I grinned, taking a moment to appreciate the breathtaking view before us.

"How did you even find this place?" I inquired.

He tilted his head in thought. "I think I was running away from some people and just ended up running through here until I got to the clearing."

"Running from some people?"

He scratched his head. "Yeah, like gang members."

My brows furrowed, and I nodded in understanding. "I'm just glad you're done with all of that."

"Me too," he sighed contentedly.

"So... how exactly did you 'stop'? Did you just walk in there and tell your boss you were done, or did you have to, like, pay him to leave, or maybe even... you know, assassinate him so that—"

"—This isn't some gang movie, Princess," he interjected with a chuckle, "But he wasn't about to let me just leave like that. The thing is, when you try to leave that world, there's a chance you might start snitching, so they usually don't let you go so easily. Your best bet is to just pack up and go to a whole other place. But, you know, I didn't want that. Jacob's got this one-sided beef with me, you saw it."

"I think he feels threatened, because I'm smart and the guys listen to me, even though I'm young. He was always turning everything into a competition between us. We had this pool game. If I won, he'd let me leave. But if he won, I'd have to stick around for less money. Well, I won, and just like that, I was free."

"Wow. You have to admit, it's a little bit like a movie." I pointed out. He laughed and looked off into the distance.

"Wanna know why I like this place so much?" he asked.

"Why?"

He turned to me, a soft smile gracing his lips. "It proves that something beautiful can grow even in the most unexpected places."

I perked up with realization. "Like lotus flowers, they grow from mud."

He nodded approvingly. "Exactly. I mean, if all this," he gestured to the flowers around us, "could bloom in a spot like this... I figured that maybe, even though I haven't been the best me I can be, there's still room for growth. There might be some good left in me. I know it sounds corny and all, but—"

"No, no, Jer, it doesn't."

He smiled warmly and reached for my hand. "Well, I want to thank you for helping me realize it."

I glanced down at our interlocked fingers and then back at him. "Me?"

He nodded. "You see the good in me, that's how I know there is good in me."

I could feel my heart soaring. "Well, I'm happy my opinion matters to you that much. You really are a good person, Jer, I know it."

He squeezed my hand in gratitude, and my heart raced as I watched his eyes drop to my lips.

I felt him leaning in, and I was so shocked that I sat frozen like a statue.

Crunch.

Jer's head snapped up, his eyes narrowing as he looked around. "Who's there?"

Anxious, I scanned our surroundings and moved closer to Jer. Was someone watching us?

Another noise, and Jer stood up, assessing the area. After a few tense moments, he let out a breathy chuckle.

I stood up too, curious. "What?"

He placed a hand on my shoulder and directed my attention to a particular spot. I squinted and barely made out a ball of grey fluff disappearing into the woods.

"Oh, it was a rabbit," I laughed in relief.

Jer nodded before his gaze returned to me, just as intense as before.

I quickly turned away, picking up his jacket. "Well, it's getting late, and I'm getting hungry. How about we start heading back?"

He looked down in what seemed like disappointment and nodded. "Yeah, let's go."

We walked in silence, the earlier moment lingering in the air between us.

I sighed in relief as we finally found the gate, and Jer opened it.

"So, do you want to grab something to eat or...?"

We stopped by his bike, and I turned to him with a slight grimace. "Actually, I was going to have dinner with my dad tonight. He's making Fajitas, so..."

"Nice," he said, clearing his throat. He handed me my helmet, and I put it on before getting on the bike behind him.

When we were about four houses away from mine, Jer gradually slowed down and came to a stop.

I unbuckled my helmet and got off the bike. "Thanks again, Jer, for everything. I'll see you tomorrow."

"Yeah, bye..." he replied as I quickly started to walk away. I felt bad but I just didn't know how to be around him. Was he trying to kiss me today? The possibility that Jer, this insanely hot guy would even think of me romantically had me wanting to pass out.

The next day, I filled Kiyana in on what had happened.

"Do you really think he was trying to kiss me?" I asked, still unsure.

"Yes, Rory, we've been over this. You guys were sitting with a beautiful view, and he basically told you that you were the most important person in his life—"

"—well, I wouldn't go that far—"

"—then he leaned in. It's obvious he was trying to kiss you. That was probably the only reason he brought you there. That stupid bunny just had to ruin everything."

"Hey! That's mean."

"Are you seriously defending him? He ruined your chance at finally, you know, kissing the love of your life."

"What? I never said anything about Jer being the love of my life!"

"L.O.M.L for short. And you didn't need to. I can see it in your eyes. I can see it in your smile." She grinned. "You're all I've ever wanted, and my arms are open wide..."

"Are you seriously singing Lionel Richie? Jer isn't the love of my life or whatever you called it, L.O.M.L?"

"L.O.M.L?"

My eyes widened as I turned to Jer.

"Yeah, it means—Ow!" Kiyana rubbed her arm where I had elbowed her, and she pouted.

"Nothing!" I smiled innocently.

"Okay..." Jer said, looking puzzled.

"Oh my God, Aurora!" a girl exclaimed, grabbing me by the shoulders.

I recognized her as Mona, the girl who seemed nice but was friends with Simran for some reason.

Wow, I never thought I'd say "Simran" and "nice" in the same sentence...ever.

"Um, can I help you?"

"No, I'm helping you!" she said, grabbing my arm. "Follow me."

"What? This better not be another one of Simran's stupid plans."

"No, it has nothing to do with her. Just trust me."

I turned to see Jer and Kiyana following me. At least I had them with me if anything happened.

She opened the doors to the school, and we walked down the stairs.

Then I saw exactly what she wanted me to see and stopped dead in my tracks.

Across the parking lot, walking towards the school, with shorter hair, longer legs, and better style in clothing, was him. Ian.

Our eyes locked, and the biggest smile broke out on his face.

This couldn't be real.

When he waved, it was like the trance I was in broke, and I ran and jumped into his arms. He caught me and held me tight before spinning me around.

I sobbed into his shoulders and squeezed him tighter.

This couldn't be real, could it?

"Ow! What the hell! Rory, did you just bite me?"

I looked at him and smiled sheepishly through my tears. "I was just making sure you were real," I sniffled.

He smiled softly at me and shook his head. "I missed you so much."

"I missed you too," I said as he gently placed me back on my feet.

"Wow," I exclaimed, grabbing his arm to steady myself. My hand traveled up his bicep.

"Like, wow."

He chuckled, flexing a little. Someone cleared their throat, and I turned to see Kiyana raising her eyebrow. I quickly let go of Ian's arm, finally acknowledging the fact that half the school had been watching us.

"Kiyana!"

"Ian!"

They hugged tightly, and that's when I noticed Simran on Ian's other side, glaring at me.

I frowned deeply. What was she doing here?

"Oh! I want you to meet my new boyfriend! Well, later, he's not here yet," Kiyana said. "Oh, and this is Jer!"

Jer looked up from scuffing his feet on the ground.

Ian held out his hand for him. "Hey, I'm Ian."

Jer stared at his hand before glancing at me. "I know."

I laughed and gave Ian a high-five on the hand that was outstretched towards Jer, to save us from any awkwardness.

"Jer isn't the most sociable person," I explained before changing the subject.

"So not to be rude or anything, but why are you here?" I asked.

"Oh well, as you know, I moved because my mom's job had her stationed in Ireland for a couple of years but now she's been stationed back here."

"It's so crazy 'cause I seemed to lose contact with all of you, except Simran. We chat from time to time."

I glanced at Simran, and she smirked at me.

I gritted my teeth.

"And Simran told me how you guys have been like the best of friends since I left. And I heard that you were having a hard time with people teasing you. Thank God Simran has been there for you."

"She what—"

"Well, now that's all over with. Let's go inside," Simran said, grabbing Ian's arm and dragging him along with her. He turned and beamed at me before following her into the school

"I can't believe she would say that."

"That bitch."

"Not to mention she had contact with him for God knows how long, while I've been miserable about the fact that I'd never hear his voice again."

"That bitch."

"You know, it wouldn't have been that bad if she just said that we were friends, but then she had to add that she's been there for me when I was bullied?"

"That bitch."

"Kiyana, could you, like, not?"

"What? She is a bitch!"

I rolled my eyes and started towards the school, then turned to Jer.

"Why didn't you shake his hand?"

He shrugged. "I don't like him."

"Why?" I asked incredulously. "You literally just met him!"

"I just don't," he said, stuffing his hands in his pockets.

"He's jealous," Kiyana whispered to me.

My eyes widened. "What?"

"I'm not jealous, Kiyana," Jer gritted out.

She smiled sheepishly and shrugged as we entered the school.

By lunchtime, I was fuming, to say the least. Simran had made sure that I had no chance at all to catch up with Ian. He was my best friend. What was her deal?

Oh, right, she hated me.

I sat down at our table and sighed.

"What's wrong?" Ryan, who was the only one who had shown up beside me, asked.

This was the first time I'd even seen him today. "Have you heard that my best friend is back in town?"

He nodded. "How could I not when Kiyana won't stop talking about him?"

"Well, I haven't spent more than three minutes with him because Simran has blocked every chance we've had at catching up. She's always ruining everything."

"Oh yeah. Didn't she tell him that you and her were like best friends?"

"Yes! Can you believe that?"

He shook his head. "Well, whenever you do get the chance to speak to him, you need to tell him the truth about her."

Speak of the devil and she shall appear.

"Hey guys!" Simran chirped with a cackle. "Mind if Ian and I sit here?"

Ian gave me a wave and sat down. "Why are you asking? This is the table you guys sit at, right?"

She cleared her throat and sat on the other side of him. "Um, yeah, I was mostly just asking for you..."

I rolled my eyes and bit into my apple.

"So how's your first day going?" I asked, having déjà vu. It felt like Kiyana moving to this school all over again.

"Well, it's been okay. Simran's been helping me out a lot."

She beamed at him and fluttered her eyelashes. Before she could speak, Kiyana plopped down beside Ryan and snorted.

"What is up with your face, Simran? Is there something in your eye? Or are you just having a spasm?"

I couldn't help but giggle behind my hand.

Simran glared at her and flipped her thick hair over her shoulder.

Kiyana offered her a fake smile as she brought out her lunch.

I and Ian gasped.

She had brought Mr. Joseph's amazing brownies for lunch again.

"Oh my God. I've missed you so much," Ian said, grabbing one.

I was right behind him, grabbing two as I laughed.

He bit into it and moaned. "Holy shit, it's even better than I remembered."

"And I thought Rory was bad when it came to these brownies," Ryan said, shaking his head.

"Can I have one?" Simran asked.

I raised an eyebrow. She had literally made fun of me for eating chocolate cake two weeks ago and called me an obese cow. Was she really gonna contradict herself by eating a brownie?

"No." Kiyana deadpanned.

Jer sat on the other side of me a few minutes later with a sigh.

"Hey, where have you been?" I asked.

"Oh I and Amy have been assigned a project in Physics so we're working together, we were just doing some work on it now."

I hummed in response and bit into my brownie harshly.

I hated that girl.

After a few minutes of Simran shamelessly flirting with Ian and Kiyana telling me about the new eyeshadow she bought, Jer placed his book down and sighed, then stood up.

"Hey Ryan, wanna go outside instead?"

"Yes please." Ryan quickly packed up his stuff and got up muttering about how this was the most awkward lunch ever.

"Bye Jeremiah," Simran said, smiling at him flirtatiously.

Was she actually being serious right now? She couldn't focus on one guy?

He walked away with Ryan without even acknowledging her.

"Well, he's an odd fella."

I laughed. "Oooh, look at you, sounding so Irish."

"Well what do you expect, I lived there for a good five years."

"We really need to catch up," I sighed.

He nodded. "Agreed."

"Tell me about Ireland," I said, placing my head in my hands.

"Sure." He threw his arm around my shoulder as he animatedly told me the story of his first day of school in Dublin.

Chapter 14

"So are you free today?"Jer asked, interrupting my conversation with Ian.

I grimaced."I'm sorry Jer, I and Ian were going to watch a movie tonight."

He nodded, his jaw ticking. "You do realize we're gonna have to continue working on our project sooner or later right? You can't just put everything on hold 'cause your buddy's back in town."

"Jer," I said, shocked.

He rolled his eyes. "Y'know what, let me know when you're out of your little bubble and you're back in touch with reality." he turned around and stormed off.

I scrunched up my eyebrows in confusion. I didn't understand what he was so upset about. Okay, maybe I had been blowing him off quite a bit. But I really just wanted to spend time with Ian and with

Simran lurking around. Outside school was the best time for us to hang out, which meant I couldn't work on the project.

"He's intense," Ian commented, with an awkward chuckle.

I gave him a tight smile and nodded. "Yeah...he is." I said watching as he turned a corner down the hall.

"Ready to go?" He asked, closing his locker.

He'd been nice enough to drive me to and from school every day since he got back which meant I didn't ride with Jer anymore. I had to admit I missed riding with him but I guess I missed Ian more.

"So what are we watching?" he asked as we walked to his car.

"I was thinking *The Little Mermaid*?"

"Of course, you'd suggest a Disney movie," he sighed.

"Hey! You used to love watching that movie with me, it was our favorite."

Ian leaned closer, speaking in a hushed tone, "Aurora, please, don't say that out loud." He glanced around nervously as we slipped into his car. "Besides, I was like six back then."

"No, you were twelve—" I started to protest but was silenced by his hand covering my mouth.

"How about we watch an action movie instead?" he asked quickly, changing the subject.

I removed his hand from my mouth, scrunching up my nose in disdain. "Ew, why would we watch a boring action movie?"

He shot me a flat look and started the car. "You're eighteen, Rory, not eight."

"I like what I like, Ian. There's no age limit on loving Disney."

"Okay, okay, fine. How about we compromise and watch something with a bit of action, like Mulan or something?"

"Yay! Sounds good to me."

I shrugged and sat back as we made our way towards my house.

When we got home, we immediately raided the kitchen cupboards for candy and then placed them all on the coffee table.

"I'll be right back, let me get the ice cream." Ian said walking to the kitchen."What do you guys have?"

"Cookie dough, mint chocolate and strawberry ripple I think."

He came back with the cookie dough and mint chocolate knowing too well not to mess with my dad's strawberry ripple.

After devouring two tubs of ice cream, sitting through three movies, and demolishing about a thousand gummy worms, my dad finally turned the key in the front door's lock.

With a brief pause and a blink, he took in the scene before him, then shook his head in mild disbelief.

"What?" I queried, eyebrows raised.

"Oh, nothing. It's just going to take some getting used to, seeing my daughter all cozy with a guy every time I come in from work."

I couldn't help but roll my eyes. "Dad, it's just Ian."

"I know, I know. That's why he isn't currently in a headlock for having his arm around you right now," he quipped, punctuating his statement with an exaggerated high-pitched laugh.

Ian's arm gingerly disentangled from around me, and he subtly scooted a bit farther away on the couch.

"Um, well, I guess maybe I should head off," Ian stuttered, his gaze darting nervously toward my dad.

"Don't be ridiculous, Ian. You're staying for dinner. Don't mind my dad – you know how overly protective he is."

I seized his arm, standing up myself. "Alright, let's cook some pasta."

"Or... we could just order a pizza," my dad interjected with a faint grimace.

"What? No way. I wanna cook for once, it'll be fun."

"Um, Rory, I think your dad might be onto something. I mean, I'm not exactly a chef, and you... well, let's just say your kitchen skills seem to have their own unique flair," Ian admitted while scratching his head.

"B-but I—"

"You tried to boil pasta without water," they chimed in simultaneously.

I gasped in mock horror. "Hey now! That was one time. How was I supposed to know spaghetti needed a water bath?"

"Darling, when you're boiling something... usually water is involved," my dad offered with a bemused grin.

I huffed and flopped back onto the couch. "Fine, fine. Pizza it is, then."

✧

I shot a glare at the back of Amy's annoying head as she tossed her hair and laughed at whatever Jer had just said.

Jer.

He'd been distant lately, spending most of his time with her.

And to make matters worse, he'd traded seats with her partner, leaving me stuck next to Jimmy Fox while he sat there with her.

Two days ago, it had felt like a punch to the gut when I walked into class and saw them deep in conversation, while Jimmy casually occupied Jer's previous spot.

I sighed and looked down, my heart sinking. I guess I was right, he wasn't trying to kiss me that day. He liked Amy.

When the bell finally rang, I got up slowly and shouldered my bag, my gaze fixed on Jer assisting Amy with her belongings.

He never did that for me.

"Hey, what's up with you?" Ryan questioned as I slumped down across from him at our lunch table.

"Nothing," I muttered, burying my face in my hands.

"Hey, guys!" Kiyana's voice chirped as she settled beside Ryan. "What's wrong Rory?" she inquired, her brow furrowed. I simply shook my head, then turned to gaze out the window, though I couldn't miss the exchange of worried glances between my two friends.

Soon, Ian joined us, with Simran trailing behind.

I let out an exasperated groan as they took their seats. I was beyond tired of hearing her relentless flirtations with him.

"Well, someone's clearly not having the best day," Ian remarked, his tone laced with amusement.

"Really? I wouldn't have guessed, isn't her face always scrunched up?" Simran quipped, her laughter ringing like she was delivering a punchline.

I brushed off her comment and let out a sigh.

I could sense Ian's concerned gaze fixed on me as I stared blankly out the window, idly poking at my food.

Simran's group of friends passed by, and they waved to her.

She playfully wiggled her fingers in response before they settled at their own table.

"You know, for supposed best friends, you and Aurora don't exactly scream friendship vibes. And what's the deal with you two only hanging out during lunch? Oh, and those girls you just greeted – who are they, what's with the multiple friend groups? And where's that girl who's always bothering you that Simran spoke about, Aurora, her name was...Gretel, right?" Ian's inquisitive voice flowed, almost like he was putting together a puzzle.

"Wow, you're on a roll with questions today. I could barely catch half of that," Simran nervously chuckled. "By the way, your shirt looks really cool, it—"

"You know what, Simran? Just shut the fuck up, okay?" I snapped, unable to contain my frustration any longer. I watched as everyone's eyes widened, and my outburst continued almost uncontrollably.

"I'm sick of you. I'm sick of your dumb face, your dumb lies, and your pathetic attempts at flirting. You and I aren't friends, never were. Ever since Ian left, you've been the one harassing me, tormenting me nearly every single day! There's no Greta or Gretel or whatever. So do everyone a favor and just fuck right off."

I took a deep breath, stood up, and collected my belongings before swiftly exiting the cafeteria. Oddly, a sense of relief washed over me. It was nice to finally get that out.

But my relief soon morphed into dread as I realized what I had just done – cursed multiple times.

"Rory! Hold up!" Ian's voice echoed after me as he hurried to catch up.

I slowed down, allowing him to reach my side as we continued down the hall.

"Why didn't you tell me earlier, Rory?" he questioned.

I shrugged. "I don't know. I guess at first it didn't bother me much. Or maybe I didn't want to shatter your perception of her, you guys seem to really get along."

He shook his head and sighed. "I should have known. I think deep down, I did kinda know - that she was exaggerating the truth. She was such a bitch to you before I left. I just thought that maybe she had changed..."

I shook my head. "Nope, she got much worse."

He draped his arm around my shoulder, pulling me in for comfort. "I'm sorry you had to go through that. I wish I didn't leave, I wish I could have shielded you from all this. I mean, I just witnessed Aurora Winter's drop the 'f' bomb multiple times. This is some serious chaos."

I glanced downward, overwhelmed with a sense of shame. "I don't even know what got into me."

He cast me a knowing glance, fully aware of the emotions that had triggered my outburst.

"What?" I asked, defensively.

"So, when were you planning to fill me in on your crush on Jeremiah?" he asked casually, as I began to open my locker. I froze.

"Huh?" I spluttered in disbelief.

He chuckled. "Come on, Rory. It wasn't exactly a mystery. Who would have guessed you had a jealous streak?" he teased, laughing again as I shot him a glare.

"I have no idea what you're talking about," I retorted, shutting my locker. I felt him fall into step beside me as I turned to walk away.

"Seriously, Aurora. I might have been away for five years, but I know you. You like him."

I frowned. "Can we please drop this?" I pleaded.

He nodded. "Sure thing." I breathed a sigh of relief. "As long as you're willing to acknowledge your feelings for him."

I abruptly halted and turned to Ian. "What? Why?"

"Because deep down, you know you like him. You just don't want to admit it."

I cast my gaze downward. "Well, it's not that simple. I already know he wouldn't feel the same way."

"I wouldn't be so sure. Haven't you noticed how much he seems to not like me? Ever wonder why?"

I shrugged, failing to grasp his point.

"It's because he thinks I'm taking you away from him. Of course, we're friends and nothing more but he doesn't know that."

I crossed my arms, teasingly retorting, "And when did you become so wise?"

"I'm just observant," he countered, his expression making it clear he wasn't letting me off the hook.

I took a deep breath, mustering my courage. "Fine, I like Jeremiah Summers," I confessed softly.

"See? Now that we've got that out of the way, we can work on getting you two together," he proclaimed.

"What? No way."

"Oh, yes way."

"No."

"Yes," he insisted, gripping my arm to halt my steps. "And step one is you actually talking to him. You can't just glare at the back of his new friends' head and hope for her to disappear. He's clearly upset because you've been blowing him off for me, and now it's time for an apology."

I nervously twisted my fingers. "That's why he's mad?"

Ian nodded like it was obvious. "Think about it. When was the last time you two spent any time together? You shouldn't have pushed him aside because of me. I'm back, Aurora, and we have all the time in the world now. I'm here to stay, so life keeps moving. That means getting back on track with your Shakespeare project and everything else."

His words hit home, and I realized he was right about everything.

"So, as soon as you get the chance, talk to him. Deal?" he pressed.

I nodded as we parted ways, heading to our separate classes.

The following day, I walked nervously toward my English class, well aware that I needed to face Jer. The challenge, however, was finding a way to separate him from Amy, who seemed to cling to him like a magnet.

Outside the classroom, I leaned against the lockers opposite, waiting with a few others for the teacher to arrive and unlock the door.

Laughter echoed down the hallway, and I glanced up to see Amy and Jer strolling towards our class, both sporting goofy smiles. A pang of jealousy gripped my chest, and I quickly averted my gaze.

Finally, Mr. Dermott arrived, and we all filed into the classroom. Jimmy took the seat beside me, his scent of chlorine as overpowering as ever. Ugh.

Hearing Amy's laughter again made me clench my teeth. I turned to Jimmy, hoping for a distraction.

"Hey, Jimmy."

He looked up, seemingly surprised by my attention. "Hey..." he responded, a hint of uncertainty in his voice.

"What's new?" I inquired.

He seemed taken aback, as if he hadn't expected me to strike up a conversation. "U-um, not much," he stammered, his dark loose curls bouncing slightly as he shook his head.

I chuckled. "Aw, you're just too adorable."

His cheeks flushed a deep shade of red, and he glanced downward. "Well, uh, is there anything interesting happening with you? I'm quite bored. Tell me something cool about yourself."

"Um..."

I rolled my eyes playfully. "Okay, do you happen to like..." I scanned the surroundings for inspiration, "...Disney? Are you a Disney fan?"

A spark of excitement lit up his eyes. "Yes! I absolutely love Disney."

I couldn't hide my surprise. "Really?"

He nodded enthusiastically. "Definitely!"

"Alright, what's your favorite Disney Princess?"

His face lit up even more. "Well, I'd have to go with Ariel."

"Hmm, predictable," I remarked, shaking my head.

He chuckled. "Predictable? How come?"

"Every time I ask a guy about their favorite Disney Princess, they almost always say Ariel."

"What? She's hot!"

"That's what they all say," I said in a sing-song tone.

"Okay, what about you?" he asked, then his eyes widened."Wait, let me guess!"

I raised an eyebrow."Okay, shoot."

"Don't give me that challenging look; it's pretty obvious you're a Sleeping Beauty fan, with your name being Aurora and all. It's cool your parents named you after her," he guessed.

"Well, actually, they were going to name me Nella, but apparently, I slept a ton when I was first born, so they went with Aurora instead."

He wrinkled his nose. "A wise choice. Nella doesn't quite suit you."

I chuckled at his response. "Do you also have a thing for superheroes?"

"Absolutely, I'm a big fan. Why do you ask?"

I gestured to his shirt.

He glanced down at his red shirt, featuring a circular logo with a lightning bolt piercing through it. "Oh, right. The Flash is my favorite."

"Why's that?"

"Who wouldn't want super speed? I could wake up just a fraction of a second before school and still get here in time, never late, always ahead."

"That does sound pretty awesome."

"Well, Mr. Brody lets me use his room during lunch to catch up on TV shows. Right now, I'm re-watching The Flash from the beginning while I wait for the new season. Wanna join me?"

I arched an eyebrow, amused. "Well, well, look at you! Going from barely being able to make eye contact to inviting me to lunch."

He blushed. "I-I just thought—"

"—Of course, I'd love to!"

"Really?" he asked, his face lighting up.

"Absolutely." I smiled. It might just provide some much-needed distance from my friends after my recent outburst and Jimmy seemed like such a sweet guy. I knew how it felt being alone at lunch.

"One thing though," I began, grimacing.

"Ask away."

"Why do you smell like—"

"Chlorine?" he asked with a sigh.

I nodded sheepishly.

He sighed. "I work as a pool boy after school every day."

"Oh, really?" I queried.

"Yeah, maybe not the most glamorous job, but it pays well, so it's alright."

Before I could respond, the bell rang, and Jimmy swiftly packed his belongings.

He turned toward me, his tall figure looming over mine. "I need to stop by my locker before we watch the show. Do you know where Mr. Brody's room is?" he inquired.

I nodded in confirmation.

"Great, see you in a bit!" he called out as he exited the class, capturing Jer's attention. I noticed his eyes flickering between me and the door Jimmy had just exited. His jaw clenched slightly, and he began packing his things.

I nibbled on my lip, recalling that I wanted to talk to him.

I followed behind Jeremiah and Amy as they left the room, my mind racing to find the right approach.

I maintained a slight distance, my eyes rolling at how Amy seemed to laugh at every single thing he said.

When they eventually parted ways, I drew nearer to Jer. He turned and arched an eyebrow at me.

"Are you following me?" he inquired.

I shook my head. "Uh, no... well, yes. I just wanted to talk to you."

"What?"he snapped.

I hesitated for a moment, gathering my thoughts. "I was just wondering when we could continue working on our project," I finally asked.

He stopped in his tracks and faced me, a humorless laugh escaping him. "You know, this situation is oddly familiar... except, I was the one asking you that same question."

Guilt washed over me, and I glanced down. "I know, and I'm sorry. I won't do that again."

He raised an eyebrow and crossed his arms. "Oh, for real? Now that it's all convenient for you, we can just start back up where we left off with the project?"

I fell silent, knowing he had every right to be upset.

He shook his head, his frustration evident. "And it's not just about the project. You pushed our friendship, your friendship with your other friends, Ryan and Kiyana, to the back burner. It was like you forgot about all of us the minute precious Ian showed up. When was the last time you hung out with anyone but him?"

I bit my lip, my own frustration rising. "Look, Jer, I'm sorry. I just wanted to spend time with my childhood friend that I missed. Why are you making this into such a big deal?" I countered.

He offered a sarcastic smile. "You're absolutely right. There's no big deal at all. That's why I'll also be spending time with my friend. Remember Amy?" he asked.

My heart tightened at the mention of her name.

"Well, I reckon I'll be 'spending time' with her before we get back to our project. But no sweat; I'm sure you'll have plenty to keep you busy," he remarked, backing up. "I overheard Jamie saying he'd link up with you soon, just another person you'd rather hang out with over me," he added with a tinge of bitterness.

"His name is Jimmy," I muttered as he stalked off.

I found Jimmy unlocking Mr. Brody's room.

"Wait, he gave you a key?" I asked in surprise.

He nodded and gestured for me to enter. "Yep, I guess I'm his favorite student."

Jimmy powered up Mr. Brody's computer and launched Netflix.

I quickly sent a message to my friends, letting them know I wouldn't be joining them for lunch today.

Once he had everything set up, Jimmy turned on the projector, casting the screen onto the whiteboard. I settled into a seat in the front row as he dimmed the lights.

"This is pretty cool. It's like being at the movies. Do you do this every day?" I inquired.

"Yep. It's pretty dope. No heads blocking the view, no kids crying, and no annoying people on their phones," he replied.

I pressed my lips together. "You come here by yourself?"

His smile wavered. "Well, yeah."

"Oh," I murmured. "You don't have anyone that joins you?" I asked.

He scratched the back of his head awkwardly. "I don't really have any friends."

I had a feeling he would respond that way.

"Well, I didn't have many friends either, until senior year. If I had known you were into Disney, we might have hit it off sooner," I chuckled. "But hey, it's never too late to make new friends."

He grinned back at me. "You're absolutely right."

With a click of the keyboard, he started the show and then settled in beside me. My face lit up when he pulled out a bag of chips and some candy from his bag.

"Yay!" I exclaimed. He chuckled and handed me the candy. I settled in, realizing that I could definitely get used to this. As the show began, I quickly got absorbed in the storyline.

Chapter 15

Jer walked into Literature class with his arm around Amy, a wide grin plastered on his face.

I had come to terms with the fact that he liked her, and that he would never have those feelings for me.

Inhaling deeply, I turned my gaze away from them as they took their seats in front of me.

"Are you okay?" Jimmy's voice broke my thoughts.

I turned to him and nodded, whispering, "Yeah."

He didn't seem entirely convinced, casting a quick glance at Jeremiah before turning his attention back to me.

"If you say so."

"Alright, class! I have assignments to grade for 10th grade. Use this time to work on your projects," Mr. Dermott announced before heading to his desk.

I let out a sigh, rolling my eyes when Amy's giggles echoed for what felt like the hundredth time since class began.

I wasn't sure what to do. Jer wasn't speaking to me, and it seemed unlikely he would work with me either.

Since Amy and Jimmy had already finished their project weeks ago, Jimmy retrieved a comic book from his bag to read.

I chewed on my lip, glancing at Jer. He was still engrossed in conversation with Amy, not even acknowledging what the teacher had said.

I picked up my pencil and started doodling in my notebook, unable to resist eavesdropping on Jeremiah and Amy's conversation. It wasn't entirely my fault, though; Amy was speaking quite loudly, and everyone else was silently focused on their projects.

"Yeah, so which movie would you like to see?" I heard Amy's voice ring out.

Were they planning to go see a movie together?

"I'm not picky, as long as it's an action movie," Jer replied.

I took a deep breath, attempting to steady my emotions. At least he always let me pick the movies.

"Alright, sounds good. I can't wait to go see something," she said, her cheeks turning a shade of pink. "Especially with you."

And just like that, something inside me snapped, echoing the way it had the previous day with Simran.

"You know what, Ava?" I said, slamming my pencil on the table, intentionally mispronouncing her name. "People are actually trying to work here. So either be quiet or get the fuck out!" I finished.

I had somehow shown some self-control in whisper-shouting, so only those closest to us could hear, and I wouldn't get into trouble with Mr. Dermott.

Jer stared at me in disbelief, Amy looked perplexed, and Jimmy awkwardly cleared his throat.

Feeling a wave of embarrassment, I looked down and noticed my pencil had snapped in half. I must have hit the table harder than I realized.

Thankfully, the bell rang, signaling the end of the class. I hastily packed my belongings and dashed out of the room.

Jimmy caught up to me quickly. "Hey, hey, hey," he said, grabbing the strap of my bag. "Calm down, Aurora."

I ran a hand through my hair, my mind racing with regret. He probably thought I was a complete jerk now. We had only just become friends, and I had already ruined it.

"What was that?" he asked, clearly taken aback.

I fidgeted with my fingers and shrugged, unable to meet his gaze.

"That wasn't like you at all. Is something going on?" he inquired.

"No," I mumbled.

"Okay, I might not know you that well yet, but that was definitely out of character."

I remained silent.

"Just tell me what's happening—"

"I have a crush on Jeremiah!" I blurted out, unable to hold it in any longer.

His eyes widened. "Oh." He grimaced as a realization hit him. "Oh."

"It doesn't matter though, he doesn't want anything to do with me."

"So you decided to take it out on Amy?" he asked.

"What? No! She's just incredibly annoying! You have to admit she's annoying."

"Well, yeah, I guess. She thinks she's smarter than everybody and she's rude but I wouldn't call her out on it. You've barely ever spoken to her so you don't even have the right to call her out on it, really."

"I feel like a terrible person."

"I can't believe you swore, really doesn't seem like you."

"Jimmy, you're not really helping here."

"I'm sorry, Aurora. I'm just really surprised," he shrugged. "But honestly, don't stress. I mean, you're too kind for your own good. Everyone has their limits."

"Will you come to lunch with me?" I asked, wanting to move past the earlier incident.

"In Mr. Brody's room, sure. But in the cafeteria? No way."

"Come on, Jimmy!"

"No!" he exclaimed.

"Jimmy, they're just my friends. There's nothing to worry about," I said while waiting for him to finish at his locker.

"I never said I was worried!"

I raised an eyebrow, skeptical of his response.

"Alright, fine. I am, okay? I just don't think it's a good idea. I'm more comfortable having lunch in Mr. Brody's class."

"But I don't like seeing you alone. Please, Jimmy? Do it for me!"

He chewed on his lip. "What if they don't like me?"

"Come on, Jimmy! They'll definitely like you. You're a great guy."

He let out a sigh. "I don't know, Aurora."

"Just give it a shot. Please, Jimmy!" I said, reaching out to grab his arm.

"Fine! But if this ends up being a disaster, it's on you."

I waved his concerns away. "Sure, sure."

"I have to admit, I like your cologne," I shamelessly said, taking a sniff.

He chuckled. "Thanks, Aurora."

"I'm just thankful that you were kind enough to point out how bad I smelled."

I raised an eyebrow. "Well, when you put it like that, it sounds like I wasn't being very nice."

He chuckled. "Fair point. But seriously, thanks. Now I make sure to take two showers after work, and I got myself a new cologne. Hopefully, the chlorine smell won't linger anymore."

When we reached our table, I cleared my throat to get everyone's attention.

"Alright, so you guys might have been wondering why I've been missing lunch for the past week. Well, it's because I've been spending it with my new friend, Jimmy!" I introduced, turning the focus from me to Jimmy as Kiyana, Ryan, and Ian redirected their attention.

I gave Jimmy's arm a reassuring squeeze as we took our seats.

"Jimmy, this is Kiyana, Ryan, and Ian," I introduced, pointing at each of them as I mentioned their names. Kiyana waved, Ryan nodded, and Ian offered a friendly smile.

"Nice to meet you," Ian greeted, extending his hand. Jimmy shook it, returning the gesture.

"Alright, so what's up with all of you—"

"Aurora?" I heard someone say, interrupting me.

I was completely taken aback when I saw that it was Simran.

My jaw dropped at her appearance. Her face was devoid of makeup, her hair was pulled back in a casual ponytail (a sight I had never seen before), and she was dressed simply in baggy jeans and an oversized graphic tee.

Gone were her usual high heels, crop tops and mini skirts.

"What the heck..."

It wasn't surprising that the cafeteria was staring at her, their reactions mirroring mine. Well, except for Ian, who seemed to be gazing at her like he was looking at an angel.

"I, um, was wondering if we could talk," she said quietly.

"Me?" I asked incredulously.

She nodded, biting her lip.

Her behavior was so unexpected. I had no idea how to respond to this.

"Sure," I said, grabbing my bag and following her out of the cafeteria, casting a perplexed look at my friends.

"I'm so sorry," she said, stopping as the cafeteria doors closed behind us.

"Sorry?"

"Yes. For everything, Aurora. I know I can never truly make it right, and you probably won't forgive me, nor should you. But I still want to try my best. First, though, I need to tell you why I did what I did, even though it doesn't excuse it."

"What exactly are you apologizing for?" I asked, crossing my arms.

She sighed and looked down. "For how I've treated you for the past five years, or really, the past fourteen years."

I cast my gaze to the side, shaking my head. It seemed very convenient that she wanted to apologize now, was this even genuine or just a ploy to appease Ian?

"Can we go to the courtyard, please?" she asked.

I nodded hesitantly, I might as well hear her out. We walked in silence, and I could feel Simran casting guilty glances at me. This whole situation was beyond strange to me.

We both settled onto a vacant bench in the courtyard.

"Okay, so I'm going to explain why I've treated you so terribly," she began, taking a deep breath.

"Do you remember when we started kindergarten and we were friends?" she asked.

I nodded curtly, already annoyed. If this whole thing had stemmed from something that happened when we were literally four, I was gonna lose it.

"And then, literally the next day, I began being mean to you?"

I nodded again.

"Well, the reason for that was that when I was trying to make friends with Ian, the moment he saw you, he walked away from me and straight to you," she said, rubbing her arm. "To be honest, everyone wanted to be friends with you. You were the unique looking, beautiful girl with a big blonde curly afro and a bright smile."

My eyebrows knitted together in confusion. I had always assumed people found me odd due to my appearance. I thought they stared at me because I looked weird.

"I know, it sounds ridiculous. We were kids, practically still toddlers. But it wasn't just that one time. Every time Ian and I would play together, you'd always show up, and then his attention would solely be on you. If we had a playdate, you had to be invited. If we played a game, you'd get to choose."

"And it wasn't that I wanted Ian all to myself or anything like that. I would have loved it if we were all friends, you know? A cute little trio. But no, once you showed it was like I was invisible. You guys would hold hands while we'd walk to school and I'd just stroll behind you with our parents. They'd gush about how cute you two were and how you'd probably get married and stuff."

"This went on all through elementary, and middle school. It was the two of you and me behind, always. The third wheel. You didn't seem to care that I was left out, that's why I'd lash out at you and—"

She took a deep breath. "I was just so jealous of you. I still am."

My eyes widened. "You're jealous of me?" I asked incredulously.

She shrugged and picked at the loose threads on her shirt.

It was a lot to process. Finally, I was understanding why she had treated me so horribly all these years. Of course I was still mad at her but I felt really bad. How did I not notice I was leaving someone out, excluding a person from our friendship. That wasn't me.

"But Simran, you're the most popular girl at school, you're beautiful and wealthy. I can't understand why you'd still be jealous of me now."

"Because money and popularity don't mean everything. You're kind and caring. You always seem so happy and carefree. You have genuine friends who care about you. You always have a huge smile on your face."

She sighed and shook her head. "When Ian left for Ireland, I was furious. I believed you'd ruined my chance of being friends with him, and it seemed too late since he was leaving. So, I started taking out my frustration on you even more," she whispered, her voice cracking.

"I'm so sorry, Aurora. I know I don't deserve your forgiveness, and Ian probably won't even talk to me. But I genuinely am sorry. And even if it doesn't change anything, I'll do everything I can to make it right," she said, tears welling up in her eyes. "I promise."

I shook my head. "Simran, I don't know what to say—"

"—you don't need to say anything. I need to make amends, not just for you but for myself as well. I hope one day I can let go of this overwhelming guilt I carry."

"So now you suddenly have a guilty conscience?" I asked, crossing my arms. "Where was this guilt when you were trying to insinuate that my mother left me purposely? You knew her Simran, your mom was her friend, saying stuff like that is just so messed up. I understand now the reason you treated me the way you have but sometimes you took it too far, Simran."

She winced, running her hand through her hair in frustration.

"Is your guilt just because Ian sees who you really are? If he hadn't come back, would you even be having this change of heart?"

"I know how it seems, and I can't deny that part of it is because of Ian, but what you said to me the other day also struck me. Your words hit home, and the looks I received from Ian and your friends when you left the cafeteria made me realize I had become someone I didn't want to be. It was all fun when the people around me supported my behavior. It didn't seem so bad, but seeing the looks of disappointment and hate. It crushed me."

"Every time I've said something to you in the past, you've brushed it off with a smile or walked away. But this time, you broke. You were angry, and you confronted me in a way I didn't even know you could.

You stood up to me, and as shocking as it was, it was necessary. I thought making you crack would bring me satisfaction, but it just made me feel awful. I never want to make you feel like that again. I appreciate your positivity and optimism, traits I wish I had. I wish I had a friend like you."

I squirmed uncomfortably. I didn't know how to respond to Simran speaking so positively about me. "You want a friend like me but it certainly seemed like after Ian left no one else did. People I'd hung out with started to disappear, everyone avoided me like the plague."

She looked down, a mixture of guilt and shame in her expression. "I'm the reason for that."

I bit my lip. I had suspected this was the case, but I needed confirmation.

"I used my popularity to isolate you. I made sure no one would approach you."

I shrugged. "Honestly, if they were true friends, they wouldn't have abandoned me based on your words. So maybe, in an odd way, I should thank you. The friends I have now are my real friends."

"I wonder what it's like to have real friends," she mused, her gaze distant. "Aside from Ian and that few years with you, I haven't experienced true friendship, if I'd even call it that. Most people despise me."

I didn't expect to feel so bad during this conversation. Knowing that her only experience of true friendship was being a third wheel and feeling ignored made me feel awful. But at the same time she could have changed things around and made friends when Ian left, in some ways she had created this situation for herself.

The distant sound of the bell interrupted my thoughts.

"Alright, well, I better get to class. So, I guess I'll see you around?" I asked. I wasn't sure if I was ready to fully accept her apology. I needed time to process everything.

She bit her lip. "I honestly don't know. I'm considering transferring schools."

"What? You don't need to leave because of this." Despite my lingering anger, a part of me felt a twinge of compassion. It was senior year and we only had a few months left, there was no reason to leave.

"I think I do, Aurora. I need a fresh start."

I nodded, understanding her perspective. "Well, take care."

She gave me the first genuine smile I had ever seen from her. "You too."

I began to walk away but turned back slightly. "Hey, Simran?"

"Yeah?" she responded, turning toward me.

"I like your new style."

Her face brightened as she looked down at her clothes, then back up at me. "Thank you."

I gave a brief half-hearted smile before continuing on to my next class.

"So, what did she want to talk about?" Kiyana asked, her curiosity evident.

I glanced at all my friends, including Jimmy, who were eagerly waiting for an update.

I rolled my eyes. "Guys, it's not really any of your business, but in short, she apologized for being a massive bitch to me all these years." We walked out of the school building, the conversation still lingering in the air.

"Oh." Kiyana's surprise was palpable.

"So, is swearing just normal for you now or?" Ryan asked, a smirk on his face.

I facepalmed, not even noticing what I had said. "Darn it."

He chuckled. "Better."

"Hey, how about we all go out for lunch?" Kiyana suggested, diverting the topic.

Everyone readily agreed, and the plan was set.

"Um, guys, I might have to pass on that. I've got work," Jimmy chimed in, starting to walk backward.

I pouted playfully. "Aw." I caught hold of his arm before he could retreat further, pulling him into a quick hug.

He chuckled and patted my head fondly, then headed off to his car.

The rest of us continued, and eventually, we made our way to Ian's car. "Cici's Pizza?" Ryan proposed.

"Sounds good," Ian agreed. "We'll meet you guys there."

After enjoying our meal, Ian dropped me off at home.

"So, you talked to Simran," he said, a hint of curiosity in his voice.

I raised an eyebrow. "Yes, Ian. We've established that."

"Did she happen to mention anything about me or our conversation?"

"Your conversation?"

"Well, if you could call it that. More like me shouting at her for an hour."

"Well, she did mention you, but she didn't go into detail about that."

"What exactly did she say?" Ian asked impatiently, clearly curious.

I crossed my arms. "I'm not telling."

He let out an exaggerated whine. "Come on, Rory, don't be like that!"

"Stop! It was a private conversation between her and me. And I'm still trying to process everything she said."

He parked the car in front of my house. "Well, whatever she said, there's no excuse for her behavior. She's been cruel to you, and honestly, I don't think I'll ever look at her the same way again."

I nodded, understanding his sentiment. But I couldn't help but think about what could be brewing between Ian and Simran, especially after all those years that he was only focused on our friendship. I wasn't ready to forgive Simran, but I also wanted to give Ian the chance to figure things out with her.

"You might not have to look at her at all soon," I mumbled, hinting at the possibility of her leaving.

"What do you mean?" he asked, curious.

"She might be moving schools, or even leaving town."

"Really?" His surprise was evident.

I gave him a knowing look. "Well, maybe someone could change her mind before she leaves..."

His eyes widened, and he turned to me, a hint of realization dawning on him. "Uh, I'll see you tomorrow, Aurora. There's something I need to do.

I got out of the car with a smile. "Okay, bye."

He quickly drove away, and I shook my head, amused by his predictability.

Chapter 16

I groaned as my phone kept ringing insistently.

"What?" I said in an annoyed tone as I picked it up.

"Oh. Sorry, is this a bad time—" came a hesitant voice from the other end.

"Simran?"

"Yeah, it's me. I just wanted to talk..."

I pinched the bridge of my nose. How did she even get my number? Ian, I guessed. Ian was the bridge between us. He was my best friend, and if he had made up with her, did that mean I had to be too? I wasn't ready for this. I took a deep breath, trying to quell my irritation. "I'm sorry for my tone. I'm not really a morning person."

"Really? I kinda pictured you as an early bird."

"Well, I kinda pictured sleeping in today, yet here we are," I replied with a touch of sarcasm. An awkward silence hung in the air.

"Um, well, I was just wondering if maybe, um, would you like to meet up for coffee?"

I let out a sigh. "What's the purpose of this, Simran? I heard your apology."

"I know, it's just that there's so much more I want to say. Give me a chance to prove to you that I'm changing."

"You don't need to prove anything to me," I retorted, holding back the rest of my sentence that would have told her to just leave me alone.

"But I want to, Aurora. Just an hour. Please."

Internally groaning, I realized I was about to agree to something I never thought would happen. "Fine," I grumbled.

"How about 3 PM? That way you'll have at least two more hours to sleep."

"Cool," I said, pulling my covers tighter around me.

"Okay, see you then."

"Yeah, good night,"I said, already half asleep.

"Um, but it's noon—"

I hung up the phone and flung it away before closing my eyes.

"Aurora!"

I groaned, burying my head under the covers.

"Aurora!"

The covers were yanked off. "Aurora, move yuh backside offa di bed right now. Yuh friend been a-wait fi yuh fi a whole hour now!"

"She's not my friend," I mumbled, then shot up in bed as I processed his words. "Wait, an hour?"

"Yes, an hour. I already came up to wake you at 3 PM, and you're still in bed," my dad scolded, drawing back the curtains.

"Dad," I whined, shielding my eyes.

"Get up. Now."

I reluctantly rolled out of bed and hurriedly got ready.

Rushing down the stairs, I found Simran in the living room watching SpongeBob.

"I'm sorry about the wait," I apologized with a hesitant smile.

"It's cool," she shrugged, giving me a genuine smile back. I noticed her casual attire - dark washed baggy jeans, sneakers, and a crop top.

"This style suits you," I couldn't help but compliment.

"Thanks. I feel so much better and comfortable in these." She said, smoothing down her outfit.

"We should probably get going. I think we'll need to go somewhere else instead of that café. It closes at 4.30 PM."

"Ooh! I know where we should go!" I exclaimed.

Half an hour later, we were walking into a nearby diner.

As we entered, a high-pitched squeal caught my attention, and I gasped as a body collided with mine.

"My baby!"

I burst out laughing as Derrick enveloped me in a tight hug, creating quite the scene.

After a playfully pushed him away. "I knew you'd be here."

He grinned and pulled me into a tight hug. "We haven't hung out in forever."

His eyes then flicked to the person awkwardly lingering nearby – Simran. His face twisted in surprise before morphing into a playful expression.

"Bitchy girl," he quipped, tilting his head. "Bitchy girl doesn't seem so bitchy anymore."

I shot him a look that said 'behave'. "Cut it out, Derrick. Simran and I are here for lunch."

His face changed to one of intrigue. "Oh, okay this should be interesting. Sign me up!"

I shook my head. " Unfortunately, you will not be part of it. Just go back to annoying Sadie. After we're done, we can catch up."

With a sigh and an exaggerated shrug, he walked away.

"Hi, Aurora," Sadie greeted with a warm smile, arriving to take our orders. Thankfully, she seemed to be in a better mood than last time today.

I returned the smile. "Hey, Sadie."

"Ready to order?" she asked, pulling out her notepad.

I nodded. "Sure. I'll go with a classic – cheeseburger and fries."

Sadie jotted it down. "And to drink?"

"Strawberry milkshake, please."

Sadie turned her attention to Simran. "And for you?"

Simran hesitated for a moment, then spoke up. "I'll have the Caesar salad and water, please."

"Sure thing," Sadie replied before turning to leave.

Simran cleared her throat, drawing Sadie's attention back. "Actually, can I change that order? I'll go for the curly fries, a cheeseburger, and a chocolate milkshake."

Sadie noted down the revised order with a nod. "No problem."

"I'm making up for lost time. I'm sick of all the diets." Simran explained as Sadie walked away, referring to the order amendment.

I nodded, not wanting to push the subject further. "So... what's the reason behind this little lunch meeting anyway?" I asked, my tone guarded.

"Well," she said, a slow smile forming. "I've got news to share and I wanted to say thank you for something."

I motioned for her to continue.

"Okay, so I'm not moving!" She beamed.

"Oh, wow. What made you change your mind?" I inquired, though I had my suspicions.

Simran's blush was obvious as she looked down. "Ian paid me a visit recently, and we had a heart-to-heart. He managed to talk me out of leaving, hence the change."

"Ah, I figured it had something to do with him," I said, trying to keep my tone neutral.

She tilted her head, giving me a knowing look. "I know you had something to do with getting him to talk to me, even if he won't admit it himself."

I couldn't help but chuckle. "Well, I'm glad it worked out, I guess."

Sadie arrived with our drinks, interrupting our conversation momentarily.

"Here you go, ladies," she said as she placed our drinks in front of us.

We thanked her before she left.

"So, apart from preventing our school from losing its resident queen bee, what else did you and Ian discuss?" I asked, raising an eyebrow.

Simran's blush deepened as she rolled her eyes. "Well, if you really want to know, Ian apologized for all those years we didn't really get to know each other. He also confessed that he has feelings for me. He said he really liked getting to know the real me when we'd talk while he was still in Ireland. And despite everything, including my less-than-stellar behavior towards you, he can't shake those feelings."

"Interesting." I mumbled.

"Yeah," she said, her eyebrows furrowing at my tone. "But of course he wanted to talk to you about this first. We're taking everything very slow. He's still angry about my past actions, but he's willing to give me a chance to make things right if you are. If so, we'll start as friends and see where it goes."

I nodded. I knew it was silly for me to be mad at this seeing as I did push Ian to talk to her. I was just so conflicted between doing what's right and being rightfully mad and bitter.

"I mean, I'm not thrilled about just being friends, but considering everything, it's more than I deserve."

I leaned back, taking in Simran's genuine remorse and the effort she seemed to be putting in to make things right. Maybe, just maybe, there was actually a decent person in there.

My agreement came out as a reflex, a principle I lived by. "Everyone deserves a second chance, Simran."

Her lips curved into a soft smile, gratitude and emotion mingling. "I'm lucky he's so forgiving. And I'm hoping that, with time, things can heal between us too." Her eyes glistened, on the brink of tears.

"Please, Simran, don't cry." I mumbled.

She let out a self-deprecating laugh. "I promise I'm not trying to turn on the waterworks to win you over. I'm just genuinely overwhelmed, and I need you to know how deeply sorry I am."

Just as the moment became emotionally charged, Sadie arrived with our food, a timely interruption that allowed Simran to regain her composure.

As Sadie left, Simran shifted her gaze toward me. "I know that if the roles were reversed, I wouldn't be so forgiving. I understand it'll take time, but I'm committed to making amends."

I stared down at my food, skepticism and uncertainty churning within me. Simran's sudden transformation was perplexing, to say the least.

"And Aurora," she added with a shaky breath, her tears falling freely. "I genuinely regret those hurtful words I said about your mom. It was thoughtless, and I truly didn't mean any of it. You were always just so happy or indifferent when I threw shit at you so every time I'd just push the limit more. And with Jeremiah, God, I hate how I acted, it was so embarrassing. I just, I felt like it was happening again. I liked a guy and suddenly you had his attention. I was just so horrible. I'm truly sorry, I really am."

I looked up to meet her tearful eyes, my own emotions conflicted. It was strange to see her in this vulnerable state, a far cry from the confident and abrasive girl I had known for so long.

"I appreciate your apology," I finally replied, my voice more even than I felt. "But actions have consequences, Simran. You can't just do hurtful things and expect them to be erased by an apology."

She nodded, her tears continuing to fall. "I know that, Aurora. I understand that I've hurt you in ways that can't be undone. I just want you to know how deeply sorry I am."

I took a deep breath. My wounds were still there, raw and painful. But there was something in Simran's expression that made me wonder if there was more to her than I had ever realized

"Look, Simran," I began cautiously, "I'm not going to pretend that I can just forget what's happened between us. Trust isn't built overnight, and forgiveness isn't automatic."

She nodded in understanding, wiping her tears with a napkin. "I know, Aurora. I'm not expecting you to just forgive and forget. I know I have to earn back your trust, if that's even possible."

We sat in silence for a moment, the weight of our history hanging in the air.

"I'll be honest, Simran," I said, my voice softening a bit. "I don't know if we can ever be the best of friends but maybe, with time and effort, we can find a way to coexist without all the animosity."

She nodded again, a glimmer of hope in her eyes. "I'd be grateful for any chance, Aurora. And I promise, I'll do my best to show you that I've changed."

"I'm doing this for Ian not to absolve you of your guilt or whatever."

She nodded with a half-smile. "Of course," she agreed. "Thank you for giving me a chance, Aurora."

I took another sip of my milkshake, savoring the sweet taste as I watched Simran enjoy her curly fries with newfound enthusiasm.

"Wow, I haven't had these in so long," she exclaimed between bites. "I didn't remember them being this good though."

Her genuine delight was contagious, and a small smile tugged at the corners of my lips as I continued to eat my burger.

"So are you sure nothing else happened with you and Ian?" I asked, raising an eyebrow.

She sighed, her cheeks turning a shade of pink. "Okay, Ian would probably be mad if I told you this but we kissed after he confessed his feelings."

"Right." I replied, with an arched eyebrow. I wasn't surprised but Ian clearly had a different definition of starting off as friends than I did.

"How did you know there was something else?"

"I can see it in your eyes," I replied with a shrug. "This is the first time I've actually seen you happy, Simran."

She giggled, and for a moment, it was as if I was seeing a completely different person. The transformation she was undergoing was more evident than ever, and I couldn't help but feel a sense of relief that she was finally letting go of the negativity that had consumed her for so long.

"This is the first time in a long time that I am genuinely happy," she admitted, her voice softening. She let out a contented sigh and took a sip of her milkshake, the corners of her lips curving upward.

As we sat there, enjoying our meal and each other's company, I realized that maybe there was a chance for us to move beyond the past. It wouldn't be easy, and there would be hurdles to overcome, but seeing Simran open up and genuinely apologize made me believe that change was possible, even in the most unlikely of people.

"Hey, Aurora," she said. "Thank you for having lunch with me today. And thank you for being honest. I needed to hear it."

I nodded. "Thank you for being honest with me too, Simran. Let's just take things one step at a time, okay?"

She nodded in agreement.

✧

I managed a tight smile as Simran joined me at my locker before school.

"Hey."

"Hey," she smiled back. "I just took the bus to school."

"Why?" I asked, genuinely puzzled. After all, she had a car she'd obnoxiously speed around the parking lot with every day.

She offered a shrug. "Just thought I'd change things up a bit."

A wry smile played on my lips. "Oh, I see. You wanted to experience life as one of us mere commoners for a day."

Her eyes widened in surprise. "No, that's not it at all. I swear, I just—"

"It was a joke," I deadpanned. As I closed my locker, I could see her realization dawning.

"Ah," she mumbled, a hint of embarrassment in her voice.

I was really trying to be civil with Simran but it was difficult for me. After speaking to Ian that evening, following Simran's and my visit to the diner, I made the decision to give her a chance. It had become clear that both Ian and I had a hand in the way things had turned out, and I couldn't deny my own culpability. Regrettably, I had no recollection of my actions in the past. In my mind, Ian and I had shared an incredible friendship, and Simran had faded into the background, a girl who had occasionally lashed out at me, driving me away from her.

"Hey, girls," Ian's voice interrupted, his arm casually draped over our shoulders as we headed to class together.

"Hey, Ian," we echoed in unison.

"I always dreamed the three of us would be like this," Simran mused under her breath.

Ian and I exchanged a glance, I could feel the guilt start to overwhelm me again. How had we shut her out for all those years without realising?

"Look at you three," Ryan cooed sarcastically as he and Kiyana caught up to us.

Before I could speak my attention shifted as I caught sight of Jer at his locker. He glanced at Simran, then at Ian's arm around me, a flicker of confusion in his eyes before he swiftly masked it. Slamming his locker shut, he walked away in the opposite direction.

I heaved a heavy sigh, frustration washing over me.

"He's still giving you the silent treatment?" Ian asked with a concerned tone.

I nodded, the weight of Jer's indifference sitting heavily on my shoulders.

Ian squeezed my arm reassuringly. "Give him some time, Aurora. He'll come around."

I shook my head, my voice tinged with doubt. "I'm not so sure, Ian. Something happened the other day, and I think it pushed him even further away."

"Ah, heard you had another one of your little outbursts," Ryan remarked.

Kiyana shot Ryan an annoyed look and turned to me. "Don't mind him, Aurora. We all have our moments."

I stared down at the ground, guilt gnawing at my conscience. "It's fine, Kiyana. Ryan's right. I don't even know what set me off. I just snapped."

A pair of arms enveloped me in a comforting hug, replacing the spot where Ian's arm had been just moments before.

"Like I've said before, everyone has their breaking point," their voice soothed, offering a reassuring touch to my turbulent thoughts. "Don't beat yourself up about it, Aurora."

I smiled up at Jimmy.

Greeting us all, he seemed genuinely happy, which warmed my heart. It seemed like he had finally found his place among us.

Walking past Simran's former clique, a thought crossed my mind about how their dynamics would shift now that she had left. Who would rise as their new leader?

"Pretending to like those girls was utterly exhausting," Simran sighed, her voice tinged with frustration.

"I'm sure they felt the same about you," Ryan retorted, with a sarcastic smile.

Simran's smile faltered, and she looked down briefly.

Ryan rolled his eyes, letting out a sigh. "Simran, that was a joke. Just a heads up, if you're gonna hang out with us, you'll have to get used to getting teased."

Surprised, Simran looked up. "Oh, okay. I'm sorry. I know I've been awful to someone you care about, and I don't expect everything to be instantly forgiven. I'm genuinely sorry, and I hope we can move forward in a better way."

Kiyana and Ryan exchanged glances, conveying unspoken understanding. "We'll see. Just don't ever hurt my friend again."

"I won't," Simran replied, shaking her head earnestly.

An awkward silence settled among us, as we navigated the new dynamic.

"By the way, I was thinking – would you all be interested in going out for lunch today? Maybe to that diner we visited, Aurora?" Simran suggested.

"Well, if you're treating..." Jimmy mumbled.

Simran's laughter filled the air as she looked around at us, seeking everyone else's agreement.

"Sure, why not. It's been a while since I left school for lunch," I responded, a small smile tugging at my lips.

Ian's eyes met mine, and he offered a proud grin, recognizing my effort.

Ryan and Kiyana, though somewhat reluctantly, chimed in with their agreement. Simran's warm and grateful gaze landed on me.

"Alright, see y'all later," Kiyana said, breaking off from the group to head to her Biology class.

"See you at lunch," Jimmy added before heading off as well.

As everyone dispersed, it was just Simran and me left, walking together to our next class.

She beamed at me. "Thanks for agreeing to the lunch."

"Like I said, I'm doing this for Ian." I said quietly.

Her smile dropped slightly but then she nodded. "Whatever your reasoning, thank you."

Walking into our classroom, it was no surprise that we attracted more than a few curious glances. After all, things were shifting, and people couldn't help but notice.

How did we transition from despising each other to the point where we could actually tolerate each other's presence?

It had me thinking about what it would have been like if we had really included Simran in our initial friendship. Maybe, under different circumstances, Simran and I could have been good friends now.

Yet, deep down, I knew I wouldn't change a thing. If our friendship had followed a different path, although I would have still been friends with Kiyana and maybe Ryan, I probably wouldn't have met Jimmy or Derrick or...Jer.

I sneaked a glance at Jer, who was immersed in his book, seemingly unaware of Simran and me entering the room.

"Hey, Simran?" I said as we settled into our seats.

"Yeah?"

"Did your feelings for Jeremiah just disappear or?..." I asked, genuinely curious.

Her eyes widened momentarily before darting towards Jer, almost involuntarily. "Um, well, yeah, I guess the feelings kinda faded away once Ian returned. I mean Jeremiah's definitely hot but Ian is, he's what I want."

"Seems like you're really into him," I commented, unpacking my belongings.

"You have no idea," she muttered under her breath, placing her binder on the table.

"Care to elaborate?" I prodded, raising an eyebrow.

She shifted uncomfortably, checking her surroundings before leaning closer to me. "I think, I think I'm in love with him, Aurora."

I raised both my eyebrows in genuine surprise. "Oh."

Simran let out a soft laugh, mixed with a hint of disbelief. "Yeah, it's a lot."

"Must be hard then, with this whole 'just friends' arrangement," I noted.

She shrugged, a look of contentment crossing her face. "I'm just grateful he forgave me. I'll take him anyway I can get him, honestly. The way he put his arm around us this morning might be a simple gesture for you, but it meant the world to me."

I nodded, empathizing with the significance of those small moments. It brought to mind the small gestures Jer used to make for me. My gaze traveled back to him.

At that moment, our eyes unexpectedly locked. In my usual clumsiness, I managed to stub my toe against the table while trying to scoot my chair closer to the desk.

Quickly averting my gaze from Jer, I grabbed my foot in slight pain.

"Sweet peas and bananas!" I exclaimed with an exaggerated groan, unintentionally prompting a chorus of chuckles from our classmates. Simran cringed and ducked her head. "You are so weird." she chuckled.

My cheeks warmed. "I'm injured, Simran. You're supposed to ask if I'm okay not to be embarrassed by me."

"You're right. I'm sorry. Are you okay?"

I rolled my eyes, still nursing my sore toe. Glancing at Jer, I noticed the slightest twitch at the corner of his lips as our eyes met again, before he quickly returned his attention to his book.

A genuine smile spread across my face. Well, at least I managed to provoke a reaction from him.

✧

"I'm too scared,"I admitted.

"To do what?" asked Jimmy, raising an eyebrow.

"To go to Lit!"

"It's lit!" Someone shouted as they walked by causing Jimmy to chuckle.

I shot him a disapproving glance. " Jimmy, pay attention, I'm in a crisis here."

"Why though?" Jimmy inquired.

"Because of Amy. I feel like I should apologize."

"Well, apologizing would be the right thing to do."

"I know, but the thing is..." I glanced around before leaning in closer to Jimmy. "I'm not sorry."

Jimmy chuckled again.

"Jimmy, stop laughing. I'm being serious here."

"Alright, alright. If you're not sorry, then don't force an apology."

"But I'll feel guilty."

Jimmy rolled his eyes. "Figure out what feels right for you, Aurora. Sometimes, apologizing when you don't truly mean it is pointless."

"Hmm, you're quite the philosopher, my friend."

"That was actually pretty basic advice but thanks," he shrugged.

I laughed. "Take the compliment, Jimmiana. Christ."

He burst out in laughter."Jimmiana? Where the hell did that come from?"

"I don't know; it just popped into my head," I giggled, with a proud shrug.

Jimmy was about to reply but abruptly stopped and cleared his throat. I followed his gaze and noticed Jer standing nearby, leaning against a locker close to our class. He must have been watching us joke around the whole time but we hadn't noticed.

His gaze was fixed on Jimmy, an unblinking glare that held an eerie intensity.

Jimmy looked away. "Just ignore him," I whispered to Jimmy, patting his arm. It was hard to dismiss Jer's glaring presence, but I said, "Don't let him get to you."

I offered a reassuring smile, which Jimmy returned with a hint of skepticism.

Finally, Mr. Dermott showed up and unlocked the classroom door. It was frustrating when teachers were late and locked the door, leaving us waiting outside. I was lost in my thoughts, only realizing I was the only one standing outside when Jimmy nudged me.

Class went by, and I contemplated talking to Amy, who seemed unusually quiet. She and Jer didn't so much as greet each other.

Ultimately, I decided not to approach her. I didn't want to apologize, and my anger hadn't entirely subsided, even though I knew I didn't have much ground to stand on.

"I can't wait for the free food," Jimmy said, rubbing his hands together with anticipation.

"Really, Jimmy? That's all you're thinking about?"

"What? How often do you get offered a free meal from the richest girl in school?" he retorted. I rolled my eyes. "Alright, I'll meet you in the parking lot. I need to use the bathroom."

Later, in the parking lot, I met Simran, and I was taken aback when I saw one of her former friends beside her.

It was the one with jet-black hair, the more pleasant one, Mona.

"Are you sure?" I overheard Simran ask.

"Yes, I should be the one asking you that, Simran," she smiled.

"Oh, hi," Simran greeted when she spotted me. "You know Mona, right?"

"Well, we've crossed paths a few times," I said, managing a polite smile.

Simran's eyes widened. "Oh. God, I'm so sorry—"

I interrupted her. "Enough with the apologies, Simran. I get it."

"I'm really sorry too," Mona added, turning her attention to me. "I did some really terrible things just to fit in with that group. And when Simran left, I started questioning why I was even part of it."

"I had the same thought," I admitted.

She looked at me in surprise. "You did?"

I nodded. "Yeah, it was clear you didn't belong with them. You're actually a nice person."

A smile formed on her face. "So, um, can I, is it okay if I..."

"If you want to hang out with us, Mona, you're welcome. The more, the merrier."

"Indeed," Ian chimed in, arriving with Kiyana and Ryan.

"Alright, folks, this is Mona, our latest recruit," I introduced her.

Mona blushed and waved shyly.

"Oh wow. Aurora's had quite the transformation, going from a bullied loner to having a massive group of friends which includes her bully—OW!" Ryan winced, rubbing his arm and giving Kiyana an annoyed look.

Simran's gaze dropped, Mona's smile faltered, and I clenched my jaw. I wished people would stop bringing that up. Ryan was like an older brother to me so the teasing was expected but it was too soon. When he realized I was genuinely upset his expression softened.

"Oh, damn, sorry, Aurora. I didn't mean to make things uncomfortable," Ryan apologized.

Thankfully, Jimmy joined us, blissfully unaware of the tension in the air.

"Jimmy!" Mona exclaimed, wrapping her arms around his neck in a hug.

Jimmy seemed taken aback but awkwardly returned the hug.

"I never see you around school," Mona continued. "We don't have any classes together, and I never see you in the cafeteria at lunch, well, until recently."

Jimmy scratched the back of his head. "Yeah, weird right."

"So, you guys know each other?" I inquired, hoping to shift the conversation away from the awkwardness.

"Oh yeah, Jimmy is our pool boy," Mona replied with a smile, looking at Jimmy.

"Oh really?" I asked, raising an eyebrow.

"Yes, I am. Can we get going now? I'm really hungry," Jimmy mumbled, steering the conversation away.

"Okay, let's go," Simran suggested.

"I'm going with Jimmy!" I declared, giving him a mischievous smile.

"I hate my life," he muttered.

I laughed and playfully slapped his arm. "Stop. You love me."

Mona glanced between me and Jimmy with a frown, seemingly questioning our dynamic.

"But you always ride with me," Ian pouted.

I shrugged. "Change is good. And I'm sure Simran would appreciate taking my seat."

Simran shot me a mock glare.

"Fine, she's more fun than you anyway," Ian said, taking Simran's hand and leading her away. Simran looked back at me, a surprised yet happy smile on her face.

I rolled my eyes. "Can't believe he's replacing me like that."

Jimmy smirked and turned to Mona, the only person left standing nearby aside from us. Kiyana and Ryan had already departed.

"Are you joining us?" he asked Mona.

"Can I?" she inquired.

"Absolutely."

I narrowed my eyes at Jimmy, seeing right through his tactic. He didn't want me to question him, so he's bringing Mona along.

I took the passenger seat, and Mona settled in the back.

Jimmy started the car, and we drove out of the parking lot.

"You think that's going to stop me?" I whispered to Jimmy, making sure only he could hear me.

"What do you mean?" he whispered back.

"Uh, I mean how you told Mona to come with us when you knew I wanted to talk to you."

"I don't know what you're talking about."

"So, how long have you had a crush on her?" I asked.

His head turned sharply toward me. "What? I do not! Please be quiet, Aurora—"

"Okay, let's give her a code name... 'the comic,' so we don't have to whisper so much," I suggested, noticing Mona's confused gaze in the rearview mirror.

I cleared my throat and leaned back in my seat.

"Alright, I'll ask again, Jimmy. How long have you liked the comic?"

He rolled his eyes. "I don't like Mo—the comic, Aurora."

"Oh, really?"

"Really."

"Then explain those lovesick glances you keep throwing at the comic."

I couldn't help but chuckle at our secret conversation. Mona must have thought we were acting really strange.

"I'm not throwing any glances at the comic," he denied and then subtly glanced at Mona through the rearview mirror.

"And there's another one."

He turned to me. "Alright, let's say I did have feelings for...the comic, what difference would that make? It's not like the comic is ever going to like me back."

"But that's where you're wrong. I can tell that the comic likes you too."

"No, it doesn't! I never admitted to liking the comic. The comic just sees me as a friend, I'm surprised it even sees me as that, let alone something more. The comic is too good for me."

"That's not true."

"Look, Aurora, can we stop talking about this? You're just giving me false hope."

"Fine," I mumbled.

We arrived at the diner soon after and joined everyone inside.

"My baby!" Derrick exclaimed, rushing over to me as he wrapped me in a hug. I laughed as he spun me around.

"I've missed you. We really need to hang out more," he pouted.

"I'm pretty sure I saw you a few days ago."

"Yeah, but we only talked for like a minute."

"Okay, how about you sit with me and my friends for lunch?"

His grin widened, and he linked arms with me. "Yay."

Thankfully, Ryan and Kiyana had chosen a large table that could accommodate all of us.

"Hey, Ryan."

"Hey, man," Ryan said, slapping his hand in greeting.

"Alright, Derrick, this is Ian, Kiyana, Mona, and Jimmy. You've met Simran."

I realized I'd been doing a lot of introductions lately.

"Hi, guys! I'm Derrick, Aurora's best friend—"

"—you're not my best fri—"

"—And Jeremiah's cousin."

I frowned. He just had to bring Jer up.

"Oh, are you two still not talking?" he asked.

I shrugged.

"Hm." He frowned. "Maybe I should talk to him."

"No, don't!" I interjected. "Just leave it, please."

I watched my friends exchange glances.

"Are you guys ready to order?" Bridgit, our server, asked with a wide smile.

Chapter 17

"Can I switch seats with you?"

As I looked up, Amy stood before me with her arms crossed. A pang of guilt hit me for my previous words.

"Sure, um, by the way, I'm sorry—"

"Don't apologize, Aurora. You meant every word you said."

I glanced down. "Um, I mean, it was uncalled for. I-I just feel really bad—"

"Of course you do, you're Aurora. The nice and sweet girl that everybody loves," she remarked sarcastically with an eye-roll. "Now, can we switch seats or not?"

I nodded, hurriedly packing up my things and taking her former desk. It was only when Jer entered the room with Jimmy trailing behind him that I realized the implications of my actions.

My eyes widened, and I turned to Amy. Why didn't she want to sit with Jer?

She shrugged. Jimmy gave Amy a tight smile before reluctantly taking his seat beside her.

He shot me a questioning look, and I mouthed that I'd explain later. Jer was busy arranging his notebook on his desk, seemingly unsurprised to find me in this seat. Being this close to him after a while made me realize how much I had missed his presence, even his scent.

After class, Jimmy caught up with me.

"So, why did you switch seats?" he asked as we left the classroom.

"Amy asked me to swap with her."

"Really?"

I nodded.

He furrowed his brow. "Why? Doesn't she like Jer or something?"

"I think they might be having a disagreement."

Jimmy raised an eyebrow. "I'm sure you're quite pleased about that."

Before I could retort with a snarky comment, our names were called from behind.

"Hey, guys!" Simran greeted us.

"What's up?"

She shrugged. "Nothing much, except for the fact that Jonah Long just asked me for my name."

"Why? Isn't he your ex?" I inquired.

She nodded. "Apparently, my appearance has changed so drastically that people think I'm a new student," she deadpanned. I glanced down at her oversized band t-shirt and Jordan sneakers, it was easy to mistake her for someone else.

"Hey, take that as a positive. This is the new you, you want others to see you differently, no?"

She nodded as we walked into the cafeteria. "Yeah, you're right."

"Hey, Ryan, where's Kiyana?" I asked.

Ryan scowled. "Just because we're dating doesn't mean I keep tabs on her. I'm her boyfriend, not her personal assistant."

"Alright then," I said, holding my hand up in surrender. "Geez."

"Why the long face?" Ian inquired of Ryan.

As Ryan started to reply, Kiyana appeared out of nowhere.

"Maybe he's upset because he's been texting other girls and I found out!" She shrieked, glaring at him.

"Baby, I was not texting other girls—"

"Yes, you were, Ryan. I saw them."

"Why do we have to do this in front of everyone? If you'd just let me explain—"

"No! I can't believe you'd do this to me. And not only that, but now you're trying to justify your actions when I clearly saw the texts myself. There were like twelve girls. What the hell?"

An awkward silence hung as everyone exchanged glances between Ryan and Kiyana.

"You know what? I thought you trusted me, but obviously you never did. Because if you truly did, you'd give me a chance to explain. Fuck this."

Ryan stormed off.

I watched as Kiyana's eyes welled up with tears.

"Alright, Aurora, let's get Kiyana to the restroom," Simran whispered.

"Oh right, yeah," I said, trying to regain my composure after that incredibly awkward experience.

Simran and I linked arms with Kiyana, leading her to the restroom.

Once we were inside, Kiyana burst into tears and clung to me. I held her tightly and gently rubbed her back.

"I can't believe this is happening," she sobbed. "I thought Ryan and I would last."

"You will, Kiyana! You and Ryan will get through this," Simran reassured her.

She shook her head against my shoulder.

"Kiyana, you and Ryan are meant to be. You'll definitely overcome this," I assured her.

"What kind of dumb-ass comforting is this? He cheated, there's no coming back from that!"

Just as I opened my mouth to respond, a few other girls walked into the restroom. I inwardly groaned as I realized they were the wannabe popular girls who often acted mean to everyone in an attempt to gain favor with Simran.

Kiyana looked up, and the girls audibly gasped at her tear-streaked mascara, smudged eyeliner, puffy eyes, and runny nose.

I couldn't help but discreetly check my dress to make sure there was no makeup transfer.

The girls started to giggle amongst themselves, their laughter barely concealed behind their hands, as they walked further into the restroom.

Simran's expression shifted from sympathy to a steely resolve, and she stepped in front of the girls before they could approach Kiyana any further.

"What do you think you're doing?" she challenged them.

One of the girls raised an eyebrow at Simran and scoffed. "Let's be real, Simran. You're not the most popular girl in school anymore. In fact, you're not popular at all. You're the opposite."

Another girl smirked and chimed in, "Exactly, so move aside, freak."

Simran's lips curled into a malicious smile, and she leaned her head back, letting out a mocking laugh.

The smug expressions on the girls' faces faltered.

"Do you actually believe that?" Simran retorted, her voice dripping with confidence. "Think about it, who is everyone talking about right now?"

She giggled mischievously. "Oh right, that would be me."

And she was right—everyone was abuzz with talk about her dramatic transformation.

She continued, her tone playful, "And what group do people stare at when they walk down the hallway?

She grinned. "Oh right, that's my group of friends again. So, girls, I suggest you rethink what you're doing here. I'm genuinely trying to be a nicer person, but I can still be your worst nightmare if you push me hard enough."

Without uttering a word, the girls exchanged glances, then turned and left the bathroom, their departure reluctant.

"Thanks, Simran," Kiyana sniffled.

"No problem. That was actually kind of fun!" Simran beamed.

I rolled my eyes. "Don't get too used to it. You're a changed woman."

Kiyana let out a sigh. "You know what, guys? I think I'm going home now."

My eyebrows knitted in concern. "Oh."

"Yeah, I don't think I can stay here knowing he'll be around."

"Okay, do you want us to—"

"—No, guys, you've done enough. You go ahead and finish lunch before it's over."

I nibbled on my lip, studying my best friend closely. "Are you sure?"

"Yes, I'm fine. Bye!"

Simran and I slowly gathered our belongings and headed out of the restroom. "Bye."

As we stepped into the hallway, we exchanged worried glances.

"This isn't good, Simran. I've never seen Kiyana that upset."

"This whole situation really sucks," Simran sighed in agreement.

Coincidentally, we crossed paths with Ryan on our way back to the cafeteria. I awkwardly cleared my throat, avoiding eye contact with him.

He scoffed. "So, I'm guessing you don't believe me either?"

I shrugged. "I don't really know what to believe, Ryan."

He shook his head. "You know, I thought that at least you would stick by me."

"Ryan, Kiyana's my best friend!"

"And I thought I was like an older brother to you."

I bit my lip and stared at the ground. He took in a deep breath before pushing past us.

I turned and watched him leave the school.

Simran rubbed my arm. "Don't beat yourself up about it, Aurora."

"But they're both so close to me. I don't want to take sides."

"You don't have to. I think the best thing for you to do is to be neutral in this situation and let them work things out themselves. But if I'm being honest, I think Kiyana needs to give the guy a chance to explain."

"Me too," I said, pushing open the doors to the cafeteria. "I just feel like if I say that to Kiyana, she'll think I'm on 'his side'. I know Ryan; he loves Kiyana so much. He would never cheat on her. I need to talk to him and find out what's really going on."

"So that was awkward," Ian mumbled as Simran and I sat at our table.

"Very," Jimmy said, grimacing.

✧

After school, Ian drove me to Ryan's house. I thanked him and waved goodbye before heading up Ryan's driveway. He opened the door after I knocked for the third time. His face dropped when he saw me.

"Hey, don't look so disappointed! Were you expecting someone?" I asked.

"Yes, my pizza." He walked away but left the door open, so I quickly came in and shut it behind me.

"Ryan, I want to apologize for before. I guess I didn't know how to react after seeing Kiyana cry so much over this. I know you would never ever do that to her. So that's why I'm here. I want to know what's going on because there has to be another explanation for what Kiyana saw."

He sat down in a recliner, and I settled across from him on the couch.

"You don't think I cheated?"

I shook my head.

"Good. At least I know someone trusts me. I can't explain how hurt I felt when Kiyana accused me of cheating, and all of you immediately started looking at me differently."

"I'm sorry, Ryan. I was just shocked. I trust you. I wasn't kidding when I said you were like a big brother to me. You are my big brother."

He gave me a sad smile. "I just wish Kiyana felt the same."

I scrunched up my nose. "You wish Kiyana thought of you as a brother?"

"What? No! I meant the whole trusting part."

"Oh."

Ryan laughed and shook his head. "Only you could make me laugh at a time like this."

I grinned. "Happy I could help!"

He smiled back at me before his expression turned serious. He stared down at his phone, which was in his hands. "Come here, I need to show you something."

I moved closer and sat on the arm of his chair. He unlocked his phone and went to the messages.

I saw numerous names of females: Kayla, Anna, Maria...

He clicked one of the chats and handed me the phone. "You can look through all of the texts from all the girls. If Kiyana had just given me a chance, I would have told her to do the same."

I scrolled through the messages.

Kayla: Hey Ryan! Sorry to bother you but there's this guy I like and he's so nice and sweet but I'm only 12 and he's 16! What should I do???

Ryan: Hey Kayla. Happy to hear from you. I think at 12 years old you shouldn't really be thinking about guys. And if you are, at least find a guy who can understand you and you can understand- someone closer to your age. You have PLENTY of time to find the right guy. Hope this helped :)

Kayla: You know what Ryan? You're right. I talked to him and he was a jerk anyway. Thanks! See you soon.

I opened another one.

Anna: Hey Ry!

Ryan: Hey Anna Banana :)

Anna: Okay so I did something really bad and I don't know what to do.

Ryan: What did you do?

Anna: I stole $20 from my mom's purse to go to the movies, that was two weeks ago and I don't know if I should tell her or just leave it.

Ryan: Anna I can't believe you stole. You know that's wrong. I think you should tell your mom what you did, you might think she hasn't noticed but maybe she never thought to ask you about it because she wouldn't even consider the fact that you would do such a thing. Tell her yourself before she finds out another way.

Anna: I told her Ryan. She wasn't too mad. She just told me to ask next time cos she'd never say no unless it's for a good reason. Cya next week Ry!

Ryan: See you!

I clicked on his chat with Maria.

Maria: Ryannnnnn

Ryan: Mariaaaaaa

Maria: I need your help!

Ryan: What's the problem?

Maria: There's this girl at school and she's not exactly bullying me but she says something nasty to me every time she walks past me and I don't know wby!

Maria: **why!

Ryan: Hmm what's this girl like?

Maria: She's pretty and popular and she has loads of friends.

Ryan: She's jealous of you.

Maria: She's jealous of me? SHE'S JEALOUS OF ME? Ryan did you not read what I just said???

Ryan: Lol I know what I said. I have a friend who's going through the same thing. She's pretty, smart and kind just like you. Trust me this girl is jealous of you.

Maria: Guess what???

Ryan: What Maria?

Maria: I talked to her! I found the courage to ask her why she kept being so mean to me and at first she acted like she didn't know what I was talking about but she finally admitted that she wanted to be my friend but didn't think I liked her! We're friends now!

Ryan: Awesome!

Maria: Thanks, Ry! you're the best!

Ryan: No problem Maria.

I looked up from the phone and smiled at Ryan. "Was the friend you were talking about in this one me?"I asked.

He glanced at the message before nodding. I beamed.

I read one more.

Eva: Hey Ryan!

Ryan: What's up?

Eva: Something happened to me.

Ryan: What happened???

Eva: My Period.

Eva: Ryan?

Eva: Bro really? Don't just leave me on read...

Ryan: Can't help! Sorry! Bye!

I burst out in laughter at that one and handed him his phone.

"So you're some kind of counselor for tweens?" I asked, smirking.

He rolled his eyes. "This is why I didn't tell any of you."

I giggled.

He sighed. "I help my older cousin with her dance class every Saturday. I just help keep things calm since she can't handle her class on her own. One day one of the girls asked me for advice on something, apparently, it really helped and ever since the girls have been asking me for advice. My older cousin, Anna, gave them all my number too"

I laughed.

He shook his head. "But I'm not gonna lie. I enjoy it, and I'm glad to know I can help them out. Y'know?"

I nodded. "You know if Kiyana actually knew the truth, I think she would love you even more."

He offered me a sad smile before looking down. "If only she had listened to me."

"Do you want me to speak to her?" I asked.

"No, it's fine Aurora. I'll give you a ride home and head over to her place. I need to talk to her now before things get worse."

I nodded. "Good idea."

I kissed his cheek. "You may act all tough and uncaring, but you're a really sweet guy, Ryan."

He blushed. "Whatever."

The bell rang. "Pizza!" I said, running to the door. Ryan pulled me back.

"Hey! I wanna get it!"

"Do you have money to pay the delivery guy?"

"No?"

"So what the hell are you going to give him in return for the pizza?"

I opened and closed my mouth a few times before stepping aside.

Ryan opened the door and paid the dude, taking the pizza and closing the door.

"Now let's eat."

Chapter 18

I was growing increasingly concerned. It had been two weeks since I'd seen Jer. We may not have been friends anymore, but I still cared deeply for him.

"Hey, Derrick!" I greeted as I approached him in the small diner. His face lit up when he saw me, and he pulled me into a hug.

"Hey, Babe, what's going on?"

Taking a seat on a stool next to him, I surveyed the place. "Do you spend all your time here?"

He shrugged nonchalantly. "Pretty much. After quitting dealing, I left my job at the bar too. So, this is where I chill."

I shifted the conversation to my main concern. "Speaking of which, have you seen Jer lately? I haven't seen him around for about two weeks."

Derrick's expression shifted to concern. "Two weeks? He's been absent from school for that long? Something's definitely up."

"Yeah, that's what I'm worried about. Do you have any idea where he might be?"

Derrick shook his head. "Honestly, Aurora, we haven't been in touch for a while. I've distanced myself from dealing, so I don't know what's happening with him."

My eyebrows raised at his remark, he spoke as if Jer hadn't quit dealing as well. I pressed him further. "But do you at least know his address?"

Reluctance crossed Derrick's face. "I do, but Jer isn't one to welcome visitors. His house is off limits, even to me."

"Derrick, please! I'm concerned he might be in trouble. I just want to make sure he's safe."

After a moment of contemplation, Derrick gave in. "Fine, I'll text you the address."

I beamed with gratitude as quickly sent it to me. "Thanks, Derrick!"

Before leaving, he raised a concern. "Wait! I should go with you. Jer's place isn't in the best part of town."

"Okay, let's go." I sighed, lifting myself out of my seat.

"Oh shoot! Can we go tomorrow? I have plans with Sadie soon."

I let out a frustrated sigh. "Fine, forget it. I guess your plans are more important than your cousin's safety."

"Aurora!" Derrick's voice called out as I stormed out of the restaurant. I was determined to find my way there on my own, thankfully he'd already texted me the address. I couldn't wait any longer; I needed to make sure he was alright.

Getting off at the bus stop closest to Jer's place, a shiver ran down my spine. Derrick's warning resonated in my mind. Maybe he was right. My heart raced as I noticed the group of older men ahead, hollering and whistling at me. Crossing the road to the other side, I quickened my pace, stealing glances over my shoulder.

It was a relief when I finally reached Jer's house. I knocked on the door, but there was no response. The door creaked open slightly.

"Hello?"

Still no answer.

I cautiously peeked inside and surveyed the empty home.

"Hello? Jer?" My voice trembled as I ventured further in.

The setting had taken on an eerie quality, and a sense of unease washed over me. Maybe I had overstepped my boundaries. Deciding it was best to leave, I turned around, only to scream in surprise as a figure blocked the doorway. The man stepped inside, his presence intimidating. He was tall, heavily built, and seemed to be in his forties. A sneer played on his lips.

"What in the hell do you think you're doing in my house?"

Stuttering, I took a step back. "I-I'm sorry, I-I was just—"

"I thought I told that fool to keep his damn friends away from here."

Was he referring to Jer?

He moved closer, and my heart raced as I stumbled over my words. "I-I didn't mean any harm, I swear."

"I don't give a fuck what you meant, you little bitch."

His speech slurred, and it became evident he was intoxicated. I bit my lip, searching for a way out.

Suddenly, the man's face contorted into anger, and he let out a scream. His fist collided with the wall in the hallway, making me jump. I instinctively brought a hand to my chest, my anxiety heightening.

"I warned him to keep people out of my house and out of my damn business. He's going to pay for this!" He shouted, his voice seething with anger.

His gaze shifted from the ground to me, and I instinctively took another step back, my eyes welling up with tears.

"You're going to pay for this," he hissed, his voice tinged with anger.

With something that resembled a war cry, he lunged toward me. Panic surged through me, and I screamed, covering my face in fear.

When the only sound I heard was a heavy thud against the wooden floor, I cautiously lowered my hands and looked up. Jer stood before me, glaring down at his father with pure hatred in his eyes. His jaw clenched tightly as he addressed me.

"What were you thinking?" His voice trembled with anger.

My lips quivered as I stammered, "I don't know." I shook my head, feeling utterly foolish. There was no justification for my impulsive actions since leaving Derrick. I should have just waited till tomorrow; I should have returned to the bus stop; I should never have entered Jer's house uninvited.

"What if I hadn't arrived in time? You're lucky my neighbor called me about a girl snooping around my house."

I looked down, overwhelmed by shame and regret.

"I don't even know what to say to you right now. This has to be one of the dumbest things you've ever pulled, and you've done your fair share of dumb things."

His words stung, but I knew I had been reckless.

"I-I just wanted to make sure you were okay—"

He cut me off, his voice dripping with frustration. "And why on earth would you do that? I thought I made it abundantly clear that I don't want anything to do with you!"

His words were a harsh blow, driving deep into my heart.

"You haven't been in school for a while—"

"Aurora, do you not comprehend what I'm saying to you? Stay the hell away from me! I don't need you checking up on me. I don't need you barging into my house, and I certainly don't need your concern. So stay away. Keep out of my life. I never want to lay eyes on you again!"

Swallowing my pain, I pulled the straps of my bag closer to my chest as tears streamed down my face. "Fine, I understand," I said, my voice breaking. With a quick, unsteady stride, I brushed past him, tiptoeing over his sleeping father, and exited the house. Once outside, I released a breath I hadn't realized I'd been holding. I dialed Derrick's number; there was no way I was going to walk alone around this neighborhood anymore.

"Hey, Derrick," I spoke shakily.

"Aurora, are you okay? Please tell me you didn't go to Jeremy's place alone?" Derrick's voice sounded worried and urgent.

"I'm sorry, Derrick. Please come quickly," I managed to say, my breath coming out in short, anxious pants.

"I'll be there in a minute. Stay calm, okay?"

"O-okay."

I nervously bit my nail, my eyes darting around the surroundings. I flinched as I heard a noise close behind me, my heart racing.

Turning quickly, I found Jer standing there, his demeanor seemingly calmer now, an undertone of guilt in his expression.

"Don't tell anyone about my dad, not even Derrick," he spoke softly, almost pleadingly.

I remained silent, my gaze averted.

It seemed that was all he wanted to say.

My body tensed as I felt his hand gently touch my shoulder. He sighed and withdrew his hand.

"I'm sorry," he murmured, a hint of regret in his voice.

Ignoring him, I sighed with relief as Derrick's car pulled up beside us. Derrick sprinted towards me.

"Are you okay?" he asked, his eyes searching my face and body for any signs of harm.

I nodded, my voice barely a whisper. "I just want to go home."

Derrick shot a final glare at Jer before opening the passenger door for me. I quickly got in and tried to settle into the seat. As Derrick started the car, I stole a glance at Jer through the window.

He was still watching me, guilt evident in his gaze. Despite everything, I couldn't shake the guilt I felt myself. No matter how poorly Jer treated me, I couldn't shake off his father's words about him paying for me showing up there. I had come to realize that Jer's involvement in drugs might not have been to pay off his father's medical bills or something similar, as I had initially suspected. It was more likely that he was covering the cost of the alcohol his father had been consuming, threatened by that monster to bring home a significant amount of money. The situation had become painfully clear – Jer's father was abusive.

I looked down and swallowed, my thoughts heavy with the weight of this newfound knowledge.

And I was the only one who knew.

✧

"Are you okay, Rory?" Ryan asked again, his concern evident in his voice.

I looked up from my untouched fries, meeting the worried gazes of everyone at our lunch table. I let out a sigh and nodded, trying to offer a reassuring smile. "I'm fine, really."

"If you say so," Jimmy replied softly, his eyes lingering on me as if trying to read my thoughts.

With their attention back on their conversations, my mind began to wander. Despite the attempts to distract myself, I couldn't shake off the emotional weight that had settled over me. The recent Jer situation was definitely contributing to my low mood, but there was something else too – a realization that had been slowly growing.

Amidst the laughter and interactions of my close-knit group of friends, I felt a sense of loneliness creeping in. It struck me that I was the odd one out, the extra wheel in a group of couples. Ian and Simran could no longer claim they were "just friends" when I and Kiyana had caught them making out in his car this morning, Jimmy and Mona were growing closer each day, and Kiyana and Ryan had thankfully got back together. So where did that leave me?

Alone.

I watched as Kiyana playfully fed a grape to Ryan, my heart aching with happiness for them but also a pang of longing for that kind of connection. Then, there was Jimmy and Mona, staring at each other after they both went for the same fry and lastly Ian and Simran, making out again. Gross.

This must have been how Simran felt all those years ago.

I couldn't help but feel a twinge of envy, even if I was genuinely glad they were all happy. Unable to bear the sight any longer, I stood up abruptly, my chair scraping against the floor. I excused myself with a weak smile and walked out of the cafeteria, needing space to breathe and collect my thoughts.

Outside, I found myself gravitating towards the bleachers, I hadn't been there in so long. However, as I approached, my steps faltered – my usual spot was occupied. Amy Finch sat there, and beside her, to my surprise, was Jeremiah Summers, his arm casually draped around her waist.

My heart sank, and I felt many emotions surge within me. As if sensing my presence, Jer's eyes met mine, and I froze in place. For a brief moment, his gaze softened, but it quickly shifted to the field, as if I were invisible to him.

My throat tightened, and I turned away, blinking back tears. Just then, my friends rushed towards me, Simran at the forefront. She read the situation without words, shaking her head slightly as if to say, "I know."

Without hesitation, she wrapped her arms around me, and the others joined in, forming a protective circle. I let out a sob, the floodgates opening as I finally let myself feel the pain that had been building up. Kiyana whispered comforting words in my ear while Ryan and the others offered their silent support.

I let it all out. I was sick and tired of this never-ending fight with Jeremiah. I was sick and tired of missing him, of longing for his presence. I was sick and tired of holding onto a hope that he would come back to me, that things would magically work out.

When my sobbing had subsided into occasional hiccups, Simran gently lifted my head. Her eyes were soft with concern.

"Let's get you inside," Simran suggested softly, her voice laced with empathy.

She and Kiyana linked arms with me, providing support that I desperately needed at that moment. As we walked back, I glanced back at Jeremiah. His gaze was fixed on me, a mixture of emotions in his eyes – a stark contrast to the unreadable mask he had worn before. I felt a flicker of something, but I quickly turned my attention away. It meant nothing, I meant nothing to him.

Back in the cafeteria, the hustle and bustle carried on as if nothing had happened, the seconds ticking away in a reality that had momentarily stood still for me. Simran's voice broke through the noise.

"Hey, I and Rory are going to head out and go to class early," she announced, her grip firm as she guided me out of the cafeteria.

Once we were outside, Simran slowed down our pace. She led me to a quiet corner of the courtyard and we sat down on a bench.

"I'm sorry, Aurora," Simran said, her tone sincere and regretful.

I looked at her, puzzled. "For what?"

"For not being there for you. For being too caught up in my own life to see something was up. You mentioned going to Jeremiah's house that day, and we brushed it off without really thinking about it."

I stared down at my hands.

Simran continued, her voice softening. "I understand if you're not ready to talk about it, but I hate seeing you like this. I wish I could do something to help."

I shook my head, my fingers tracing patterns on my arms. "Honestly, Simran, there's no need for that anymore. I'm done with this. I'm done with holding onto something that's just hurting me."

Simran's brow furrowed in surprise. "You're giving up on him just like that?"

I looked at her, my expression resolute. "It's not about giving up. It's about choosing myself. I can't keep holding onto someone who isn't willing to hold onto me."

Simran studied me for a moment before nodding slowly. "I see."

A weight lifted off my shoulders as I said those words aloud. I was taking back control over my own emotions, over my own life.

Simran put a hand on my shoulder, offering a reassuring squeeze. "Just remember, whatever you decide, we're here for you."

I managed a small smile, grateful for her unwavering support. "Thank you, Simran. I really appreciate that. And thank you for being there for me and Kiyana, you're an amazing friend to have in a crisis."

"I meant it when I said I was changing," Simran replied with a gentle smile. I nodded, letting my head rest on her shoulder.

That evening, Derrick came over after hearing about what had gone down today from Ryan. He had invited all our friends in hopes of cheering me up.

Ian and Simran arrived first, then Kiyana and Ryan, and finally, Mona and Jimmy showed up.

"Oh my God, this is going to be the best sleepover ever!" Derrick exclaimed as we all huddled together on the couch or on the floor nearby.

My head snapped towards him. "Sleepover?"

"Yeah... didn't you notice we were all in our pajamas?" Ian asked.

"What? Guys! I can't have guys sleep over, my dad would kill me!"

"Well, it's a good thing I called him and made sure it was okay." Kiyana grinned, holding up her phone.

"You asked him?" I asked. She nodded. "And he said it was okay?"

She nodded again. "So now that that's settled, go get into your pj's, Rory, and let's have some fun!"

"Hey, do you have anything I could wear? I have no pajamas." Derrick said.

I nodded. "One sec."

I walked up the stairs, changed into my princess-themed pajamas, and got some sweatpants for Derrick from my dad's room.

"Okay, what are we watching?" Mona asked.

"A horror movie!" Ryan grinned.

"No! A superhero movie! Preferably DC," Jimmy suggested.

"Uh, no way! We're watching a Disney movie. Right, Aurora?" Kiyana chimed in.

"Right—"

"No! Let's watch Mean Girls!" Simran interjected, clapping her hands in excitement.

"How about a comedy?" Ian proposed.

"Fine, what movie?" I asked. Can't go wrong with a comedy.

Once we had agreed on a movie, we settled down to watch, with candy and snacks that Mona and Jimmy had picked up on their way over. I smiled as Ian wrapped his arm around me and Simran leaned her head on my shoulder.I was so lucky to have these guys. Only my friends could make me smile when I felt like this.

Chapter 19

"Alright, class, you're aware that you've got roughly four weeks remaining for this project. I've given you ample time, and I expect you all to be well on your way. But for those who aren't, I suggest you get a move on."

Mr. Dermott's gaze lingered on us with anticipation as we stared at him blankly. "I said, get started."

Without delay, everyone pulled out their materials and began their work. Mr. Dermott sighed and retreated to his desk.

Jimmy glanced at me. "What's your plan?" he asked.

I shrugged. "No idea."

My gaze flicked towards Jeremiah, who was absorbed in his phone.

It had been another two weeks since I witnessed him and Amy on the bleachers. They were officially a couple now, a topic that had been circulating throughout the school for days. Amy, the girl who had apparently won over Jeremiah Summers.

ADE OLUOKUN

Amy had gained popularity and reveled in the newfound attention.

Interestingly, despite their "relationship," I had yet to see them share a kiss or even hold hands. If I dared mention it, people would probably think I was jealous.

Oh, by the way, in addition to drawing everyone's attention, Jeremiah and Amy's love life had solidified my reputation as the girl deemed unworthy of Jeremiah's affections.

Perfect.

Jeremiah turned his focus to me, his eyes still fixed on his phone screen. "I completed the project on my own. Don't worry, your name is on it."

"But—"

He pivoted away and slipped on his headphones before I could respond.

I sighed and rested my head on the table.

Jimmy gave my shoulder a comforting pat.

"So, something interesting happened in the hallway today, guess what?" Simran said as she joined me at our usual spot in the cafeteria.

"What?" Jimmy inquired, biting into his apple.

"Someone bumped into me, and guess what? They didn't cower in fear or immediately start begging for forgiveness. They didn't even bother to apologize. They were about to, but when they saw it was me, they just rolled their eyes and walked away."

I let out a sigh. "It's my fault."

Simran shook her head. "Don't go blaming yourself for everything. How could this possibly be your fault?"

"Simran, don't you see? Everyone else views me as a loser, so by extension, you're dragged into it too," I said, putting a reassuring hand on her arm. "No offense."

She stayed quiet, contemplating my words.

"Well, I couldn't care less," she replied, stealing a few fries from my tray. "In a few months, we'll be out of here, and those idiots won't matter anymore. So screw them."

"Hell yeah!" Ian chimed in as he took a seat beside her.

"Yeah, maybe you're right," I admitted, feeling a little lighter.

Derrick's voice interrupted our conversation as he sat down across from me. "Hey, guys!"

"Derrick, what are you doing here?" I questioned.

"Is it against the law to come and visit your friends? Don't worry, I'm pretty good at blending in," he replied with a dismissive wave.

"How are you holding up?" he asked, genuine concern in his eyes.

I rolled my eyes playfully. "I'm fine, Derrick."

"Okay, just checking in," he said with a warm smile.

"I appreciate it, really. I'm just tired of people constantly asking me how I'm doing. It's not like I'm going through a breakup or mourning a pet. Someone I liked doesn't feel the same way about me. It's not a monumental crisis."

"Liked, as in past tense?" Derrick quirked an eyebrow. "So you're over him?"

I nodded, looking down at my food. "Yeah."

Derrick's eyes suddenly widened, and he leaned down to check under the table. I stared at him, puzzled.

"Why are you wearing jeans?" he exclaimed, with shock on his face. "What happened to your signature sundresses? I don't think I've ever seen you in jeans before!"

I groaned. "Derrick, don't start. I just wanted a change for a bit, alright? Besides, these jeans have been in my closet since like ninth grade."

Derrick grinned mischievously. "Well, look on the bright side – you still fit into jeans from when you were fourteen!"

I shot him a deadpan look.

Kiyana and Ryan joined us at the table. "Hi, Derrick!" Kiyana greeted cheerfully.

"Hey, Kiyana. Hey, bro," Derrick replied, giving Ryan a fist bump.

Ryan raised an eyebrow. "What brings you here, man?"

"Just hanging out with my friends," Derrick said casually.

"You should probably find some friends your own age, dude," Jimmy quipped, giving Derrick a friendly pat on the back.

Derrick shot Jimmy a mock glare. "We're only like a year apart, comic nerd."

Kiyana intervened with a stern look. "Hey, hey, hey, no need to throw insults around."

Derrick playfully pouted. "Fine, fine. I can take a hint when I see one." He started to get up.

"Derrick, stop being ridiculous and sit down. You know we all love having you around," I said.

As the bell rang, signaling the end of our cafeteria break, we bid our goodbyes to Derrick...or so we thought.

While waiting for Kiyana to finish at her locker, we heard some commotion coming from around the corner.

"Just talk to me, Jeremiah! I don't get it."

"Derrick, let's not do this here—"

"—Then where, Jeremiah? Because the last time I checked, you've been avoiding me."

Jeremiah sighed. "It's complicated."

"Wow, you know that sounds very familiar. Remember when we were younger? When the drug shit started? What's going on? I thought we stopped keeping stuff from each other."

Jeremiah looked down.

"It's bad enough what you did to Aurora, and now you're not talking to me either."

I glanced down at the mention of my name.

Thankfully, there weren't many people in the hall, and most had already headed to class.

"I'm sorry," I heard Jeremiah say to Derrick, but when I looked up, his gaze was fixed on me.

He turned around and walked away, looking back at me one more time before disappearing out of sight.

I let out a sigh.

Walking over to Derrick, who looked upset and confused, I gave him a comforting hug. He returned it, burying his face in my hair.

Rubbing his back gently, I eventually pulled away. "I have to get to class now, Derrick. I'll see you later, okay?"

He nodded. "Bye, guys."

Our friends echoed their farewells, and we all headed to our respective classes.

✧

"Hey, honey."

"Hey, Dad," I replied, making my way downstairs.

"Are you okay?" he asked, concern in his eyes.

I offered a nonchalant shrug. "Yeah, I'm fine."

His narrowed gaze hinted at his skepticism. "What happened to your sundresses?"

I reached for a banana from the fruit basket. "What do you mean?"

"I mean you wore jeans to school, and now you're in sweats."

"I just wanted to be comfortable, Dad. What's the big deal?"

He fixed me with an intent look. "You tell me, Aurora. What's really going on?"

"Nothing," I said, my tone deflecting his inquiry. "I'm going upstairs."

His sigh lingered behind me as I made my way to my room.

I settled down with my laptop to watch a show, only to be interrupted by a tapping sound on my window. I paused the show, straining my ears to catch the sound again.

When there was nothing but silence, I shrugged off the noise and resumed my show.

However, a few seconds later, I heard another tap. Then, almost immediately, another.

I paused my show and approached the window cautiously. Opening the curtains slightly, I looked down to see Jer standing there. Relief washed over me, knowing it wasn't some stranger or a sinister presence.

"Wait, what's Jer doing here?" I muttered to myself, opening the window a bit more.

"Aurora!"

"Yeah?" I asked, my confusion evident.

"I need—" he began, but his words were cut off by a groan as he doubled over. When he straightened up slightly, I noticed he was clutching his side.

"Jeremiah, is that blood?" I asked, my anxiety spiking.

"I need help."

"Why on earth did you come around here? Have you not heard of using the front door?"

"I was going to climb up," he managed to say, his breaths uneven.

"Jeremiah! What do you think this is? Do you think you're a ninja?"

"Well, I..."

"Go to the front door. I'll open it."

I hurried downstairs and swung the front door open.

"Aurora—"

"Oh my God, what did you do to yourself, Jeremiah?" I exclaimed, my eyes fixed on his stomach.

"Put your arm around me."

He complied, wrapping his right arm around me for support as I helped him inside.

"You need to lie down."

"But I don't want to make a mess on your couch."

I halted, realizing he was right. "Can you manage to get upstairs?" I inquired.

He winced but nodded.

With careful steps, I assisted him up the stairs and into my room. It was a miracle my dad couldn't hear all the commotion.

"Nice room."

I shot him a look. "This isn't the time, Jeremiah," I chided as I guided him toward my bed.

"Jeremiah?"

"Yes," He answered, settling onto the bed.

I crossed my arms, exhaling heavily. "Why would you come here like this? What exactly am I supposed to do?"

He let out a weak chuckle. "Um, fix me? Where's your first aid kit?"

"I don't know! Who keeps a first aid kit at home, anyway?"

"Actually, a lot of people do."

"Do you?" I inquired.

"Well, no, but—"

"Why didn't you just go to the hospital, Jeremiah? Even if I owned a first aid kit, I'm not a doctor and judging by the blood, that's a deep wound."

"I can't."

"Why not?" I asked, my frustration growing.

"Because I'd have to explain what happened," he replied quietly, avoiding my gaze.

I took a deep breath and sat down next to him. "Jeremiah... did your dad do this to you?" I asked gently.

He nodded, his attention fixed on a loose thread on my comforter.

I ran my hands through my hair, feeling helpless. The situation was far more complicated than I could handle.

Then I heard my dad humming outside my door.

"Who's that?" Jeremiah panicked. "Your dad's home and you let me in the front door? I'm not tryna get stabbed twice tonight, Aurora!"

"Stabbed?" I shrieked in shock, staring at the blood oozing out between his fingers. "You know what? You're right! My dad's home and he can help!" I rushed to the door.

"Wait, Aurora, don't!"

"Dad!"

"Yeah? What's going on? I heard some noise earlier. Did you fall down the stairs again?"

I swallowed hard. "No, but..." I said, my fingers twisting nervously. "My friend is in my room, and he's really hurt. I need your help!"

His eyes widened. "Did you say 'he'?"

I bit my lip.

My dad lunged for my room's door, but I quickly pulled him back.

"Dad, wait! He's hurt. Like, badly hurt."

"Hurt? How?"

"He's wounded, Dad, on his side."

"Why didn't he go to the hospital?"

"Oh Lord Jesus," he muttered, running his hands through his hair.

"Dad, calm down—"

"Calm down? How mi fi calm down when there's some boy inna yuh room who really mash up and can't reach nuh hospital because of it? That usually means they don't want the authorities involved."

"I know how it sounds, Dad, but he's my friend and I need your help. Please. I'm scared." I begged with tears in my eyes.

"Okay, okay. Let me go get the first aid kit," my dad sighed, kissing my forehead.

"We have one?" I called out.

"Of course we do," he said, rushing down the stairs.

I returned to my room to check on Jeremiah.

"How are you feeling?" I asked.

"Honestly, I feel lucky," he mumbled.

"Lucky?" I asked incredulously.

"Yeah. It could have been way worse. This cut could have been so much deeper if I hadn't been quick enough."

I shook my head, gently rubbing his chest. "I hate that this happened to you."

He shrugged, laying his hand over mine. "Me too. But it is what it is, bound to happen sooner or later."

My dad walked into my room, and I quickly moved away from Jeremiah and stood up.

He slowly approached the bed, his gaze fixed intently on Jeremiah.

Jeremiah gulped. "H-hi, Mr. Winters."

"Hello," my dad said shortly. He took a seat beside Jeremiah and instructed him to remove his hand from where he was clutching his side.

He was at least being somewhat civil.

With the scissors, he cut through Jeremiah's shirt and then carefully examined the wound. He shook his head before searching through the first aid kit.

"You lucked out, kid. The wound looks nasty but it isn't deep enough to be too alarmed about."

I recalled my dad mentioning that he had wanted to become a doctor when he was younger. It was strange, but he seemed to be quite invested in the task at hand. On the other hand, Jeremiah appeared visibly in pain.

My dad efficiently stitched up Jeremiah's wound and tidied up the area.

"I don't know you or why you felt the need to come to my daughter for help, but I'd appreciate it if you kept any criminal activity away from my family. Now leave."

My eyes widened.

I understood that look in Jeremiah's eyes once again. That expression he wore when he was being unfairly judged. He appeared shattered, as though he was on the verge of giving up.

He took a deep breath and nodded. "Okay. Thank you for your help."

"No! Stay there!"

"Aurora, it's fine," he began.

"I said stay there." I gritted out.

He immediately eased himself onto my bed.

"Dad, can I talk to you outside?"

My dad let out a sigh and nodded.

He followed me out of the room. "Dad, how could you say that? You don't even know him."

"Aurora, I understand that you're caring and kind, and I truly appreciate that, but you can't always trust folks like this guy. He might just end up bringing you trouble. I mean did you see that wound? And you let him into our home!"

"This is exactly what I'm talking about! I'm fed up with it, Dad! I'm tired of witnessing him being unfairly judged time and time again. And if I've had enough of it, I can't even imagine how he must feel."

"Sweetheart, listen to me—"

"No, Dad, you listen. Jeremiah is the most intelligent guy I know. He cares about his schoolwork more than anyone I know and possesses so much potential. But because of people like you putting him down, he won't even have faith in himself." I said, my voice quivering as tears welled up. "Dad, his father is abusive!"

My dad's expression changed, and I could tell that my words had struck a chord. After all, he had also experienced childhood abuse.

"So the wound is from...."

"His dad hurting him," I whispered.

He shook his head. "I'm sorry. You're not a naive little girl anymore, and I should have known you wouldn't have let him in if he was dangerous. It's just that you're growing up so fast and this, this a lot."

I offered him a sad smile and leaned in for a hug. He hugged me tightly and then pulled away with a sigh.

"Of course, you'd be the one helping someone who's in need, just like your mom. The poor kid, though."

"Dad, can he please stay here?"

"Fine, I'll get him some blankets so he can sleep on the couch—"

"Dad, no! I want to keep an eye on him."

My dad bit his lip and sighed. "I'll get the airbed," he said reluctantly.

I grinned. "Thanks, Dad!"

I walked back into my room to see Jeremiah looking off into space.

"How's your stomach?"

"Feels a bit better."

"Good."

My dad came in with the airbed, sheets, and blankets as well as painkillers and a water bottle for Jer.

He dropped them by my bed.

"Hey, I just want to apologize for what I said earlier. I should know better than to judge someone like that. I'm just trying to keep Aurora safe."

Jeremiah half-smiled. "I understand, sir."

"Aurora told me about...your situation. You can stay here as long as you like, but I think you and I need to have a talk about what's happening at home in the morning."

Jeremiah's throat bobbed as he swallowed down his emotions, and he nodded slightly. "Alright."

"What's your name, son?"

"Jeremiah."

He inflated the airbed and brushed off his pants.

"Alright then. Good night, honey," he said, kissing my head. "Night, Jeremiah."

"Good night, sir. Thanks a lot for patching me up and letting me crash here. I really appreciate it."

My dad chuckled softly. "No worries, Jeremiah. Get some rest, alright?"

"Yes, sir."

Once my dad left the room, I turned to Jeremiah with a guilty expression. "I'm sorry for telling him about it. I was just so angry, and I—"

"It's all right, Aurora. I don't even know why I'm still covering for my dad, been doing it since I was a kid, just a reflex. Plus, it's humiliating, you know? I'm supposed to be the big tough dude, but I'm getting roughed up by my own pops when I step through my front door. Makes me look weak and pathetic."

"Jeremiah, don't worry about how it makes you seem. You're always so hung up on what others think. But who cares? This is your life. And right now, you need help."

"You're right, I know. And after tonight I realize it's time to open up about everything. I could have been seriously injured or worse, even dead."

Sitting down next to him on the bed, I asked in a low voice, "He did it 'cause of me, didn't he?"

He sighed and gently placed his hand on my thigh. "Yeah, partly. But don't blame yourself! You were just trying to watch out for me."

"That's not what you were saying that day," I mumbled.

"I'm sorry about that."

"Why didn't you go to your girlfriend's place tonight anyway?" I asked, pushing his hand off me and turning away.

He carefully scooted closer. "Look Aurora, she's not my girlfriend."

"What?" I turned back to him. "You guys broke up?"

"No, we were never even together."

"What?" I asked again, confusion swirling within me.

"It was all an act. Frankly, I'm surprised how well we pulled it off. We didn't really act like a couple."

"Why would you pretend to date her?"

"Truth is, I wanted you to stay away. After you showed up at my house and my dad almost attacked you, I was scared. I was worried you might try something again, and since you're not Amy's biggest fan, I thought it might be a good move... I don't know, just to keep you safe."

"Ah," I replied, subdued. "And what did Amy get out of it?"

"Popularity."

I rolled my eyes. "I might not have been her biggest fan, but I thought she was better than that."

"Same here, but she's not who I thought she was. She spends her time judging everyone around us, acting like she's better. It's the same way other people judge me, I don't like that. One time she said something about you and I lost my cool and blew up at her."

"The time when she swapped seats with me?"

He nodded. "We stopped talking, but then I asked her to help me out and pretend to date me, and she said she'd do it for popularity."

"But tonight made me realize something else," he chimed in, shifting the topic. I looked up to meet his gaze, a look I'd never seen before graced his face.

I shifted uncomfortably. "And what's that, Jeremiah?"

"At one point tonight, I seriously thought I might not make it out alive, and oddly enough, you were all I could think about, Aurora."

I sat still.

Taking my silence as an encouragement to continue, he said, "Aurora, instead of pushing you away, I should have been pulling you closer. You're the one person who's always believed in me, the one who helped me believe in myself."

"I know I've been pretty shitty to you lately, even before you came to my house. But when Ian came back, and you were so close to him, I couldn't help feeling jealous. And then there was that Jimmy guy. It seemed like you didn't want me around, like you had so many other people in your life. I missed the times when it was just the two of us."

He shook his head. "I know it's not an excuse. I seem to mess things up all the time, especially when it comes to the whole emotion thing. But the truth is, I have so many emotions when it comes to you. I guess what I'm trying to say, Princess, is that I love you."

Chapter 20

"You love me?" I asked, my disbelief evident.

"Yes, Aurora, I do, with all my heart."

"Fuck."

Jeremiah laughed, taken aback, but his amusement soon turned into a wince.

"Are you alright, Jeremiah?"

"I'm okay, now stop calling me Jeremiah, would you?" he said, gently holding my hand. "I prefer it when you call me Jer."

I furrowed my brows, slowly slipping my hand out of his. "Jeremiah, I don't even know how to respond. You can't just go from treating me like dirt to dropping the L-word. Do you expect me to just forgive and forget?"

His smile faltered. "I-I guess, I don't know what I expected. I just needed to be honest with you about how I felt."

I shook my head. "Jeremiah, you really hurt me. You can't expect me to brush that aside."

"I know, Princess, and I'm sorry. I was an idiot, letting my jealousy mess things up. I shouldn't have taken my frustrations out on you, and I definitely shouldn't have punished you for trying to help me." He sighed. "But Aurora, you hurt me too. You're one of the very few people I'm close to, and when you seemed to drop me the moment your friend returned, it hurt. It made me feel like I was just a replacement, like you didn't really care."

"I'm sorry, Jeremiah. It wasn't fair to you, but my actions were more about Simran taking up all his time than about you, I promise. I do care about you, Jeremiah. You know that."

"Yeah, I know that now. Suburban girl ventured into the hood just for me," he chuckled.

I wrinkled my nose. "Ew, I'm not a fan of that nickname."

"Can you find it in your heart to forgive me, Princess?"

I bit my lip as I considered his words.

"Jeremiah, I dunno. The words you said and your actions keep replaying in my mind. I know I shouldn't have dropped you like that when Ian came back and really regret it, but the way you treated me was cruel," I said, trying to steady my emotions. "You said you never wanted to lay your eyes on me again."

"I didn't mean it though, I just wanted to say something to get you away at that moment. If my dad had hurt you, I don't even know what I'd do. I'd rather you away from me than you hurt. I regretted it as soon as I said it, seeing the pain on your face tore me apart."

"Okay, I understand why you did it. I do and I know you didn't mean that stuff but I don't think I can just move past it."

He closed his eyes and sighed. "Please give me a chance, Aurora. I promise—"

"Jeremiah, can we just put this on hold for now, please? I'm emotionally and mentally exhausted. And you need to get some rest."

"Of course, I'm sorry, Aurora."

"I'm sorry too. I want you to know that. For now, let's just focus on getting you better."

He nodded in understanding.

"Ugh, now I need to change my sheets 'cause there's blood on them from your wound."

"Sorry," he said, carefully swinging his legs off my bed.

"It's okay, I'm just relieved you're alright."

He gave me a grateful smile before settling onto the airbed.

I changed my sheets and found one of my dad's shirts for Jeremiah to wear, since his was torn and stained with blood.

I turned out the lights and got under my covers.

"Good night, Jer."

"Good night, love."

Despite the situation, I couldn't help but smile at his term of endearment.

✧

"Dad, can I stick around too?"

"No, sweetheart. You've got to head to school."

"Dad, please? I want to be a part of this."

"Don't worry, you and Jeremiah can discuss everything once you're back home, alright? Right now, I need to talk to him about the situation and figure out what steps he's going to take. I think the first step is taking him to see an actual doctor to make sure his wound doesn't get infected and all that. "

Jer walked into the kitchen, still looking half-asleep.

"Morning," he muttered drowsily.

"Good morning." I greeted him quietly, memories of our conversation from the previous night flooding my mind.

"How's your stomach feeling?" Dad inquired.

"It's much better."

Dad settled at the table with a bowl of cereal. "Glad to hear that. Grab some food, take an Advil and then get back to bed, okay?"

Jer nodded, slowly shuffling towards me.

"What kind of cereal do you want, Frosted Flakes or Lucky Charms?" I asked Jer.

"Lucky Charms."

After I finished my breakfast, I stood up and grabbed my bag. "I'm heading out now."

"Alright, have a good day, honey," Dad said, giving me a hug.

"Goodbye, Dad," I replied.

Jer walked me to the door.

"See you later?" he questioned.

"Yeah, later. And don't hold back with my dad, he..." I searched for the right words, "he understands what you've been going through."

Recognition flickered in Jer's eyes, indicating that he grasped my meaning. "Well, maybe it'll be easier to talk to him."

I nodded in agreement. "I hope so. Bye."

"Bye, Princess."

"Hey," I mumbled as I approached my friends, who were waiting by Ian's locker.

They turned their attention to me, their faces marked with concern.

"What?" I asked, perplexed by their reactions.

"Kiyana said she saw you and Jer at your front door this morning, is everything okay?" Ryan observed.

"I was gonna come over but I didn't want to interrupt, it seemed like an intense conversation." Kiyana whispered.

I let out a deep sigh and cast my gaze towards the ground. I had no clue what to say, of course I wanted to tell them that Jer was in trouble and he'd been through so much but I couldn't, it wasn't my story to tell.

"What's going on?" Ian asked, closing his locker.

I shrugged nonchalantly. "It's nothing, really..."

"Don't hold back, Aurora. Tell us what's up," Simran urged, her eyes reflecting her worry.

"Alright, fine. But it's a long story..."

"I've got time," she responded, crossing her arms.

"Babe, no you don't, the bell's about to ring," Ian reminded Simran gently.

"Oh." She glanced at the clock, then shifted her gaze back to me. "We'll resume this conversation at lunch."

During lunch, my friends sat around the table as I shared the details of the previous night's events. I decided to leave out the fact that Jer had been stabbed, focusing on him confessing his feelings for me.

"Oh. My. God." Simran practically shrieked. "I'm so happy for you!" She seemed ready to leap across the table to hug me, but she stopped herself just in time.

"But then why did you seem so upset this morning?" She asked.

"Do you really expect her to just forgive him after everything he's done?" Ryan chimed in. "He's been such an ass."

Kiyana nodded in agreement. "Exactly. Even if he had his reasons, whatever they might be, his actions weren't fair to Rory."

"Aurora messed up too though; if she had never drifted away from him, they'd still be close," Ian interjected, shrugging. "No offense, Aurora. I'm going to play devil's advocate here because I really think you hurt the man."

"You can't put all the blame on her for his actions. Sure, she made mistakes, but that doesn't excuse everything he did," Ryan countered firmly. "Like if he loved her why try to make her jealous with Amy? It's just stupid and cruel."

I focused on controlling my breath as my friends continued to go back and forth on the situation between me and Jeremiah. The thing was, none of them were aware of the complete story. They didn't really know what happened when I tried to visit him or about his efforts to protect me by moving on with Amy. They didn't understand his reasons for showing up the evening before or the complexities of his relationship with his father. I was grappling with conflicting emotions—I felt hurt, yet I understood him, and my heart ached for him.

"Guys, let's not debate Jeremiah and Aurora's love life. It's not our place, especially when he's not here to defend himself," Simran interjected, noticing the expression on my face. "By the way, where is he?"

"He's not feeling well, so he's at home."

"Your home, right? I saw you leave him there." Kiyana said.

"Yeah, he's at my place."

"I'm so confused." Jimmy mumbled, speaking for the first time during this whole conversation.

"Yeah, are you cool with him or not?" Ryan asked.

I shrugged. I was just as confused honestly.

"Wait, your usually overprotective dad let Jer into your house that late, let him stay over, and then allowed him to skip school and stay after you left?" Ian questioned, I could tell he knew there was more to the story from the way he studied my expression.

"What can I say? He actually likes the guy," I shrugged. "They unfortunately have a few things in common."

Chapter 21

When I arrived home, Jer and I settled on my front steps so he could enjoy some fresh air after being cooped up due to mandatory bed rest, courtesy of the doctor.

As I sat beside him, the events leading up to his injury replayed in my mind. "I'm confused," I began, "when I came to your house, your dad said he'd 'make you pay.' But why would he wait so long to do this to you? I mean, that was weeks ago."

Jer let out a sigh. "I had been crashing at a friend's house. I only came home to get more clothes. He arrived just as I was leaving."

"And he was drunk?" I inquired.

He nodded. "And angry. He smashed his beer bottle against the side of his car and tried to stab me with it. Fortunately, I reacted quickly enough, so he didn't cut too deep."

I winced at the brutal image. "Jesus, Jer."

"When I fell to the ground, he actually seemed scared and remorseful for a moment, but then a neighbor came out, and he got in his car and drove away," he explained.

"And what did your neighbor do?"

"She wanted to call the cops, but I asked her not to. Instead, I asked if she could drop me off at your place."

"So that's how you ended up here," I realized.

He nodded in confirmation.

"There's something else I need to tell you," he added, his gaze dropping.

I furrowed my brows. "Alright, go ahead."

He took a deep breath. "I don't know if you've noticed, but I don't talk about my mom. There's a reason for that."

Honestly, I hadn't even picked up on that, as I hadn't discussed my own mother either.

"She's in jail," he whispered.

My eyes widened in surprise.

"She's in jail because she loves my dad," he continued, shaking his head and clenching his fist, the bitterness evident in his voice.

I placed my hand on top of his.

"My dad has been abusive ever since I was small. He abused my mom and when I was around five or six he started hitting me too. Despite that my mom loved him, like really loved him. I didn't get why. I still don't."

"When I asked, she said she loved him for the man he used to be.

In fourth grade, I had this teacher, Ms. Morley. She was the first teacher to actually do something when she saw the marks on my body. One day I came to school with a black eye and that was it.

She called the cops on my parents. They were going to arrest my dad since they noticed my mom also had bruises but my mom took the fall for him. She told them that it was her who had been hitting me so that my dad wouldn't go to jail.

I was young but that was when I realized my mom loved my dad way more than she loved me. If she really loved me she wouldn't leave me with that freaking monster. She would let him go to jail for what he did to me. To us."

"I'm so sorry, Jer, that's horrible,"I said, shaking my head.

I wrapped him up in a hug and he buried his face in my hair and sighed.

"So she's still in jail now?"I asked.

He nodded against my shoulder.

"Do you visit?"

He shrugged, pulling away."No."

"So what are you going to do?"

"I'm going to the police station. I need to tell them about my dad."

"Maybe you should also talk to your mom? Maybe convince her to admit it was your dad abusing you all along."

He shook his head."She's a lost cause. I never want to see her again, she can rot in jail."

I looked down and wrung my fingers.

"What?" he asked, raising an eyebrow.

"I just...well I..."

"You what, love? Just say it."

I blushed and sighed."I just feel like you should talk to your mom. First."

"Why?"

"Maybe we can snap her out of whatever trance your dad has put her in. If you convince her to confess she'll probably have a chance of being released."

"No." he stated, his jaw set.

"Jer."

"What? I don't want anything to do with her. Drop it."

I bit my lip and looked away but felt his eyes study me.

"Okay, Princess. What's this really about?"

"Nothing," I said quietly.

"Aurora?" he said, taking my hand. "What's wrong?"

"I haven't mentioned my mom either and there's a reason for that too."

His eyebrows scrunched and he nodded for me to go on.

"I-she...She..."

"If you're not ready to tell me—"

"I am! Just give me a second. This is the first time I've actually told someone about her or about what happened to her."

"It's okay. Take your time."

I took a deep breath, gathering my thoughts. "My mom died when I was around nine...I think, I can't remember exactly. I've kind of blocked out most of those memories until now," I admitted, shaking my head slightly. He wrapped his arm around me in support. "My mom was a missionary."

"A missionary?" he asked, his interest piqued.

I nodded, a mixture of emotions welling up. "Yeah. She traveled all over the world, to places in the Middle East, sometimes Africa, China, India," I explained, my voice tinged with both sadness and nostalgia. "My mom was deeply religious, and from a young age, all she wanted to do was travel and connect with people, share her faith, and give them hope. Whether it was helping children in India or building houses and teaching kids in Mexico, she was all in. Her passion led her to some really challenging places. She believed in rescuing people, whether from difficult circumstances or just giving them a message of hope."

Jer nodded in understanding, his eyes locked on mine as I spoke. "Your mom sounds incredible," he said softly.

I managed a small smile. "Yeah, she was. And she believed so strongly in what she was doing. She met my dad on a plane coming back from one of her trips in Mexico, actually. She was trying to talk to him about Jesus, and all my dad wanted was her number," I chuckled through a tear that escaped. "But they hit it off and got married. My dad was cool with her traveling because he loved that she was so devoted to her calling. After I was born, she started to go on fewer trips and tried to focus on local ministries and her blog to connect with people. But then...she decided to go on one last mission."

A heavy sigh escaped me. "They killed her," I whispered, my voice breaking. "They killed my mom."

Jer pulled me into his lap, holding me gently yet firmly, providing a comforting anchor. I buried my face in his chest and let myself cry, letting out all the pent-up sorrow and frustration that had been hidden away for so long.

"I can't even describe how she died, it was just horrible, so brutal but they found her body a month later. A whole month, she was just left there!" I sobbed, my voice shaky with grief. "No one deserves that fate. Especially not her."

Jer's soothing touch continued as I released my emotions. When my sobs subsided into hiccups, I looked up at him, sniffling. "I'm not exactly religious like she was, but I've always admired what she did, you know? It takes a special kind of person to dedicate their life to helping others, to spreading hope and compassion, even in the face of danger." I paused, trying to steady my voice. "She always put others before anything else."

"Your mom sounds like she was amazing."

"She was. And to me, she died a hero," I managed to say, biting my lip to stop the tears from overwhelming me again.

"I can see why you're so determined to stay positive. She sounds like she was always hopeful and optimistic. You're carrying on her legacy in your own way," Jer said gently.

"Yeah, I try to. I just want to live my life the way she did and stay connected to her memory."

"I get it, Princess."

I leaned my head against his chest again and sighed.

"That's why I want you to talk to your mom, Jer." I said, playing with the hair at the nape of his neck. "You have a mom, she might have made some mistakes but just give her a chance. Please?"

He paused for a second before nodding. "Okay, but only for you. I'd do anything for you."

My breath caught as his words hung in the air, and I suddenly became acutely aware of our proximity. I was sitting on his lap, his hand gently rubbing my thigh, and his gaze on me was so intense that I could practically feel his emotions radiating from his eyes.

It made my heart swell. Before I could fully process what was happening, I realized that our faces were inches apart, and we were leaning closer to each other.

As our faces drew even closer, his hand moved from my thigh to gently brush my hair away from my eyes, his touch sending shivers down my spine. His warm palms cupped my face tenderly, and then our lips met.

The kiss was soft and unhurried, a delicate dance of emotions that words couldn't properly describe. With one hand on my face and the other curving around my back, he pulled me closer, deepening the kiss with a growing intensity that left me feeling like the rest of the world had melted away.

His lips were warm against mine, and there was a faint taste of mint that added a touch of sweetness to the moment. We eventually parted, both of us needing to catch our breath, and he rested his forehead against mine. I caressed his cheek, our close proximity allowing us to share the same breath of air.

"Wow," he breathed, and a soft chuckle escaped me in response.

"I've been waiting to do that since we met," he confessed, in both sincerity and playful amusement.

"Since we met? Really? Because all I remember is you telling me to leave you alone," I teased, raising an eyebrow.

He let out an exaggerated scoff, his lips curling into a mischievous grin. "I mean, yeah, I was rude but in the back of my mind all I was thinking about was how soft your lips looked," he admitted, his tone suggestive and his grin growing cheekier.

I couldn't help but roll my eyes at his audacity, but there was a warmth in my chest that I couldn't ignore. The tension that had been building between us seemed to have found its release, and it left me feeling surprisingly content.

✧

I glanced at my phone, then took another look around the hallway. With a sigh, I closed my locker and leaned against it, feeling a little irritated that Jer hadn't shown up yet, despite his promise to meet me there.

"Why you mad?" A whisper brushed against my ear, and I jumped slightly before turning to find Jer there.

"I'm not angry. I was just annoyed because you told me you would meet me here like ten minutes ago," I said, trying to sound less flustered than I felt.

"Actually, four minutes and twenty-two seconds ago," he replied, checking his phone. "And I just stopped to admire my beautiful girl."

Heat rushed to my cheeks as I protested, "I'm not your girl. You have a lot of making up to do."

Jer chuckled, a hint of mischief in his eyes, and he pulled me closer. "Of course, and I'm ready to put in the work. You're worth it and I want you more than anything."

My breath hitched at his words and I noticed his eyes drop to my lips. Leaning in, our lips met, and my back pressed against the locker as his hands traced down my back.

I gently pushed him away when his hand brushed against my butt. "Okay, let's not go crazy," I told him, tugging at my dress to adjust it.

He flashed a cheeky smile, his eyes dancing with playful energy.

As we walked past, I couldn't help but notice a few glances and whispers from our peers. "Ugh, not this again. I was just getting used to not being gossiped about."

Jer shrugged, his arm slinging over my shoulder. "I don't mind. I want everyone to know that we're together."

"We're not together," I retorted, my tone firm.

"Not yet," he sang, his arm comfortably draped around me.

I sighed. "This is so weird."

"What?" Jer asked.

I hesitated before admitting, "I dunno, I just don't think I've ever seen you this...happy."

A genuine smile played at the corners of his lips as he looked at me. "Well, I guess there's a first time for everything. I truly am happy though," he said thoughtfully.

I beamed at him. "Well, that makes me happy."

"You make me happy," he said, pecking my lips again. I knew that for someone who was trying to resist him, I was doing a pretty bad job but I couldn't help it.

"Hey, whatever happened to your 'happy song'?" he asked.

"Happy song?" I asked, puzzled.

"Yeah, remember when we met? You kept singing this song, and you said it helped you stay positive when someone was annoying you or something."

"Oh, that!" I laughed. "Yeah, that isn't really a thing."

"What?"

"I made it up. To annoy you."

He rolled his eyes. "Of course, you did."

We stopped in front of our friends, who all stared at us curiously.

"Oh my God, you guys are so cute!" Kiyana squealed as she hugged us both. "Hey, Jer! Haven't talked to you in a while. I'm happy you decided to stop being such an ass. Don't you ever break my best friend's heart again." She finished with a tight grip on his shirt.

"Okay, down, tiger," I said, gently prying her fingers from Jer.

"Hey man, happy to see you." Ian greeted.

Jer greeted him back with a nod while Simran waved timidly.

"Hi! I'm sorry for being a... um, you know... and hitting on you all the time. I don't even know what I saw in you." Jer raised an eyebrow.

"No offense!" She exclaimed after realizing what she had blurted out.

"None taken, I guess," Jer mused.

"Hi, I'm Mona." Mona extended her hand, and Jer shook it.

"Jeremiah."

"Hey."

"Hey, Johnny," Jer spoke half-heartedly.

"It's Jimmy." He frowned.

"Whatever." Jer shrugged.

"Jeremiah," I warned.

"Sorry, Jimmy."

We all directed our attention to Ryan, who had remained silent.

"Hey?" Jeremiah's voice carried a hint of uncertainty.

Ryan fixed him with an unyielding glare. "What? Do you expect me to just ignore everything you've done?"

I closed my eyes momentarily, a plea escaping my lips. "Ryan, please, not now."

"No! I'm sorry, but I'm not going to pretend like what you did wasn't messed up."

"What I did? You don't even know the full story."

"I know enough. You're not the person I thought you were."

Jeremiah's eyes burned into Ryan. "You know nothing. How could you possibly pass judgment on me when you haven't tried to speak to me since Aurora and I stopped talking?" Jer's words held frustration and a desire for understanding, as he stepped closer to Ryan.

"Why would I talk to you? You hurt her—"

"No, I'm talking about before that, Ryan. I thought we were friends, but the moment Ian showed up and Aurora distanced herself, so did you!"

Ryan's eyebrows knitted together as Jeremiah continued.

"I could have used a friend, I could have used someone, but I ended up feeling alone." Jeremiah's voice cracked on the last word. "It's clear that our friendship was conditional on whether I was on good terms with Aurora, so maybe we were never truly friends to begin with."

"That's not true," Ryan retorted.

"It is though, Ryan. Where have you been?" Jeremiah's words hung in the air as Ryan remained silent. "So, don't judge my actions when you don't know shit."

Jeremiah began to move past us. "Wait, Jer," I interjected, grabbing his arm.

"I'll catch you later," he responded, gently shaking off my hand. The expression in his eyes conveyed that Ryan's words had touched on deeper resentments.

I turned to Ryan, my voice firm. "Ryan, there's more to this whole thing with Jer than you know. He's been through a lot. I really appreciate your concern for me, but I can handle my own issues. You focus on your own relationship with Jeremiah, not mine." With that, I walked away.

Later as the lunch bell rang, I caught up with Jer at his locker.

"Hey, are you okay?" I asked, concern lacing my voice.

He shrugged. "I'm fine."

"Are you mad at me?" I inquired, a tinge of guilt coloring my words. It was obvious that he partially held me responsible for Ryan's distance, and I felt a pang of regret. Jer had started the day in such a good mood, only to fall into brooding a mere twenty minutes in.

"I don't know, Aurora. I'm feeling pretty conflicted right now." he sighed. "I don't want to be mad at you, though."

"I truly am sorry for how things went down when Ian came home. I promise, I'll make it up to you."

"So, I guess we both have some making up to do," he replied, a half-smile forming.

I crossed my arms. "You've got a lot more to make up for than I do."

He scoffed playfully. "This isn't a competition, Aurora."

"Just saying," I laughed. "Coming to lunch?"

"With you? Of course," he grinned, our fingers intertwining.

"You're unbelievable," Amy's voice cut through the air, catching us off guard as we made our way to our lunch table.

"What the—" I began, taking a step back at the intensity in her expression.

"You can't do this to me, Jeremiah! We had a deal. I don't care if you finally got a clue and realized your feelings for her. You didn't even bother telling me about you guys!"

"Jer? You didn't tell her?" I asked, surprised. While I wasn't fond of Amy, it still felt odd that he hadn't called her to let her know their little arrangement was over.

He shrugged.

"I assumed she'd find out today, and she did," he said with a nonchalant tone, turning to face her. "So, see ya."

"You're such an ass! Just when I was finally getting some attention around here, you ruin everything!"

"Honey, you're still getting attention. Just not for the reasons you'd prefer. What are people calling you now? Oopsie? Since Jeremiah clearly made a mistake choosing you." Simran chimed in, joining us with her characteristic sass.

Amy snapped her mouth shut, glared at Jer, then at me, and stormed out of the cafeteria.

"That girl needs help," Simran said, shaking her head as we continued to our table.

"How's your stomach, Jeremiah?" Mona asked once we were seated.

Jer looked at me briefly before turning to Mona. "My stomach?"

I shifted uncomfortably in my seat. I hadn't told our friends what had happened.

"Um... yeah," Mona continued, raising an eyebrow at our awkwardness. "You said he didn't feel well, that's why he hasn't been at school."

I stared at her, still wondering how she had deduced it was stomach troubles that he was suffering from.

"I guessed it was a stomach ache 'cause I noticed Jer grabbing his stomach a few times this morning," Mona clarified.

"Oh," I laughed nervously. "Yeah."

Jer and I exchanged relieved glances before focusing on our food again.

"Guys, we should celebrate," Simran suddenly suggested.

"Celebrate?" I questioned.

"Yeah! I mean, you guys are together, and everyone seems happy. Why not?" Mona chimed in.

"We're not together," I mumbled.

"Are we going to ignore the whole blow-up with Jer and Ryan this morning?" Jimmy added.

Jer let out a sigh. "Y'know what? I want to celebrate. Or at least do something fun. I'm tired of always being the one dampening people's moods."

"You don't dampen moods, Jeremiah. Don't say that," I reassured him.

"How about we do something tonight?" Simran suggested.

"Yeah, we can go to my uncle's restaurant," Jimmy offered.

"Your uncle owns a restaurant?" I asked, surprised.

He nodded. "Yep, Italian cuisine."

"You're Italian?" I raised an eyebrow.

Jimmy nodded. "Yeah, half."

"Cool, so it's settled," I said, clapping my hands together.

"So, is Ryan invited? I noticed he and Kiyana didn't even show up for lunch," Mona inquired.

Jer shrugged with his jaw set. "It's up to them whether they show up or not."

Chapter 22

"Jimmy, Il mio amore!" a voice called out, and we looked up to see a chubby lady running towards Jimmy. Instinctively, we all took a step back as she barreled toward him.

His eyes widened. "Oh Lord, let me live through this," he muttered. I had to bite my lip to stifle a laugh. He let out an 'oof' as she enveloped him in a tight hug.

"Tesoro, please. Let go of the boy. You will hurt him," a man's voice interjected from behind her.

"Okay, okay," she relented, grinning. "How are you?"

"I'm good, Zietta."

"That's wonderful, Bello. I'm so happy you decided to visit."

"Jimmy, it's so good to see you," the man said with open arms as his wife, I assumed, stepped aside.

"Hey Zio Antonio," Jimmy replied, embracing him.

"Introduce us to your friends, Jimmy. I'm happy you finally made some. I remember when your only friend was your action figure of the Flash—"

"Zio! Please," Jimmy gritted out, his face turning red.

The man laughed. "Okay, okay. Who is this bella ragazza?" he asked, smiling at Mona.

"That's Mona," Jimmy said, his eyes filled with adoration.

After a solid five seconds of just staring at her, his uncle playfully nudged his arm. "And the rest?"

"Oh, um, this is Ryan, that's Jeremiah, then there's Ian, Simran, Kiyana, and Aurora," Jimmy introduced, gesturing to each one of us. "And guys, this is my uncle and aunt."

"Nice to meet you all! So many beautiful young faces. Come with me," his aunt warmly invited.

We followed her, drawing curious glances from most of the elderly folks there.

"I know this place doesn't seem that exciting, but we get free food and as much as we want," Jimmy whispered to us.

"Here we are." She said, gesturing to a massive table away from the other guests.

"Thanks, Zia."

"No problem, Tesoro. Someone will be back to take your orders."

I picked up the menu and licked my lips. Italian food was always a treat.

"Oooh, carbonara!" I exclaimed excitedly. "What are you getting, Jer?"

"Oh, I dunno, maybe a few slices of pizza—"

"No, Jer! You can get pizza anytime. Try something you've never had before."

He rolled his eyes. "Fine."

"Jimmy!" A girl's voice squealed.

"Franci," he said with a touch of distaste.

She hugged his neck and planted a kiss on his cheek, causing Mona to raise an eyebrow.

Franci giggled. "I know you missed me, Jimmy."

"Whatever you say," he sighed.

"Well, are you going to introduce me to your friends?" she asked.

He shot her a look. "No."

She giggled again. "Don't mind him. This is just how we interact with each other. We've been friends since birth, my parents are really close with his aunt and uncle. I'm Franci, in case you didn't already know."

We all stared at her blankly, and she gave us expectant looks. She seemed overly familiar for someone we had just met, and Jimmy didn't seem too thrilled about her presence.

"What are your names?" she inquired after a moment of silence.

"Look, Franci, I really don't feel like dealing with you today, so could you please just go?" Jimmy's tone was direct.

She pouted. "Jimmy, don't be like that. I'm just trying to get to know your friends," she said, running her hand through his hair. I noticed Mona's face turning slightly red. I could tell from the look on her face that things were about to heat up.

Mona jumped up and swatted Franci's hand away. "Don't touch my man."

My eyes widened, Ian sniggered, Kiyana and Simran grinned with excitement at the impending showdown, and Jimmy choked on the water he was sipping, coughing profusely.

Franci stared at Mona in shock. "Excuse me?"

"I said don't. Touch. My. Man. Or is that too hard for you to understand?"

I jabbed my elbow into Jer's side to suppress his laughter.

Franci gasped. "Look, I don't know who you think you are, but you can't just waltz in here and talk to me like that. And sorry to burst your bubble, but Jimmy and I are already together," she declared, placing her hand on his shoulder.

"No we are not, Franci. Stop telling people that!" Jimmy said in frustration, trying to shrug her hand off.

Mona smacked her hand away once more. "I told you not to touch him."

"Stop hitting me!"

Mona crossed her arms, speaking slowly. "It's simple: you stop touching him, and I stop hitting you. Got that?"

"Don't talk to me like I'm an idiot," Franci said through gritted teeth.

"Then stop acting like one. And while you're at it, maybe try being less desperate."

Franci gasped. "Vaffanculo a chi t'è morto," she shot back, just as Jimmy's aunt returned to our table. She let out a startled exclamation and covered her mouth. Franci's eyes widened, and Mona smirked before calmly sitting back down.

"Francesca Ernesta Romano! Did you just tell Jimmy's lovely friend to engage in inappropriate activities with her deceased family members?"

Jer and Ryan burst into laughter, while everyone else stared awkwardly at the scene.

"I-I—" Franci stammered.

"Leave. Your mother will hear about this."

Franci slinked away, her head down, but she shot one last glare at Mona before disappearing.

"I'm very sorry about that, my friends! Now, are you ready to order?" Jimmy's aunt asked as she returned to the table.

Mona's victorious smirk remained as we all turned our attention to Jimmy's aunt.

"I'll have the spaghetti carbonara," Mona said sweetly, her tone shifting instantly from confrontation to politeness.

Jimmy cleared his throat. "I'll go with the margherita pizza, please."

Kiyana followed. "I'll have the eggplant parmesan."

We all placed our order with me going for spaghetti carbonara and Jeremiah getting the same.

"Alright, I'll have those orders placed for you. Enjoy your time here!" his aunt said with a wink before heading off.

"I've heard some wild insults, but what even was that?" Jer mused.

Jimmy sighed. "Ugh, that's like the least offensive Italian insult, trust me."

"So what was it like having two girls fighting over you?" Ryan asked, breaking his silence since we had all gathered. It was surprising that he had even shown up, especially given the effort everyone was making to ignore the tension between him and Jer.

Jimmy blushed and waved off the notion. "Come on, they weren't exactly fighting over me."

Jer chimed in with a proud nod. "They were pretty much duking it out, and I must say, Mona held her own. Impressive, really." Mona offered him a smug smile in response.

"I've heard about this Franci girl before. Jimmy's too nice to shut her delusional ass down, so I thought I'd help." Mona explained as she speared her pasta with her fork.

"Fair enough," Jer mumbled, apprehensively.

Ryan added with a smirk, "Who would've thought, our man Jimmy, a ladies' man."

"Who would have thought he'd be pulling more than any of us," Jer mused. They both laughed, and a look passed between them before they glanced away. I hoped that meant there was still hope for their friendship.

The restaurant was alive with the sound of cutlery clinking, conversations in the distance, and the mouthwatering scent of Italian dishes wafting through the air. As our orders landed on the table, the plates were placed in front of us, each one more enticing than the last. We wasted no time in digging in.

Jeremiah and I shared a laugh as we twirled spaghetti onto our forks at the same time. When I was about to take a bite, I spotted a little sauce smudge on the corner of his mouth. Trying not to laugh, I subtly gestured to my own face. He got the hint and wiped his lips with a bashful smile, which made me chuckle.

With full bellies and high spirits, we hung out at the table even after we'd polished off our meal, enjoying each other's company and the laid-back vibe of the place.

As the restaurant slowly emptied out and the sun started to set, we eventually decided it was time to call it a night and head back home.After saying our goodbyes to everyone else, Ryan held Jer and me back.

"Hey, Jer, can I speak to you?"

He took in a deep breath before nodding. He kissed me on the cheek, and he and Ryan wandered away from us. I turned to Kiyana.

"Think they'll be okay?" I asked.

"They'll be fine. Don't worry," she assured me, hugging me to her side. Once they were done talking, they walked back over to us, and Ryan offered me a tight smile.

"Hey, Rory, I'm sorry about earlier. It wasn't my place to get in between you two like that. You know how much I care about you, and I just want to protect you."

"I know, Ryan, and I love you for that. You have to remember I'm a big girl, and I know what I'm doing, okay?"

He nodded, holding out his arms for a hug, which I gladly accepted. "So, you guys are good now?" I asked.

They exchanged glances, and Jer nodded. "We will be."

We said our goodbyes, and Jer and I made our way back to my house.

"I don't know why you insist on walking so much." he muttered, shivering a little.

"Oh don't be a baby! It isn't cold. It's basically spring now and besides, how else would we get home? You didn't bring your bike."

"You could have just asked your dad to pick us up or one of the guys to give us a ride."

"Well, tough luck. Let's just enjoy the fresh air," I said, lacing our fingers together. "So, how did that conversation with Ryan go?"

Jer shrugged. "We're guys, you know, we get over stuff quickly."

"But you seemed really hurt, Jer," I noted. "Do you think you two can get back to where you were before?"

Jer looked into my eyes. "Look, I understand we've kinda got this whole friend group now, but I want you to know that you're my priority. If people want to keep things superficial with me, that's okay. At least I know what to expect. I have you and that's enough."

"Jeremiah, I don't like that," I replied. "I appreciate how much you value me, but I also want you to have friends outside of us."

"I tried that, Aurora, didn't work out," Jer said. "Why would I willingly put myself in that situation again? If anything happens between us, they'll all choose you, and honestly, I can't blame them. You're like the most amazing person I know."

I stopped in my tracks, gently pulling him back. "You know, it means the world to me that you think so highly of me, but I really think that your friendship with Ryan is worth the effort. You two are so similar, you get along really well and I can see that you care about each other. Please, give it another try, not just for me, but for the friendship itself."

Jer sighed, a hint of a smile playing on his lips. "Fine, beautiful, anything for you."

I beamed at him and planted a sweet kiss on his cheek. We walked in a comfortable silence for a while before Jer spoke up again.

"Will you come with me to talk to my mom tomorrow?" Jer's voice was soft, almost hesitant.

"Of course, Jer," I replied immediately.

He breathed out a sigh of relief. "Thanks, Princess, I don't think I'd be able to do this without you. But I know I have to give her a chance."

I smiled."Good."

"Do you think she'll confess?" he asked.

I nibbled on my lip. "I can't say for sure, Jer, but I hope she does."

His jaw ticked."Me too."

"I think we also need to swing by your place, Jer."

He stiffened."Why?"

"Because Jer, you've been wearing my dad's old clothes for the past few days. You need to get your stuff."

"You're right. I'm just not sure if he'll be there. I mean he took off that day but he might have come back."

"Well, considering your neighbor pretty much witnessed him stabbing you, I doubt he'll be back any time soon."

He furrowed his brows and hummed.

"Don't worry, Jer. If you want, my dad can come too."

"I'm not worried." He snapped, going rigid.

"Okay Jer, I'm just saying."

He looked down.

"Jer, in this situation, anyone would feel scared. I mean, he stabbed you with a broken beer bottle." I gently lifted his chin, aligning our eyes. "You don't have to put on a tough act with me, Jeremiah."

"I'm sorry, you're right." He said as I unlocked the front door. "It'll take time before I can fully let my guard down, though."

"That's completely fine. I'll be here, waiting," I reassured him. We stepped inside, and my dad sat lounging on the couch with Netflix playing on the TV, looking like he was about to doze off.

"Hey, guys. How was dinner?" my dad asked, yawning as we walked into the house.

"Wonderful. I had the best carbonara ever."

"Carbonara? Man, I'd love some of that right now."

"We should all head down to that restaurant sometime, it's pretty good." I said

"Sounds great. Jeremiah, how are you doing?"

"I'm fine, sir."

My dad smiled. "Good. I'm gonna head to bed guys. See you tomorrow."

"Good night, Dad.

"Good night Mr.Winters."

"Night."

I turned to Jer. "Movie?"

"Sure."

✧

"Just breathe," I said, gently squeezing his hand.

We observed as a woman was led into the visitor's room, and Jer's demeanor stiffened.

She was of shorter stature, her tight black curls bouncing as she walked. As she drew nearer, I noticed two fresh red marks on her cheek, stark against her dark skin.

"Jeremiah," she whispered.

There was an unmistakable love in her eyes as she looked at her son, and a sense of warmth filled my chest. It felt like this visit was already worth it, just to see that expression on her face.

"Mom."

I was taken aback by the tremor in his voice.

I smiled, finding it ironic how much he had resisted coming to see her, and now he was regarding her as if he wanted to jump across the table and embrace her.

She took a seat, her gaze never leaving Jeremiah, her eyes glistening with tears. "Hello, baby."

"You recognize me?" he questioned, voice cracking.

"Of course, my love. I haven't seen you in years, but I'd never forget my baby. Never."

She made a subtle move to reach for his hand, but a nearby guard spoke up.

"No touching."

She withdrew her hand, letting out a sigh, then shifted her attention from Jeremiah to me. "And who might this be?"

"I'm Aurora. Pleased to meet you, Mrs. Summers."

"Nice to meet you too, dear."

"So, uh, how have you been?" Jer asked, nervously scratching the back of his head.

She shrugged and chuckled. "As well as one can be in here. I'm just really grateful to see you. This is the first time I've seen you since..." Her voice trailed off, and she pursed her lips.

Jer inhaled sharply.

"Baby, I'm so sorry. I know you're angry at me, I know you feel betrayed. I would too. I would hate me. I can't fathom why you even came here. I was certain I'd never see you here."

"Well, Aurora suggested I give you another chance," he admitted. "So, I decided I would. I just want to understand why you would do that to me, why you would do that for him."

"Baby, I know. And I believe it's time for me to explain everything."

"Maybe I should go—" I began, feeling like I was intruding.

"No, stay," Jer said, his grip on my hand tightening.

I swallowed hard and nodded, our fingers interlocking as I placed our hands in my lap.

She smiled at us fondly before looking down and taking a shaky breath. "Jeremy, when your dad started hitting you, I was scared and horrified. I tried to take the heat off you by making him angry with me, hoping he'd only hurt me and not you. But it didn't work, it just made him want to hit you more.

So, I switched up my approach. Even though I hated him so much, I started pretending he was a great husband and dad. It's weird, but it actually made him hurt you less. I kept it up as long as I could, until we got reported to the police by one of your teachers, they saw all your bruises. At that point, it wasn't an act anymore; he had threatened me, Jeremy."

She paused, her voice shaking with emotion. "He told me that if I didn't confess, once he got out, he'd kill the both of us. I saw it in his eyes, and I knew he meant it. I really didn't want to leave you alone with him but back then I felt like I had no choice. I know now that there are steps I could have taken to prevent him from coming anywhere near us when he got out, but back then his threats felt real. He manipulated me into believing them."

Her eyes welled up with tears as she continued. "I'm so sorry, Jeremiah. I'm sorry for making you think I didn't care, for leaving you alone. It was to protect you. Back then, I couldn't imagine explaining it to you; I didn't think you'd understand."

Her voice was full of sincerity as she went on. "I love you more than I can say, Jeremiah. Not a day has gone by without me thinking about my wonderful son. I've worried about you, your safety, and how you've grown. Please know that."

Tears formed in her eyes, and I found myself wiping my own cheeks, deeply touched by her words and the emotions behind them.

"I love you too, Mom," Jer said, his voice trembling. "I knew it. I knew there was no way you'd do that to me."

"I would never," she said. "I would have to be a damn lunatic to still love that bastard. No, I knew for years I had to leave, I just didn't know how."

Jer let out a strangled laugh and sighed. "Mom, I can't leave you here. Not after what you just told me."

"Don't be silly, baby. What are you going to do? Break me out? I have a couple more years and I haven't caused much trouble so I should be seeing you soon."

"No, I want you out of here now. I'm going to the cops about Dad, and I'm telling them the truth. I want you to confess that he was the one who hurt me."

Her eyes widened. "Oh, I don't know, Jeremiah."

"What do you mean? You think I just randomly decided to tell the cops now? No, Mom, he tried to kill me a few days ago."

"What?" she breathed out.

"He broke his beer bottle against a door and stabbed me with it," Jer stated, bluntly.

His mom placed her hand over her mouth. "W-what? A-are you okay? Why? I mean, what?"

"I'm fine, Mom. Calm down, calm down."

"That son of a bitch needs to pay for what he's done," she said menacingly.

"Damn right he does," Jer nodded.

"So what happened after he hurt you? Did you go to the hospital? Because you'd have to tell them what happened. Wouldn't he be in jail already?"

"No, I wasn't going to do this at first, so instead of the hospital, I went to Aurora's. Her dad stitched me up. I've been staying with them ever since that night."

"Thank you for taking care of my son," she said to me.

"No problem, Mrs. Summers." I laughed. "I wouldn't say I was taking care of him though."

"You're giving him a place to sleep and food to eat, that's taking care of him, honey," she laughed. "And you're the one who suggested he come talk to me. I will forever be grateful to you for bringing my son to me."

I smiled.

"Mom, what happened to your face?"

She laughed and waved him off. "This is nothing, honey. I just got on the wrong side of some powerful people here."

"I thought you said you were staying out of trouble? We need to get you out of here," Jer said with wide eyes. She laughed again.

I watched as the guard came to our table.

Mrs. Summers turned to see what I was looking at and sighed. "Well, I guess our time is up. It was so great to see you, Jeremiah."

"You too, Mom."

"I'll see you soon?"

"No doubt about it." he smiled.

"See you later, honey," she said, smiling at me.

"Bye, Mrs. Summers."

She was escorted out of the room, and we got up to leave.

Once we were outside, Jer stopped me.

"Thank you so much, Aurora," he said.

I shook my head. "I didn't do anything, Jer."

"But you did, Princess. If it wasn't for you, I would never have gone to talk to my mom. Never. And I wouldn't have found out that she actually did care about me. I would never have been able to mend things with her."

"Well, I'm just happy you did. When your mom got up just then, I saw a light in her eyes that wasn't there when she came out."

Jer smiled with tears in his eyes. "I love you so much, Aurora."

"And I love you, Jeremiah, with all my heart," I said, cupping his face in my hands.

His eyes widened before he grinned at me, dipping his head to kiss me passionately, right in the middle of the parking lot of a prison. And it couldn't have been more perfect.

Chapter 23

"And now I'm turning him in." Jeremiah finished with a big breath.

Everyone stared at Jeremiah in pure shock.

"S-so your dad stabbed you?" Simran asked, her voice trembling.

Jeremiah nodded.

"And you were a drug dealer?" Mona inquired, her eyes wide.

Once again, Jeremiah nodded.

"Jeremiah, man, I'm truly sorry you had to go through all that abuse for all these years. You don't deserve that. No one does," Ian said, shaking his head in sympathy.

"I'm sorry your mom had to take the blame for it. All this time, you two could have had some kind of relationship. God knows I wish I could," Ryan mumbled, his voice heavy with sadness. I rubbed his shoulder, sharing the same sentiments.

Jeremiah furrowed his brow. "What do you mean? I thought your mom was still around."

Ryan sighed deeply. "Well since we're sharing, um, m-my mom got into a car accident a few years ago. She had just lost her job, and she and my dad weren't in a good place. I guess she felt kind of empty or something. She decided to go to a bar to drink and then tried to drive herself home after drinking non-stop for hours. She ended up crashing into a stop sign. She's currently in a coma."

"Ryan, shit, I'm so sorry. I didn't- I didn't know," Jer shook his head, visibly moved.

Ryan shrugged. "It's cool, man. I know."

Kiyana wrapped her arms around Ryan and planted a supportive kiss on his cheek.

"This sucks," Simran sighed.

"Life sucks," I mumbled back, and Simran raised her glass of orange juice in agreement.

"Well, thanks for sharing, Jer. That must have been difficult. You too, Ryan," Jimmy said with a warm smile.

I was genuinely proud of Jer for opening up about his experiences. It was a significant step, and I wanted him to feel like he truly belonged in our group, knowing that everyone was there for him. He deserved that.

"No problem," Jer said. "It actually feels good to get it off your chest."

"True that," Ryan agreed with a nod.

I swallowed wondering if I should tell my friends about my mom.

"Babe, I know what you're thinking. You don't have to if you're not ready," Jer whispered to me, caressing my hand in his.

"I don't think I'll ever be ready, telling that story once was enough for me" I whispered back.

He shrugged. "And that's fine."

I let out a breath and smiled.

"Alright, you know what? We need some ice cream. I'm gonna hit up the convenience store," Jimmy announced, getting up.

"Oooh, yes! Cookie dough please!" I requested with enthusiasm.

"No way, let's go with mint chocolate chip," Ryan countered, offering his own suggestion. However, his proposal was met with stark silence. It was like he'd just committed ice cream heresy.

"Uh, let's go with the cookie dough," Mona chimed in, shooting Ryan a mildly disgusted look.

We all mumbled our agreement, making our preference clear.

"Hey, what's wrong with mint chocolate chip? It's fantastic," Ryan defended himself, with a hint of defiance in his voice.

"Oh honey," Kiyana said, patting his head with a loving yet firm smile.

"Pick up some candy too," Simran called out from her seat.

"I'll go with!" Mona said, standing up.

"Okay, guys, I have the perfect idea!" Simran said after Mona and Jimmy had left.

"What is it?" Kiyana asked, getting excited.

"Okay, so Mona's birthday is coming up soon, and I was thinking we should throw her a surprise party."

"Yay, a party!" Kiyana clapped.

"And we can plan it for after things play out with Jeremiah's father. Hopefully, if he goes to jail, it can be like a celebration for that too."

Ryan raised an eyebrow. "A celebration...for his dad going to jail?"

"No, I like it. I mean, that's what I want. For him to go to jail and for my mom to be released, so if things do go that way, then I wanna celebrate," Jer nodded.

"Great!" Simran clapped. "We need this, guys. We need to have some fun, y'know? What do you say, Aurora?"

I smiled. "Why not?"

✧

"Silence. All stand," called the Clerk.

The judge and commissioners entered the room and took their seats at the bench.

"Calling the matter of Jason Summers, Marie Summers, and Jeremiah Summers," he said.

"Very well," said the Judge.

"Your honor, my name is Mark Putt, and I will be representing the complainants, Marie and Jeremiah Summers."

"Your honor, my name is Patricia Weatherill, and I will be representing the accused, Jason Summers, at this hearing."

"Thank you. Mr. Putt, would you like to begin?" the judge asked.

"Thank you, Your Honour. You see," Mr. Putt began, outlining the harrowing details of the case. He described the years of abuse that Jer and his mom had endured at the hands of his dad, detailing incidents of physical violence, emotional trauma, and the perjury that had led to Mrs. Summer's false confession when the abuse was first reported all those years ago.

As Mr. Putt continued, he presented evidence, including medical records, photographs of injuries, and statements from neighbours who had been witnesses to the abuse firsthand. The courtroom was filled with a palpable sense of tension as the full extent of the abuse came to light.

Throughout the proceedings, I couldn't take my eyes off Jer, I knew it must have been hard for him to relive all this trauma.He clutched his mother's hand tightly, his eyes fixed on his father.

On the other side, Patricia Weatherill, Jason's defense attorney, attempted to counter the allegations. She argued that the evidence was circumstantial and lacked concrete proof of Jason's guilt. However, her arguments seemed feeble in the face of the overwhelming evidence presented by Mr. Putt.

As the proceedings continued, it became increasingly clear that justice was finally catching up with Jason Summers, who had managed to evade the law for far too long. The courtroom awaited the judge's decision, hoping that it would bring closure and healing to the Summers family after years of suffering.

"Do you promise to say the truth, the whole truth, and nothing but the truth? So help you, God?"

"I do," Jer said.

"Please state your full name for the court."

"Jeremiah Summers."

I nervously shifted in my seat as I awaited Jer's testimony.

my dad grabbed my hand and squeezed it.

I looked over at Jer's mom and bit my lip. I really hoped this worked and she got out.

She must have felt my eyes on her because she turned, and when our eyes locked, she offered me a reassuring smile. I smiled back before she was distracted by her lawyer.

I looked to the other side where Jer's father sat, and shivered.

I couldn't stop replaying the moment he lunged at me in his house every time I saw him.

When he had taken off after stabbing Jer, it turns out he had been staying at a motel in the next town over.

Thankfully the odds didn't seem to be in his favor, seeing as he was hiding out, making him look suspicious.

Not to mention Jer's neighbor who had witnessed the stabbing was testifying, and a lot of other people in his neighborhood who had heard or seen him abusing Jer.

I couldn't help but feel a little angry at them that they were only saying something now.

"The jury has reached a verdict. Jason Summers is found guilty on the account of attempted murder, household abuse, and perjury."

"Marie Summers is found not guilty. All previous charges will be dropped."

I couldn't help the big smile that broke out on my face as the Judge slammed his gavel down.

My dad gave my hand another squeeze, and we all got up to leave.

Jer hugged his mom tightly as she cried tears of joy.

Later that day, Jer and I lay cuddling on his bed.

"I'm so happy for you, Jer," I said, caressing his face.

He beamed at me and shook his head. "I can't believe he's actually gone, I can't believe my mom is actually home, I can't believe I'm actually free."

"Aw, baby," I giggled, wiping away a tear that escaped his eye.

He laughed then sniffed. "Tell anyone you saw me cry, and it's over between us."

I laughed in shock. "Oh really? Don't you have to ask someone out to be able to break up with them?"

"Well, I mean—" he started.

"Uh-uh, I don't remember being asked out or saying yes. I will be waiting though."

"It'll be worth the wait, my princess. I promise," he said gently tugging one of my curls.

I grinned and rested my head on his chest. "I just realized this is the first time I've been in your room."

Jer shrugged. "There's not much to it anyway. And it's not like I'm gonna be here for much longer."

"What do you mean?" I asked, my eyebrows furrowed.

"Well, it's getting closer to graduation, and after graduation, most people go to college so that they can get a job and then they can—"

"Okay! Okay! I get it," I said, smacking his chest.

He laughed.

"I just didn't know if you were still going."

"I am. And... I just got accepted to my dream university."

I sat up. "Wait, what?"

"Yep. Came in the post today," he stretched across me and grabbed a letter from his bedside table.

"Here."

I grabbed the letter and read it. "Wow, Jer, I'm so happy for you! You didn't even tell me you applied."

"Yeah, I know. I just didn't really think I would get in, so I didn't see the need."

"You're amazing, Jer; of course, you'd get in."

"So is this where you're going?" I asked.

"I'm not sure," he said.

"You know, we haven't really talked about college and us."

"Well, we have plenty of time to figure it out. All I know is that I want to be with you, no matter what. Even if I have to make some sacrifices."

"Jer, don't be ridiculous. I would never want you to put your future at risk because of me. But of course I want us to be together, even if we're not official yet," I added playfully.

He groaned. "Aurora! It'll happen. I just want to make sure it's special."

"I know, I know." I laughed, flashing a teasing smile.

"You know I love you," he said, giving me a sweet peck on the lips.

"I love you too."

"You ready for the party tonight?"

I nodded. "I'm just glad we got a pass on helping out because of the whole court thing."

"Lazy," he teased, playfully poking my arm.

"I am not. It's Simran! Have you met her? She's such a perfectionist and she's so bossy. I feel sorry for anyone who had to help out."

Jer laughed. "True."

We looked up when we heard a knock on the door.

"Yeah," Jer called.

"Hey, kids! I made some snacks!"

We sat up as his mom brought a tray with drinks, chips, and candy.

"Oh God, I've missed this," Jer said, grabbing a chip.

His mom laughed and placed the tray on the bed.

"Okay. I'm gonna go catch up on Grey's Anatomy. I've missed a lot. Shout if you need me." She chuckled.

"Sounds good, Mom."Jer replied with a sad smile.

Once she had left, I turned to Jer, ready to ask him a question that had been weighing on my mind for a while.

"Hey Jer?" I began.

He hummed, lying beside me.

"That whole thing with Ryan's uncle... what went down there?"

He frowned and stared down at the chip in his hand. "Okay, so when I was about fifteen, a rival drug dealer approached me. He said he liked how smart I handled things and wanted me to work with him. I turned him down, but someone saw us talking and ratted me out to Jacob."

"Jacob insisted that I had to prove my loyalty to him, and the only way to do that was by fighting someone for him. We had to battle it out until one person stabbed the other. It was really stupid, and I was terrified, but if I didn't do it, he'd have had a bunch of guys seriously mess me up. So, I had no choice. Ryan's uncle was one of the few guys I actually liked that I worked with, and he felt bad for me, so he offered to be the guy I fought."

"He let me stab him so the whole thing could just be over. It was a quick, shallow jab, and I rushed him to the hospital right after, so he was fine. Jacob left me alone after that, thankfully."

"Oh, wow, Jer," I said, shaking my head. "It pains me to think you went through all those crazy, traumatic experiences, especially at such a young age."

He rested his head against my shoulder. "Sometimes I can still hear the knife piercing into him and see the wide-eyed look he gave me. Stabbing someone is just so personal, you're so close to them. I hated it."

I ran my hand through his hair and kissed his forehead.

"Did you ever talk to Ryan about it?"

He nodded against me. "Yeah, when we started hanging out more, I explained what happened."

My eyebrows furrowed. "Why didn't you tell me?"

He groaned and buried his face deeper into my neck. "I don't know, Aurora. I just didn't want you to see me in that light. I was hoping you'd forget, honestly. I'm obviously not proud of it, and telling that story isn't fun."

"I get that," I whispered. "Just know that there isn't anything you've done that would make me look at you differently. I know things aren't black and white, and sometimes you can't avoid doing certain things even if you don't want to. I adore you, and nothing will ever change that. Okay?"

"Okay, baby," he said, his voice muffled by my neck.

We lay together for a while, with me cuddling him, before I left for Kiyana's to get ready.

"Wanna ride to her place?" Jer asked.

"Yes, please! Take me on your bike."

"As you wish, my princess," he said in a decent English accent.

I giggled, clapping excitedly.

I watched cartoons on Kiyana's TV as I waited for her to find a perfect outfit for the party.

"Okay, so how about this one?"

I looked up to see her dress.

"Sure."

"Rory!"

"What? This is like the fiftieth time you've asked! Just pick a dress!"

"Fine. No need to be so rude about it."

I rolled my eyes.

"And by the way, instead of lying on my bed, maybe you should be looking for a dress too."

"But I don't wanna!"

"Too bad." She deadpanned. "You need a nice outfit."

"I'm already wearing a dress though. Can't I just keep this one on?"

"Aurora, of course not. Sundresses won't cut it for this kind of party!" She yanked me off the bed and hustled me into her closet.

"Ugh."

"You always wear dresses like this," she said, nodding at the one I was currently wearing. "So how about tonight you mix it up a bit?"

"What do you mean?"

"I mean..." she said, lifting the skirt of my dress, "Instead of going for something cute and safe, let's aim for something sexy and hot."

She plucked a red, low-cut satin dress with a daring slit on the left side that ran up to mid-thigh. "Like this!"

My eyes nearly popped out of their sockets. "You want me to wear this?"

"Come on. Jeremiah thinks you look good now, imagine how he'd react to you in this dress?"

"Um..."

"Come on sis, you gotta step out of your comfort zone a bit, and it's not that bad."

I bit my lip and sighed. "Okay."

"Yay! Yay! Yay!" Kiyana squealed, jumping up and down.

"Could you please stop screaming? The neighbors might call the cops or something."

Kiyana scoffed. "They're used to this. Anyway, I'm going to straighten your hair, do your makeup really well. Red lipstick would look amazing with the dress. Oh, and these black heels."

I rolled my eyes as she ushered me to her dressing table.

"Holy cow," Simran whispered when she saw me.

"Who knew Aurora Winters could look so hot?"

"Oooh Simran, don't tell me you've got a thing for her now."

"Maybe," Simran said, winking at me.

I shook my head and pushed her shoulder. "Cut it out, guys. Or I'll run back home and change."

"Okay, okay. Let's get going. The boys are meeting us there." Simran informed us.

I chuckled. "I can't believe Mona thinks she's just having dinner with your family."

"Just? Uh, you obviously don't know my parents. We had Tyga at my sister's middle school graduation party. They go all out for everything."

I nodded, impressed.

"Sorry, you had to come pick us up. My car just wouldn't start." Kiyana told her.

"It's fine, as long as I'm not late to the party I'm hosting."

"What's on your mind, Aurora?" Kiyana asked when she saw my frown.

"Jer said he can't make it." I said, staring at his text message.

"What? Why not?" Simran asked.

"He said he'd explain later."

"Oh, sorry Rory, that sucks."

I shrugged. "Yeah. I was actually excited for him to see my outfit."

Kiyana rubbed my arm in comfort before we had to quickly rush out.

"Okay, girls, let's hustle. We've only got ten minutes before she arrives," Simran told us as she pulled up to her house.

"Ten minutes?" Kiyana asked. "Why did you pick us up so late?"

"Sorry, I had to get ready," Simran shouted back as we jumped out of the car.

We shuffled into her house quickly.

"Okay, guys, she's going to be here really soon. Everyone take your positions and be quiet."

Just then, we heard a car pull in outside.

"Jimmy just texted me that they're here! Shhhhh."

We all hid in our respective places and stayed silent as the door opened.

"Why is it so dark? Where is everyone?" Mona whispered.

"I'm not sure. Switch on the lights, would you?" Jimmy asked.

"Sure."

"SURPRISE!!!" Everyone shouted, jumping out.

Mona screamed and fell into Jimmy's chest, who was laughing.

"Oh my God, guys," she said, her hand on her chest.

"Happy Birthday!" Simran said.

Mona smiled thankfully at her and gave her a hug.

"Thanks, everyone!" She said, with a huge grin.

After that, everyone went off to do their own thing, and the party was in full swing.

"Happy Birthday, Mona."

"Thanks, Aurora," she said, turning to me, and then her eyes widened as they traveled down. "Holy..."

I laughed and waved her off.

"Seriously, Rory, you look amazing."

"Thanks," I beamed.

"Damn," I heard from behind me.

Derrick, Ryan, and Ian stared at me, their jaws hanging open in disbelief. I couldn't help but roll my eyes.

"This was a terrible idea, Kiyana," I whispered.

"Maybe so," Kiyana said back. "I don't like how my boyfriend's looking at you."

"You clean up nice," Ryan said.

"I don't think I've ever seen you in a dress like this," Ian mumbled.

"Girl, you look fine," Derrick said, shaking his head.

I laughed, rubbing my arm consciously. "Thanks, guys."

"Where's your man at, anyway?" Ryan asked.

"He couldn't make it," I replied

"What? But he told us—" Derrick began, but a sharp elbow from Ian cut him off.

"So, who's up for a drink?" Ryan asked, trying to change the subject.

I stared at them suspiciously.

"Me!" Kiyana said, raising her hand. "Let's get this party started."

Silently, I slipped away, making my way outside.

I had almost forgotten how much I hated parties. As bubbly and social as I was, big crowds just wasn't my thing.

Thankfully, Simran's beautiful backyard provided a pleasant distraction. I wandered around, admiring the array of flowers, and eventually stumbled upon a charming little pond with ducks.

"How cute!" I squealed.

"Not as cute as you."

Startled, I spun around.

"Jer?" I stammered in disbelief.

"Here in the flesh," he said, gesturing at himself. Jer looked great tonight. He wore a pair of light washed baggy jeans with black cat Jordan 4 sneakers. His black short-sleeved button-up shirt was casually unbuttoned to reveal a white tank top, showing off his fit body and adding some extra style to his relaxed vibe.

"But—" I stammered, snapping out of my trance.

"You look so fine," he complimented me, slowly letting his eyes travel down my figure.

I blushed and replied, "Thank you."

I took a step closer, completely forgetting my confusion about him showing up out of nowhere. He gently placed his hands on my waist.

"It's incredible how you can be both adorable and incredibly sexy at the same time," he smirked, as I placed my arms around his neck. "Get you a girl who can do both, huh?"

I giggled, giving him a cheeky grin. "And don't you dare forget it."

"And your hair... it's straight," Jeremiah pointed out with a furrowed brow.

"Thanks, I hadn't noticed," I teased with a laugh.

"No, sorry. It looks amazing. I just really love your natural hair," he clarified with sincerity in his eyes.

"You're so sweet, Jeremiah. I just wanted to try something different," I explained. "Okay, how about we head back to the party?"

Jeremiah grinned mischievously as he declared, "Nah, I have another idea."

I quirked an eyebrow and asked, "Oh? What's that?"

He extended his hand towards me and said, "Follow me."

Confusion crossed my face, but I took his hand without hesitation. "Where are we going, Jer?"

"You'll see, my princess," he replied, squeezing my hand. "The fact that you're already outside makes this a lot easier."

We ventured deeper into Simran's expansive garden, and my steps slowed when I noticed the enchanting glow of fairy lights ahead.

"Jer..."

"We're almost there."

I gasped, instinctively covering my mouth in astonishment when we reached our destination. I looked up, captivated by the pretty lights that adorned the gazebo. Delicate vines and flowers adorned the railings of the stairs, small candles lined the way, and a red carpet led to the center of the gazebo.

Jeremiah led us up the stairs and positioned us in the heart of the gazebo. He took a deep breath and gazed into my eyes.

"Aurora, when you walked into my life, everything changed," he began.

Although he hadn't said much, tears welled up in my eyes.

"I've never had many friends, always kept to myself," he continued. "As a kid, I avoided people because I didn't want them to ask about my bruises. And as I got older, I thought I didn't need friends or anyone else. I had myself and my books. With all the rumors and everyone being scared of me, it was easy to stay that way."

"Then, one day, I decided to spend my lunchtime at the bleachers. I'd always hung out with some of the guys I dealt to at the back of the school, but that day, I had this urge to sit at the bleachers."

"I was glad I did. It was nice and peaceful, but then you showed up. I was honestly in shock when I saw you. Your massive curly blonde afro, your bright blue dress with white daisies, and yellow Converse. Your energy. Everything about you intrigued me. As I got to know you, I realized you were just as beautiful on the inside as you were on the outside."

"I knew that I wanted you. I knew that I needed you, but I tried to fight it so many times because I was an idiot. I'm done fighting, Aurora. I want you. I need you. I love you. I've always called you Princess, but now I want to make you my queen."

Overwhelmed with joy, I couldn't help but squeal as tears of happiness streamed down my face.

Jeremiah chuckled and said, "So, Aurora, will you be my girlfriend?"

I nodded fervently, tears of joy still flowing. "Yes, of course. I love you so much, Jeremiah."

"I love you too, baby."

I reached for his face and, on tiptoe, kissed him passionately and deeply, trying to convey my feelings through the kiss. One of his hands gripped my waist firmly, while the other cradled my neck, kissing me just as intensely.

His lips then trailed to my neck, and I tilted my head to grant him access, my eyes opening slightly and widening as I shrieked in shock.

Jeremiah jumped, quickly followed my gaze and reluctantly let me go. Our friends had been watching us from one of Simran's many windows.

Derrick mimicked our make-out session, and he and Ryan burst into laughter, while the others grinned and cooed.

I hid my face in embarrassment as Jeremiah laughed. "They kind of helped me plan this."

"That's so sweet," I said, fanning my face. "They might be really annoying sometimes, but I love our friends."

"They're the best," he agreed.

"We should probably go inside," I cleared my throat.

"Sounds good; I haven't even said 'happy birthday' to Mona yet," he replied.

Jer took my hand as we made our way back inside.

"I probably won't be drinking tonight, by the way. It's not really my thing in general," I informed him.

"Fine with me. If you're not then I'm not," he agreed.

"Really?" I asked, pleasantly surprised.

"Yeah, I'd rather not get high off alcohol," Jer explained with a teasing smile.

"Haha, so I made a mistake," I blushed.

"You were so innocent and naive back then," he remarked.

"I just didn't know any better," I defended myself.

"How? You watch TV shows, no?" he inquired.

"Um, Disney shows?" I replied with a sheepish smile.

He shook his head and groaned, "Lord, help me."

Chapter 24

"I need to talk to you about something," my dad said, his expression serious.

I furrowed my brow. "What's wrong?"

"Nothing's wrong, baby. I just have something to share with you," he clarified.

"Alright," I responded, taking a seat across from him at the kitchen table.

"So, there's this lady at my workplace," he began, "and we've known each other for quite a while. We weren't particularly close until one day her car broke down, and I gave her a ride home. After that, we started talking more."

"Okay?" I replied, still uncertain.

"The thing is, me and her, we're... dating," he finally admitted.

My eyes widened in surprise. "Dating?" I repeated, trying to process the information.

He nodded. "I don't want you to think I'm trying to replace your mom or anything. I will always love her, and she'll always be in my heart. But I think... I think I'm ready to move on."

"Oh," was all I managed to say. I stood up abruptly. "I need to... go."

"Wait! Aurora? Sweetheart!" My dad called after me.

I rushed up the stairs and into my room, closing the door behind me. Sitting on my bed, I stared at the wall in a state of shock. The truth was, I hadn't seen this coming at all. The thought of my dad dating again had never even crossed my mind.

It wasn't that I didn't want him to be happy. I was just genuinely taken aback. I didn't know if I could bear to see my dad with anyone other than my mom.

"Honey? Are you okay?" My dad's concerned voice came from behind the door.

"I'm fine, Dad. I just need some time to think," I replied softly.

"Alright, baby, take all the time you need," he said, understanding in his tone.

✧

"Hi, Dad," I said, taking a seat beside him on the couch.

"Hi, honey."

"I'm really sorry for how I acted earlier," I began to apologize.

"Rory, you don't need to apologize," he reassured me

"But I was being kinda selfish and rude. Here you are, telling me one of the most amazing things that has happened to you in a while, and I..."

"It's fine, Aurora. I expected you to react like that or even worse, honestly."

"I'm happy for you, Dad. I really hope it works out because you deserve it. You really do," I sincerely told him.

He beamed at me. "So... how do you feel about her coming to dinner tonight—"

"Whoa, let's not push it," I interrupted with a playful grin.

He laughed. "Okay, maybe another time."

I nodded in agreement.

"I was actually thinking we could have Jer and his mom coming for dinner?"

"Oh, okay. Sounds good," I agreed, grabbing my phone to text Jer.

Later that evening, our guests arrived.

"Hey, Jeremiah, nice to see you again," my dad greeted Jer warmly.

"You too, sir," Jer replied respectfully.

"Hi, Marie," I said, turning to Jer's mom.

"Hey, honey," she replied with a warm smile.

"This is my dad," I introduced them. "I know you two haven't formally met yet."

"Hi, nice to meet you," my dad said, shaking her hand.

"You too," she replied with a friendly tone.

"So, what's for dinner?" Jer asked, plopping down on our couch and propping his feet up on our coffee table.

"Jeremiah!" his mom gasped, chiding him for his lack of manners.

"It's fine," my dad laughed. "Jer lived with us for quite a while; this is like his second home."

Jer smiled at my dad, and he returned the smile before heading to the kitchen.

"We're having homemade pizza for dinner by the way," he called out.

"Yes!" Jer exclaimed.

Marie sat down in the armchair and shook her head at her son.

"Anything to drink?" I asked.

Jer stood up. "I'll get it. You sit down."

"But—"

"Just chill, Rory. Sit down," he insisted, gently pushing me back onto the couch.

"What would you like to drink, Mom?" Jer asked.

"Water is fine," Marie replied.

"Cool," Jer said before heading to the kitchen.

"We'll, he's in a good mood," I remarked.

Marie laughed. "He sure is. I don't even know what to do with him. He's basically bouncing off the walls at home."

"Aw, he's happy his mom's home," I gushed. "He's really come a long way. I'm not used to seeing him so excited and happy."

"And he has you to thank."

I waved her off. "I didn't do anything."

"Oh, yes, you did. Don't think he hasn't told me everything you've helped him through."

"Everything?" I asked, wondering just how much he'd actually told her.

"Yes, he told me about the drugs," Marie confirmed.

I gave her a sheepish smile. "Oh."

"I was saddened, but not surprised. He was covering the mortgage, all the bills, school supplies, groceries, plus having to come up with extra cash whenever his father demanded it, or else he'd face the consequences. I just don't know what I was thinking when I took the fall for his dad. It was so foolish."

"Marie, you can't blame yourself. He manipulated you, and you felt like it was the only way. It's really tough, but what's done is done. Focus on the present and the future you now have with Jer," I encouraged.

"You're right. I'm just relieved he's moved past all that now," she added.

"Me too," I wholeheartedly agreed.

Jer finally returned from the kitchen, carrying a tray of glasses and water bottles.

"Boy, how long does it take you to get some water?" Marie teased.

"Sorry, Ma, I was just talking to Mr. Winters," Jer replied.

"Winters. Isn't it funny how your last name is Winters, and ours is Summers," Marie mused with a smile. "You know what they say, opposites attract."

I exchanged a knowing glance with Jer, and we both smiled.

"Okay, people, the pizza is ready!" my dad announced from the kitchen.

"Yay!" Jer exclaimed, dashing off to the kitchen.

I giggled at his enthusiasm and followed him.

"Wow, Dad, that's a big pizza for only four people," I pointed out. He tilted his head to the side, and a bright smile crossed his face. "You know what? You're right. How about you invite all your friends over?"

"My friends? It's a little short notice, don't you think?" I questioned.

"Oh, gwan, you never know if you don't ask," he encouraged.

"Yes, please do. I want to meet Jeremiah's friends once and for all," Marie pleaded.

"I'll reheat the pizza when they get here."

"Okay," I agreed. I stepped out of the kitchen and texted all my friends to come over. Surprisingly, they all agreed, and Simran even thanked me for getting her out of golfing with her family.

"Hey, angel!"

"Hey, Derrick!" I greeted him with a hug. "How've you been?"

"Awesome. Just excited to see my favorite aunt. Where is she?" Derrick asked eagerly.

I heard Marie laugh as she approached. "Oh, shut it, Derrick. I'm your only aunt."

He smiled sheepishly and they shared a warm hug. "I missed you," he whispered, holding her tightly.

"I missed you too, honey," Marie replied affectionately, her eyes filled with warmth. "You know, Derrick was my only visitor when I was in prison?"

Jeremiah's eyebrows furrowed as he walked closer. "You visited my mom?"

Derrick shrugged sheepishly. "I'm sorry, Jeremy. I know you were mad at her for lying for your dad, but I felt bad, and I missed her, so I've been visiting her ever since I turned 18."

Unexpectedly, Jeremiah enveloped Derrick in a grateful hug. "Thank you for being there for her and letting her know someone cared, even when I couldn't."

I couldn't help but gush at how heartwarming this moment was.

"Of course, anything for family," Derrick replied, returning the heartfelt embrace before pulling away. "Maybe you and aunt Marie could come to my place for dinner sometime.

Marie cringed slightly. "I don't know about that, sweetheart. I mean, I just put your Dad's brother in jail."

"And he deserved it. Look, my dad hasn't even talked to him in years. He couldn't care less about the deadbeat. Plus, they kinda asked me to invite you," Derrick explained.

Marie's eyebrows raised in shock. "Really?"

Derrick nodded with sincerity. "I know both my family and yours turned their backs on you guys when you and Jason got married, but after the trial and everything my dad feels horrible. He had no clue what you and Jeremy had been going through. They want to be there for you, Marie. And you too, Jeremy. I've tried to talk to them about this so many times but they never listened until now, I'm sorry it took so long—"

"Better late than never, honey." She beamed as a tear of joy escaped her eye, and she embraced Derrick once again.

The doorbell chimed once more, prompting me to hurry to answer it.

"Hey, little sis," Ryan greeted me with a warm smile.

Returning his smile, I gave Ryan a hug before ushering him inside. "You didn't come with Kiyana?"

"Um, she lives across the road. Shouldn't she be here by now?" Ryan pointed out.

"True," I acknowledged, my brow furrowing in thought.

"So, what's on the menu for dinner?" Ryan inquired.

"Homemade pizza," I replied.

Ryan pumped his fist in excitement and headed off to join the others. I opened the door once more to see Ian's smiling face with Kiyana and Simran standing behind him.

"Hey, Ian," I welcomed them all inside.

"Hey, best friend," Ian said, giving me a warm hug.

"Hola, Rore-whore," Simran said with a smirk.

I rolled my eyes playfully. "I'm glad that is something we can laugh about now, Sim-ran-through."

She stuck her tongue out at me and walked past, leaving Kiyana left to walk in.

"Kiyana Deshane Joseph, how come it took you so long to get here?" I teased, crossing my arms.

She smiled sheepishly. "Well..."

Simran backed up, chiming in, "She stayed over at mine after last night."

My eyebrows furrowed. "Oh. What happened last night?"

"You see, we might have, uh, gone clubbing and got super drunk," Kiyana confessed, a hint of guilt in her voice.

My eyes widened in disbelief. "But you guys aren't even old enough, how did you even get in?" I pointed out.

"Oh, you know Simran, she has connections and stuff," Kiyana whispered with a mischievous grin.

"I mean Simran, I'm not surprised about – no offense, girl – but you, Kiyana? Underaged drinking? In a club?"

"And that's why we didn't invite you," Kiyana blurted out, her eyes widening in shock at her own words. I took a step back, and Simran's eyebrows raised in surprise. Kiyana quickly slapped her hand over her mouth.

"I'm so sorry, Rory. I didn't mean that! At least not in a bad way anyway," Kiyana apologized, realizing her slip.

"I'm gonna go," Simran said awkwardly, making her way to the living room.

"I'm really sorry, Rory," Kiyana apologized again.

I shrugged, concealing my hurt. "I get it. I'm too much of a prude for you. Now that you have Simran, you can do all the wild things I never agreed to."

"Drinking and dancing at a club isn't exactly wild, Rory, and that's not how it is," Kiyana defended herself.

"Drinking?" Ryan asked, walking up to us.

"You didn't tell him?" I asked incredulously.

"Kiyana, you know what happened to my mom!" Ryan said in disbelief.

"You two do realize most people our age drink, right? It's not a big deal. I just wanted to have some fun for once," Kiyana admitted.

"For once?" Ryan probed. "What's that supposed to mean?"

"Oh, don't worry, it's nothing to do with you, Ryan. She's just finally happy that she has friends who aren't all buzzkills," I interjected.

"Rory, that's not it—"

"Okay then, is it me?" Ryan asked.

"No, baby, no. Guys, please! I'm sorry, Rory, for what I said, and Ryan, I know how much you detest alcohol after what happened. But there's nothing wrong with drinking if it's done responsibly, okay?"

"I just needed to let loose. I... I didn't get into the fashion college I wanted to go to and Simran was with me when I got the letter, she suggested going out to cheer me up." She sighed.

"What?" I asked, my heart going out to her.

"Babe, I'm sorry," Ryan said, giving her a comforting hug.

She hugged him back tightly. "I just can't believe it. All my life my plan was to go to this one school and now that's gone. What am I supposed to do now?" She asked in a muffled voice.

When Ryan pulled away, he lifted her chin and wiped her tears away.

"Kiyana, you are amazing. And if they can't see that, then fuck 'em," he reassured her. " I know no matter what school you end up going to, you'll be great."

Kiyana managed a smile, and I rubbed her arm in support.

"I'm sorry, hon, I know how much you wanted to go there," I told her sympathetically.

She nodded, and just then, the doorbell rang again. I opened the door for Jimmy and Mona.

"Hey, people!" Jimmy greeted as he walked in.

I laughed and hugged him, then greeted Mona warmly.

"Hey, guys! Mona, how does it feel to be an adult?" I asked with a smile.

Mona shook her head with a laugh. "Seeing as my mom still wakes me up every morning and cleans my room, I wouldn't really consider it adulthood."

"That's the last of them," I informed my dad, following them into the living room.

He nodded and headed to the kitchen to reheat the pizza.

"I'll help!" Jer offered and followed my dad into the kitchen.

"It's really nice to meet you all," Marie chimed in, offering a warm smile to everyone.

"It's nice to meet you too," they all chorused in response.

I was about to switch on the television when I stopped. Everyone was already enjoying themselves just talking to each other. We didn't need TV to entertain ourselves.

"Aurora," Marie called, waving me over.

I walked over and sat beside her on the loveseat

"Y'know, when I asked, Jer told me your mother passed away," Marie began, her tone gentle.

I looked down and nodded. "Yeah, a couple of years ago."

She nodded in understanding. "And I might have asked your dad if he was seeing anyone. I know, I'm a bit nosy, but I couldn't help it! He told me he had just started seeing a lovely lady."

I nodded in acknowledgment.

"Now, honey, I know this is none of my business, but your dad is amazing. He works full-time and takes care of you with no help. And he's actually doing a good job! Do you know how rare that is these days?" Marie asked, her tone kind and supportive.

"I know, and he deserves to be happy, so not to be rude, but what are you trying to say?" I inquired.

She smiled warmly. "I'm saying that you should give this lady a chance."

I nervously wrung my fingers. "I don't know how to."

Marie nodded thoughtfully. "Well, maybe you should start by inviting her to this dinner party."

My eyes widened with surprise. "Now?"

"Well, think about it. Would you rather meet her another night when it's just you, your dad, and her, having an awkward dinner or now, when we're all here?"

"You're right," I admitted, realizing the wisdom in her suggestion.

She smiled reassuringly. "And don't worry, we'll be here for support."

Feeling more at ease with the idea, I nodded and got up from the loveseat. I entered the kitchen and burst into laughter when I saw Jer wearing an apron. I hugged him from behind and playfully looked around him to see what he was doing.

"Don't laugh at me!" he said, his tone playful. Then he leaned in closer and whispered, "I know you think I look sexy."

I giggled. "I'm not gonna even reply to that."

"Y'all can relax with all that, I don't need to see it," my dad muttered.

"Oops, sorry dad." I chuckled awkwardly, quickly letting go of Jer and walking closer to him. "What are you doing, anyway?"

"I decided to make more food since I hadn't really thought about just how many people were coming. You have a lot of friends," my dad remarked with a grin.

I smiled back and flipped my hair. "I know, it's so hard being this popular."

They both chuckled.

"Anyway, I think you might need to make even more," I suggested.

My dad's eyebrow raised in surprise. "Why? Isn't that all of them? How much bloodclaat fren yuh have?" he asked, sounding exasperated.

Jer burst into laughter at his last remark and I chuckled, shaking my head. "Actually... I was hoping that maybe you'd invite your girlfriend."

"What? Really?" he asked, his face lighting up with excitement.

I nodded, my heart swelling at his reaction. It was clear that he really cared about her.

"But I thought you said—"

"I changed my mind. I'm sure she's amazing."

"She is," he confirmed with a smile. "Okay, you hold down the fort, Jeremiah. I'll go call her. And please, I beg you in the name of God, do not let Aurora near any food."

"Hardy-har-har," I said dryly, while Jer laughed.

I felt Jer pull me towards him once my dad had left, and he smiled at me, shaking his head with admiration. "You are incredible, do you know that?"

"Well, yes, of course. But may I ask why I received this compliment?" I replied, teasing him.

He chuckled. "I mean about inviting his girlfriend. I know it must be hard, but you're putting his feelings before yours, and I'm proud of you for that."

I smiled at him, appreciating his support, and he gave me a gentle peck on the lips.

"Hopefully, she's nice," I said, feeling anxious.

"If she's with your dad then she will be," Jer assured me.

Taking a deep breath, I steeled myself. "Alright."

My dad returned with a bright smile. "She'll be here soon."

"Great," I replied with a nervous smile.

I walked out of the kitchen and into the living room. "Hey, guys, my dad's girlfriend will be joining us for dinner, so try to make her feel welcome."

Marie nodded and gave me a proud smile. I sat down on the floor since all the seats were taken, and Derrick joined me.

"Hey, cupcake."

"Hey."

"I just wanted to thank you."

"Thank me? For what?"

"I never thought I'd see Marie outside of prison again. But thanks to you, here she is," Derrick said with gratitude.

"I don't know why everyone keeps thanking me for things. I don't really think I did anything."

"Except for being an amazing friend, girlfriend, and daughter."

"She's just like her mom," my dad remarked from above us.

I looked up at him and gave him a bittersweet smile. "Thanks, Dad."

The doorbell rang, and I eagerly volunteered, pushing my dad aside.

"Geez, okay," he chuckled

I slowly approached the door, my heart racing with anticipation. I took a deep breath and opened it. At the door stood a stunning woman in her thirties, with a graceful stature. Her loose, curly hair framed her face, and her flawless, radiant caramel skin added to her striking beauty. She stared at me in complete shock.

"Aurora?"

"Evie?"

"Wait, you two know each other?" my dad asked, sounding surprised.

"Um, yes!" I laughed. I ambushed Evie with a massive hug, and she took a step back, laughing in return.

"I haven't seen you in so long," she said, her eyes filled with warmth. "My girl's all grown up."

I grinned at her, closing the front door behind her.

"Wait, wait. Evie? As in my boss's previous assistant? The one you made friends with?" my dad inquired, realization dawning on him.

"Yes! Exactly!" I laughed.

"You've always gone by Lynn with me; I would have never imagined," he said, still in shock.

"I'm so lost," Derrick mumbled from behind my dad. We all turned our attention to him, and he raised his hands in a surrender. "Sorry, I'm being nosy."

I chuckled. "It's fine, Derrick. Basically when I was like eleven, I got super sick at school, like really bad, but my dad was at work, so he had to come pick me up and then take me back to work with him."

"Yeah, I had a really important meeting, so I couldn't take her home, and I had to beg my boss to let Aurora stay with him," my dad explained.

"He had no interest in watching a sick child, so he dropped her off with me. We had a blast, actually," Evie finished, her voice filled with fond memories.

"And we've stayed in contact this whole time. We used to email and then exchanged numbers when I got a phone," I explained. "We text every now and then."

"Funny how time flies. Back then, I was an assistant, and now I have my own assistant."

"Evie, I can't believe you didn't tell me you were seeing someone!" I exclaimed, playfully slapping her arm.

She smiled sheepishly. "I know, I'm sorry. But I haven't really told anyone. I didn't want to jinx it. It never even crossed my mind that the man I'm dating would be your father, though, Aurora. What are the chances?" She chuckled.

"I never made the connection either; I don't think we ever interacted when you were Josh's assistant," my dad shook his head. "Wow, well, this is going way better than I thought it would. I can't believe you two already know each other."

"Seeing you two beside each other, it all makes sense. Even your personality. She's basically the female version of you, Aaron!" Evie teased.

We headed into the living room, where everyone had been eavesdropping on our conversation, no doubt.

"So, guys, this is Evie...or Lynn, I guess, my dad's girlfriend and also my friend?" I introduced with an awkward laugh.

Evie laughed and greeted everyone. "Nice to meet you all."

They all exchanged pleasantries, and my dad ushered us into the kitchen to eat.

"Wow, Aaron, did you make all of this yourself?" Evie asked, admiring the spread.

"I did. Well, with the help of Jeremiah," my dad admitted.

"Oh no, I'm not taking any credit for this. All I did was chop stuff."

"Well, you chopped them very nicely," I said, patting Jer on the shoulder.

"So, Aurora, is this the hot, sexy bad boy—" Evie began, but I interrupted her in embarrassment.

"Evie!" I exclaimed through gritted teeth, my face heating up.

My dad choked on his salad, and everyone else burst into laughter.

"Oh my God, someone kill me," I mumbled into my hands, feeling utterly mortified. His mother was literally in the room with us.

I felt Jer rub my back comfortingly. "Don't worry, babe, we all know you think I'm sexy."

"Shut up," I said, elbowing his stomach playfully.

He let out a small groan and leisurely picked up his slice of pizza. However, when no one else was paying attention, I shot an annoyed glare at Evie and mouthed the words, "I can't believe you."

In response, Evie flashed me a sweet smile.

"By the way, why do you go by Lynn instead of Evie now?" I inquired.

Evie placed her fork down and began to explain, "Well, my full name is Evelyn, but I've never been a fan of it. I went by Evie for most of my life. But when I got promoted to a new position at our company, I decided it was time for a change. I wanted to be taken more seriously, and I felt like 'Lynn' had a more mature ring to it."

"That makes sense," my dad nodded, taking a sip of water. "But honestly, I think Evie is perfectly fine. You shouldn't have had to change your name to be taken seriously."

She rolled her eyes. "Well, my dear, as a woman in a high position, especially a black woman, you often have to demand respect. Unfortunately, people don't always treat you with the seriousness you deserve."

"That's true, and I'm sorry. I know it's not easy for women in the workplace. But I want you to know that I would have taken you seriously," he reassured her.

She laughed, affectionately placing an arm around his neck. "I know you would have."

Her eyes shifted to my arm. "Ooh, Aurora, I like your bracelet. What are those?" she asked, referring to the charms.

"Disney princesses."

"Of course," she chuckled.

"She loves her Disney princesses, that's for sure," Derrick commented.

"The fact that she won't even watch anything but Disney is so crazy to me." Ian laughed.

"Did you know we were watching Cinderella the other night, and she covered her eyes when Cinderella and the prince kissed?" Jer shared, prompting laughter from everyone.

I tried to defend myself, but my words were muffled as I spoke with my mouth full of pizza. "I did not! He's joking."

"So what if she did? Disney is awesome!" Kiyana defended. "I love it as much as she does."

"Do you recite the words to The Princess and The Frog in your sleep?" My dad asked.

"Well, no, but—"

"Are your walls painted with Disney characters?"

"No..."

"What's so bad about that?" Marie chimed in.

My dad decided to drop another bombshell, saying, "She got it painted this year for her 18th."

Marie's eyes widened in surprise. "Oh."

I rolled my eyes, feigning annoyance. "You guys are making me sound crazy."

"I'm beginning to realize that you are," Simran teased.

"Disney crazy, anyway," Jer added with a grin.

I shook my head and sighed as my dad launched into another story about my "crazy" love for Disney.

As I glanced around the table, I couldn't help but smile. This was my family now. It was funny how not so long ago, I had felt so alone, like I had nobody. Jer might see me as some angel who came into his life and turned things around for the better, but he was that for me too. Without him, I wouldn't have been friends with any of these amazing people. I wouldn't have met Marie.

This time last year, I was miserable, and now, look at me. I am happy. So happy.

They were right about my obsession with Disney. I used to wonder why I couldn't let go of it, but now I know. All these princesses had gotten their happy endings, and I was waiting for mine, wondering what I was doing wrong.

The truth is, I just had to be patient. I just had to wait for my happiness, which came in the most unexpected way— in a brooding, angry, anti-social guy, who might also be a hot and sexy bad boy.

Epilogue

One Year Later

"Do you take Aaron Winters to be your lawfully wedded husband?"

"I do."

"And do you take Evelyn Adekoya to be your lawfully wedded wife?"

"I do," my dad said with the biggest smile on his face.

"You may kiss the bride."

I clapped as they kissed, feeling a surge of happiness for my dad and Evie. I was thrilled that these two were finally getting married. I couldn't have wished for anyone else for my dad. And I was honored to be Evelyn's maid of honor.

We had thirty minutes before the reception for wedding photos, so we all headed out.

"Hey, babe."

I looked behind me to see Jer looking incredibly handsome in his tux.

"Hey."

"Are you happy?" he asked, interlocking our fingers.

"Very."

"Good," he said.

After taking the photos, we headed to the reception venue, which was thankfully only ten minutes away. I didn't think I could stand any longer with all of Evie's other bridesmaids. They were quite the gossipers.

"Hey, honey," my dad smiled at me.

I smiled back. "Hey, Dad, I haven't seen a smile that big on your face since, like... you know—"

"Yeah, I get you," he nodded. "I haven't seen you this happy in a while either."

I rolled my eyes. "You haven't seen me at all in a while, Dad."

"Exactly!" he said, pointing at me playfully.

"Hello, you gorgeous people," Evelyn beamed, looping her arm with mine and my dad's.

"Hey, love."

"Hey, Evie."

"You know, Aurora, I have to admit, I'm a tad envious of how stunning you look in that dress," Evelyn confessed. "And those braids? Girl, you look so good."

I flipped my waist-length blonde braids and giggled. "Thanks Evie, I love them so much."

"They suit you so well."

"They really do, you should braid your hair more often. You look so beautiful," my dad chimed in with a proud smile. He noticed Jer talking to his mom and called out.

"Jeremiah!"

Jer furrowed his brow upon seeing my dad and mumbled something to his mom before he approached us slowly with his arms crossed.

"Oh, come on, Jer, you're not still upset, are you?" my dad implored.

"Yes, I am, and you no longer have the privilege of calling me Jer. It's Jeremiah to you," he announced.

"I said I was sorry," my dad offered. "My brother said he couldn't make it which was really upsetting but then when he found out he could—"

"So I was just a backup plan?" Jer interrupted.

"Jer, you gotta let this go, it's his wedding," I told him.

Jer gasped dramatically. "Aurora, I thought you were on my side."

Evie laughed. "As entertaining as this is, I think I'll go mingle with our guests."

My dad addressed Jer as she walked away. "Jer, I really wish you could have been my best man, but Jonathan's my brother, and it meant a lot to him to be here today," my dad explained.

Jer sighed. "I understand that, but you only told me ten minutes before the ceremony!"

"I didn't know how to break it to you, and I didn't want to hurt your feelings."

Jer folded his arms. "Well, consider them hurt," he said before turning and stomping away.

"I think he's actually upset about this," my dad mumbled.

"You know Jer, dad, he's always been the jealous type."

We laughed and he shook his head."Okay, I guess I have to go talk to people with Evie. I mean this is my wedding and all." He said reluctantly.

I laughed."Have fun with aunt Melanie!"I said, pushing him in her direction.

He groaned."Not that old hag. She gwine start cuss 'bout how mi get big and fat."

I offered him a sympathetic smile as he reluctantly walked away. I looked around and saw someone waving wildly at me.

"Kiyana!"I said, hugging her tightly.

"Hey Rory, I'm sorry I couldn't get back sooner."

"It's fine. I know how busy you are with school."

Not getting into her top-choice school didn't stop Kiyana from pursuing her dream; she chose another university with an amazing fashion program instead.

"The ceremony was absolutely beautiful." she said.

"It was. Where's your boyfriend, by the way?"I asked.

"Oh, Hector's getting us drinks."

"Oh, okay. Can't wait to see him."

"So you and Jer seem to be as strong as ever."

"Yeah, we sorted things out after our argument, but let's keep this between us. I'd rather my dad not know. Jer was his best man until ten minutes before the ceremony, and he really likes him. No need to tell him we almost broke up."

Kiyana nodded. "But did you guys really work things out? You never filled me in on the details."

I took a deep breath and sighed. "Well, honestly, it was the whole long-distance thing that got to me, you know?"

Kiyana nodded in understanding. "Oh, trust me girl, I know. It's tough out here."

I nodded in agreement "The main issue for us was me just being really in my head about things and projecting them on to him y'know? I was worried that Jer might meet someone new and exciting at his college and forget about me. I was always calling him and texting, asking who he was with."

Kiyana frowned, "That doesn't sound like you at all, Aurora. You know you're the only one Jer has eyes for."

"I know, I know, but being in college really opened my eyes, Kiyana. For example, my roommate, she's so...active and outgoing when it comes to guys. I realized that maybe there were things Jer wanted to do that I wasn't—"

"Oh," Kiyana said, raising her eyebrows.

I continued, "Yeah, we barely saw each other, and when we did, we always kept it PG. I just got paranoid. I mean, have you seen him? He could literally have any girl he wanted."

"One night, he texted me that he was heading out to a party with his new friends, and I just couldn't shake the paranoia. I ended up calling him multiple times, demanding to know where he was and who he was with. It turned into a huge argument over the phone, and he was so fed up with my jealousy that he suggested we take a break."

Kiyana winced. "Aurora, you know what happened with me and Ryan in high school. You can't always think the worst; you have to trust him, or it'll ruin the relationship."

"I know, I know. That's why I called him the next day, apologizing for the way I acted and I told him I loved him too much to let go. He told me he loved me too but couldn't be with me if I didn't trust him. We eventually agreed to give the long-distance thing another chance and work on our trust and communication."

"So, how are you two now?"

"We're great. We talked about all my insecurities in detail, and he made it clear he doesn't expect anything from me. We're taking things at my pace. He was actually pretty upset that I even worried about that kinda stuff with him. He said he's not with me for physical...stuff; he's with me because of who I am and because he loves me."

"I love how you're jumping through hoops just to avoid saying the word 'sex'," she laughed.

My cheeks heated up."Okay, enough about me, how're things with your man?" I asked, changing the subject.

"Great! Hector is being an amazing boyfriend as usual."

I smiled.

"Stop calling me that!" someone whined from behind me.

"Ryan!" I squealed and hugged him.

"Hey little sis." he laughed, hugging me back.

"What's up?" I asked.

"Well, I'm just super annoyed because she keeps calling me Hector."

"It is your name," I pointed out.

"My middle name!"

"No, it's your first name. You just begged your mom to list Ryan as your first name when you got to high school."

He turned to Kiyana and gave her a look. "You had to tell everyone, didn't you?"

"Yep," Kiyana smirked. "I love the name Hector, anyway. It's so cute."

"No, it's not," he said, crossing his arms.

"How are things at college?" I asked Ryan.

"Good, I mean as good as they can be. I'm just happy to be home."

"Spending time with your mom?"

Ryan nodded with a big smile.

His mom had thankfully woken up from her coma about five months ago. But being in a coma for such a long time had left her with some side effects that might make life more challenging.

"How's she holding up?"

"You know, she's trying. It's been tough, I can't lie. But physiotherapy has really been helping her. I just wish there was more I could do to help, especially since I can't be with her all the time."

I nodded in understanding. "Just knowing you're there for her is enough, don't worry. You've been a great son."

"Thanks, Rory. How about you though, how's the big shot doing at her prestigious university?"

I rolled my eyes. "Not this again."

"What do you mean? You were holding back how smart you are the whole time, of course I'm bringing it up," he said.

"I wasn't holding back. It just never came up," I shrugged.

"Jer used to complain to me about how indifferent you seemed during y'alls senior literature project or just with your studies in general. Do you remember that? The fact that you're just as smart as he is, or maybe even smarter, is just so shocking."

I shrugged. "I was indifferent; that stuff just comes naturally to me, but I don't really care for it. I wouldn't really call myself smart, you know. There's a lot of stuff I space out on."

"She's what we'd call academically smart but not street smart," Kiyana added.

I gasped, hitting her arm. "That was so unnecessary. And what do you even mean? I'm definitely street smart."

"Oh really? Does getting high on alcohol ring a bell?" she asked, trying to stifle a laugh.

"Or maybe getting drunk off weed?" Ryan smirked.

I groaned. "Stop, guys, that was years ago! I'm never gonna live that one down."

They both laughed in my face.

"Okay, we're gonna go sit down," Kiyana said, leaning on Ryan. "My feet hurt."

"Okay, see you."

I wrapped Simran in a hug from behind, and she heaved.

"Hey, Aurora," she choked, and I laughed.

"Hey, Simran," I said, jumping in front of her. "I love your hair."

"You do? I don't know if cutting it short was a good idea."

"It looks amazing."

"Thank you! Wait, have you seen Ian?"

"Um no. Why?"

"He went to get a drink twenty minutes ago and he hasn't been back," she shrugged. "You look hot in that dress, by the way."

"Thanks," I said, giving her a little twirl. "So how's modeling going?"

"Great! I mean, my parents are still upset that I didn't go to college, but this was a once-in-a-lifetime opportunity. This scout from an agency literally approached me at the mall, telling me that I was perfect for one of their client's clothing line!"

"Yes, Simran. I know what happened. I was with you."

"Oh yeah!" She laughed. "I just never get tired of telling the story."

"I can see that."

"Although Ian isn't thrilled with how little time we get to spend together these days," she remarked.

"Really?" I inquired.

She nodded. "It's challenging, but I believe we'll make it through."

"Me too," I replied. "I'll catch up with you later, alright?"

"Sure, babe."

I strolled away and unexpectedly ran into Mona. "Oh, Mona... hi."

She nervously bit her lip. "Hi."

"How have you been?" I inquired.

She shrugged. "Okay, I guess. It's tough having to see Jimmy every day on campus."

I nodded and started to walk away, realizing I couldn't handle this conversation.

"Aurora, wait!" she called out.

"What?" I asked, turning back to her.

"I'm sorry."

I shook my head. "I don't think I'm the one you should be apologizing to. Honestly, I don't think you should have come, I forgot you were still invited. This is supposed to be a happy event, and you're putting a damper on it for me."

I walked away and found Ian by the lake.

"Hey, Ian."

"Hey."

"Are you okay?" I inquired.

"I'm fine, I suppose," he said with a shrug.

"Come on, Ian. Talk to me."

He sighed. "I don't know. This wedding has me thinking, you know? I want to spend the rest of my life with Simran, I'm sure of that, but I'm not sure I can handle her new job."

I tilted my head. "Ian, aren't you happy for her?" I asked.

"Of course I am. This is everything she's ever wanted and more."

"Exactly, and she's over the moon. So happy."

"I know. I just... she's my girlfriend. I don't like the idea of sharing her with all these people."

"I get that. I mean, Jer's modeling too, not as exclusively as Simran, but I totally understand."

"I don't want her to forget about me."

"She won't. I mean, right now she's wandering around looking for you."

"She is?"

"Yup."

"I should probably go find her then."

"You definitely should," I said, and he turned to walk away.

"And Ian?"

"Yeah?"

"Tell her how you feel, work through this together. Trust me, communication is key."

He nodded with a look that told me he understood that I was speaking from experience.

I turned toward the lake and then screamed in shock as someone pushed me. Just before I hit the water, two arms grabbed me by the waist and stopped me from falling.

I was lifted up and spun around.

"Derrick! You idiot!"

"Nice to see you too, babe."

I pushed him away. "You scared me half to death."

"That was the plan. How's college treating you, smarty-pants?"

I rolled my eyes. "It's fine. How's life treating you, loser?"

He gasped and placed a hand on his chest. "So hostile. Going to one of the country's top colleges is changing you, Aurora. What a snob."

"Shut up," I laughed.

"Hey, guys."

"Hey, Jimmy," I said, giving him a warm hug.

"How are you holding up?" Derrick asked, his concern evident.

Jimmy shrugged, and I couldn't help but notice the dark circles under his eyes and his growing beard.

"I'm doing alright, I guess. I'm just grateful for the distraction. This is a really beautiful wedding."

"You know she's here—" Derrick began.

"Yep, I saw her. It's fine; I see her in class all the time. This isn't any different."

Jimmy and Mona had broken up about a month ago when he had discovered her cheating with one of her professors in her dorm room.

"On the bright side, I just secured an internship at Google."

"What? No way!"

"Yup," he nodded. "I'm pretty excited."

"I've heard their offices are amazing," Derrick chimed in.

"They are. I attended an event at one of their offices a few months ago. It was pretty awesome," Jimmy said.

"Good for you," I said, offering a supportive smile.

"Thanks."

"Oh my God," Derrick exclaimed, grabbing onto my arm for support.

Jimmy and I followed his gaze, and my eyes widened as I saw a group of waiters carrying trays of delectable food. From what I could see, there were ribs, chicken, burgers, and more.

"I was so disappointed when I saw the menu and realized the best option was 'Nemo and Dory,' but just look at this! Incredible food."

"Nemo and Dory...?"

Derrick and Jimmy darted off before I could even finish my sentence

"Boys," I shook my head in amusement.

I made my way to find my dad and inquire about the surprise food, waving to Marie as I went.

"Hey, Dad, what's going on?" I gestured to the people clearing the tables of food and replacing it with the new dishes.

"Ask Evie."

Evelyn smiled sheepishly and shrugged. "What? No one seemed to be really enjoying the seafood, and my uncle owns a restaurant that just catered for a big party today, but they didn't have a big turnout, so he offered to have the rest of the food delivered here."

"Wow, okay."

"I just want this to be perfect!"

"Well, I'll tell you something," Jer said as he walked up to us. "These ribs are definitely perfect."

"See?" Evelyn smiled.

"Aurora, you should get some food before it's all gone. These people are savages," Jer told me

I looked up and noticed everyone rushing to grab food, and I stood. "You're right. I'll be back."

I walked up to the serving table and filled my plate with all kinds of delicious, greasy food.

"Aurora."

I frowned. "What?"

"Please, can we talk? I need to tell you—"

"I really don't want to know."

"Please, Aurora," Mona said. "I thought we were friends. If the tables were turned, and Jimmy was the one who cheated, would you treat him like this?"

I bit the inside of my cheek and didn't answer.

"Exactly. I knew none of you really liked me—"

"That's not true."

"Then please talk to me. I need someone right now."

I nodded and sat beside her at her table.

She sighed. "I know what I did was wrong, and I regret it every day. Lately, I haven't felt as close to Jimmy, which doesn't make sense to me since you and Jer have been miles apart and seem stronger than ever. Then there's Kiyana and Ryan, Ian and Simran. Maybe we should have tried the whole long-distance thing too."

She shrugged. "Jimmy really wanted me to go to IUP with him, and even though I didn't want to, I went. I think that's what caused us to drift apart. We forced it."

I nodded.

"But cheating on him with my professor was so stupid. It just kinda... happened. I was struggling with my studies and with Jimmy, and he was just there. I just wish everyone didn't hate me now."

"You're our friend, Mona. I'm sure we'll be able to forgive you eventually. I mean, Simran and I were enemies, and now look at us.

She offered a sad smile. "Thanks. I'm sorry to do this at your dad's wedding. Go enjoy yourself."

I smiled at her, returning to my table.

After the reception, my dad and Evelyn were off to the airport for their honeymoon in Bali, and Jer took me home.

"Will you stay over?" I asked tiredly.

"Of course."

"Will you carry me in?"

"Anything for you, Princess."

He parked the car and got out, coming over to my side and lifting me in a bridal-style carry. With his pinky fingers, he deftly grabbed the straps of my heels and shut the car door.

He carried me up to my room and gently laid me down.

I stretched out and sighed.

"Today was fun."

"It was," he replied, unbuttoning his shirt.

I sat up and grabbed my pajamas.

"Hopefully, I'll have a little sibling soon enough," I said, removing my dress.

"You think?" Jer asked, lying down on the bed. "Isn't your dad a little old."

I gasped playfully and got under the covers with him after changing.

"He is not. And Evelyn definitely isn't."

"True. She's, what, ten years younger? Your dad's still got it."

I laughed and nestled my head on his chest.

"Hopefully, that will be us one day," he whispered, his fingers gently playing with my curls.

"What do you mean?" I asked, curiosity piqued.

"Married."

I looked up at him, surprised. "Married?"

"Yeah, married. And then we'll have beautiful children. Maybe even twins – a cute little girl and a strong, brave boy who'll protect her..."

"I like the sound of that," I said, snuggling closer to him.

He wrapped his arms around me tightly and planted a tender kiss on my forehead. "It's funny because I used to think my future was going to involve dealing drugs, running from the cops, and dealing with my father. But here I am, dreaming about having a family of my own."

I smiled. "Amazing, isn't it?"

"Yes, you are."

I grinned and cupped his face. "I love you, Jeremiah."

"I love you too, Princess."

In that moment, as I gazed into his eyes, I realized that I had found my own happy ending, just like the Disney princesses I had always admired. And it was even better than I had ever imagined.

Read More From This Author

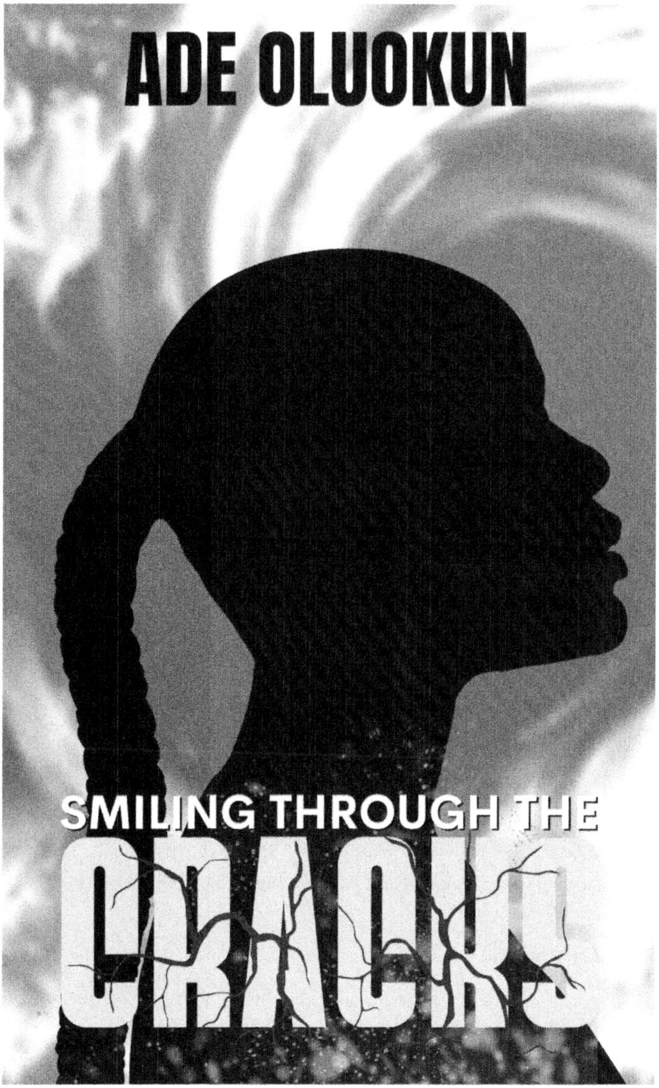

ADE OLUOKUN

SMILING THROUGH THE
CRACKS

Chapter 1

Flashback

I looked up at Cole, a loving smile on my face. I had finally mustered the courage to say it—I told him I loved him, and it felt amazing. It had been almost a month now since he had dropped the 'L bomb' himself and even though I hadn't reciprocated then, he continued to remind me daily how he felt. I'd been feeling guilty about not saying it back but I wanted to be sure of my feelings. A crooked smile stretched across his face, "I have a surprise for you!" Anticipation swelled within me, causing my eyes to widen with curiosity and delight.

"Really? What is it? When do I get it?" I couldn't help but ask, bouncing like a child eagerly anticipating a present.

He chuckled, a mischievous glimmer dancing in his eyes. "Soon, babe, you'll get it soon," he replied, his voice laced with a devious tone.

Despite the unusual undertone, I leaned into his embrace, enveloped in a wave of happiness. His touch, his words, and the promise of something special filled me with a sense of excitement.

The Present

"Amira!" A shrill voice pierced the air, jolting me awake. I groaned, standing straight reluctantly. Kaitlyn stood before me, her expression filled with disbelief. "I asked you to make that iced coffee like twenty minutes ago!" she yelled. Her silk-pressed hair was styled in a low bun, and she confidently stood tall in her heels, despite their inconvenience for our job. Her flawless brown skin contrasted nicely against our white uniform tops. I rolled my eyes in response.

"Calm your non-existent tits, I'll bring it over in a second," I growled. She gasped, opening her mouth to reply, but no words came out. Instead, she huffed and walked away from the drinks station. I stretched my limbs and let out a tired yawn.

I quickly prepared a cappuccino on ice and brought it to Kaitlyn, who promptly handed it to an annoyed customer. During a lull in the rush, I snuck into the break room, hoping to catch a moment of rest on the worn-out couch. But the door swung open with force before I could even close my eyes. "Amira!" My name was shouted for the second time in ten minutes. Once again, I groaned, glaring at whoever was calling me. It was May.

"What?" I snapped. I loved May like a second mother, but that didn't mean I treated her any differently than everyone else. She sighed, her green eyes accentuated by prominent bags, a clear sign of exhaustion from managing a diner staffed mostly by college students. She shook her head at me, her ginger curls bouncing, and pursed her thin lips.

"Aren't you supposed to be at the drinks station today?" she asked, running her hands through her graying hair. I shrugged nonchalantly.

She rubbed her hands over her face in frustration. "Amira, what am I going to do with you? I ask you to do one thing, just one thing, and you can't even make an effort?" she exclaimed.

I rolled my eyes, resting my head against the arm of the chair. "May, you're overreacting. I do make an effort. I got up this morning. That's something," I retorted. She glared at me, her patience wearing thin.

"I've done so much for you since what happened, and you haven't shown any signs of trying to move on. It's been a year,

Amira. You have responsibilities that need to be taken care of!"

❧

Flashback

"Hey, Cole, what were you talking about with Nikki and Richard?" I inquired. I secretly hoped their conversation had something to do with the surprise Cole had mentioned a few days ago, which I was still eagerly awaiting. He offered me a tight smile.

"Oh, it's nothing. Um...how about we go bowling?" he suggested.

"What? Right now? Cole, you have a shift!" I reminded him. If he wanted to be promoted to assistant manager, he couldn't afford to miss a work day without prior approval. But one thing I adored about Cole was his knack for doing fun things at the most unexpected times. He rolled his eyes.

"Who cares about a silly shift or this dumb job? All that matters to me is you, Amy," he declared. I giggled, relishing that he called me Amy —a special nickname only he could use.

"You're not going to report me, are you?" he asked, raising an eyebrow. "Richie can cover my shift."

As a manager myself, I knew I shouldn't have allowed him to swap shifts on such short notice. But he was my boyfriend, how could I possibly resist?

"Of course not, Cole. You're so sweet!" I exclaimed, hugging him tightly. We stood near the diner's front window, embracing each other. As I held him, I caught a glimpse of Nikki's reflection behind us, smirking at Cole. I wasn't sure what that was about, but I brushed it off as mere imagination. It was probably nothing.

The Present

"Hey, are you okay, Amira?" May asked, concerned as she stood over me, a hand on my shoulder. Blinking, I snapped out of my trance and shrugged her hand off.

"Fine, I'll make your dumb drinks," I snarled, storming out of the room. May had no right to dictate when I should or shouldn't move on from my trauma; it was completely unfair.

On my way out, I collided with Natalie, her blonde hair smacking me in the mouth. "Oh, are you okay—" she started, but I pushed past her and returned to my station.

"Que pasa, Mira?" Jonah, another coworker, hollered from the kitchen through the serving hatch. He grinned at me, his lip ring gleaming in the light as he did, and pushed his long black curls out of his face. Although his hair should have been tied up or covered with a hair net, he loved showing it off. I grunted in response, clearly displaying my mood. He winced and sheepishly went back to work.

"I got it," I told Eli, letting him know I was back at my station. He handed me the mug he had just grabbed and put on an apron to continue taking people's orders.

"Are you good?" he asked, concern evident in his brown eyes. I nodded stiffly, not wanting to discuss it further.

The rest of my shift was spent making drinks and passing them to the servers. Before we knew it, closing time arrived, and we began cleaning up the diner after a long day's work. However, all I had done was make drinks —bad ones at that.

Eli had been pestering me about what was wrong all day, which was becoming annoying. I struggled to keep my temper in check, knowing he was one of the few people I tried to keep my cool with. He had been a true friend since I moved here, standing by me even when I pushed him away.

"I'm fine, Eli. Just give me some space," I muttered through gritted teeth, my voice carrying the weight of weariness and frustration. It was a response I had found myself repeating over and over again throughout the day.

Kaitlyn sauntered over with Natalie following behind. "Natalie, stop doing that. You're irritating me," I snapped as she bounced up and down. Sometimes I couldn't stand her—she reminded me of who I used to be.

"Guess what?" Natalie exclaimed, unbothered by my words. "I'll tell them!" Kaitlyn hissed.

Natalie huffed and crossed her arms. "Tomorrow," Kaitlyn paused for dramatic effect, "There's going to be a—"

"A new employee!" Natalie blurted out, bouncing with excitement again. Kaitlyn glared at her.

"Yes, because someone won't do her job, we needed more help," Kaitlyn said, staring pointedly at me.

Eli wrapped his arm around my shoulder. "Hey, leave Amira alone. She does her job."

"So, sleeping on the couch in the lunchroom and snapping at people is doing her job?" Kaitlyn asked, her arms crossed. "We all know that May would never fire her precious little Amira, so more help it is."

Kaitlyn's final remark stung, causing my jaw to tense. She could never understand my relationship with May or why she let me get away with so much. Regardless of her prying, I kept my mouth shut. Nobody here needed to know about my past.

"Don't listen to her, Amira, he's kitchen staff so it has nothing to do with you." Natalie assured me. I rolled my eyes at her, I didn't need her to try and make me feel better. I was fine.

"Who the fuck even cares about a new employee, anyway?" I asked.

"Yeah, we get new people everyday," Eli added, with a shrug.

"Oh, I forgot the most important part! He's hot! He actually went to high school with us. Literally everyone had a crush on him. He was like 6'6" with the sharpest facial features ever, he had amazing hair and he was genuinely kind to everyone, not to mention the star of the basketball team," Natalie babbled.

"I doubt he was that amazing..." Eli mumbled, crossing his arms. I raised an eyebrow at him, knowing he secretly had feelings for Natalie. It wasn't surprising, they were a perfect match, both having a positive outlook on life, and Eli being the only one who could handle Natalie's energy. But then as I actually took in the description of the guy Natalie was talking about, my heart began to race. I remembered a guy from high school who fit that description perfectly.

"What's his name?" I asked, trying to keep my voice steady.

"Jabari Brooks."

The moment Kaitlyn uttered that name, I froze.

Jabari Brooks, the guy I had a raging crush on when I was sixteen? The dipshit I had embarrassingly made a fool of myself in front of? The bastard I had shamelessly asked to prom only to be rejected? No fucking way.

I still cringed at the memory from time to time. Back then, I was a different person, living in a fairytale world. I convinced myself that he loved me just as much as I was infatuated with him, simply because he would smile at me in the halls and we'd occasionally engage in conversation.

He was on the boys' basketball team, while I played for the girls' team. Sometimes, the girls would watch the guys practice and vice versa. I remember him making a passing comment about how he liked my height, standing at 5'11" and from then, I was instantly smitten.

For an entire year, I fantasized about us being together until around April of his senior year and my junior year, when I mustered the courage to ask him to prom. I thought it was the perfect opportunity to declare my love before he graduated and disappeared from my life. Long story short, he said no. It was the most crushing experience of my life, and one would think it would have taught me not to fall head over heels for men at the slightest display of kindness, but here I was.

He couldn't possibly work here. It was just inconceivable.

"Amira!" Natalie said, her face uncomfortably close to mine. I pushed her face away with the palm of my hand.

"Huh?" I asked.

"Ow!" She groaned, rubbing her nose.

"You zoned out. Are you sure you're okay?" Eli asked. I nodded before shrugging his arm off me.

"I'm fine," I said, biting my lip.

I didn't need any more reminders of my past and how foolish I had been. I just hoped I could avoid him.

SCAN TO READ MORE

Buy Book ♡

About The Author

Ade Oluokun

Ade Oluokun is a Toronto-based content creator, business owner, and devoted fashion enthusiast. From her early years in high school, she embarked on a creative journey, immersing herself in various forms of expression, be it through the written word or captivating visuals. Ade's profound love for storytelling has fueled her interest in writing, which she skillfully combines with her photography prowess and boundless creativity.  Through her unique blend of inspiration and artistry, she crafts compelling content that resonates deeply with her audience. Ade Oluokun is a true visionary who continually pushes the boundaries of her craft, leaving an indelible mark on the world of creativity.

Acknowledgment

Reflecting on my journey, writing a book with diversity and a strong Black female lead has been a long-held dream. Today, as I write, I'm filled with joy and a sense of accomplishment.

I want to thank my friends and family for their unwavering support and encouragement. Your love and guidance made this book possible. To my family, your encouragement and sacrifices shaped me as a writer, and I'm forever grateful for your belief in my dreams. Friends, your encouragement and feedback have been invaluable.

I also appreciate the authors, poets, and storytellers who paved the way for diverse voices. Your work inspired me and highlighted the importance of representation.

To the readers who embraced stories featuring Black characters living everyday life, thank you. Your support fuels my passion to create more stories celebrating the Black experience.

This book is a testament to representation's power and the potential in our stories. I hope it inspires more diverse storytelling and a richer literary landscape. Thank you for joining me on this journey. Your support means a lot.

Printed in Great Britain
by Amazon

32428963R00202